SLEEPING WITH THE ENEMY

Also by Wahida Clark

Thug Matrimony

Every Thug Needs a Lady

Payback Is a Mutha

Thugs and the Women Who Love Them

And by Kiki Swinson

Wifey

I'm Still Wifey

Life After Wifey

Published by Kensington Publishing Corporation

SLEEPING WITH THE ENEMY

WAHIDA CLARK

KIKI SWINSON

Dafina
Books

KENSINGTON PUBLISHING CORP.

DAFINA BOOKS are published by

Kensington Publishing Corp.
850 Third Avenue
New York, NY 10022

ISBN: 978-0-7394-9882-8

Printed in the United States of America

CONTENTS

ENEMY IN MY BED

by Wahida Clark   1

KEEPING MY ENEMIES CLOSE

by Kiki Swinson   141

Enemy in My Bed

Wahida Clark

To my Uncle John. R.I.P.
They don't make them like you anymore.
If they did, the world would be a better place.

Chapter 1

Kreesha had just finished fluffing up her king-sized pillows when she heard her doorbell ring. She looked at the clock on her nightstand, which read 8:49 A.M. She peeked out her bedroom window and saw a high-yellow sista wearing a white Nike sweat suit and sneakers. Her hair was in a ponytail, and she looked agitated. With her hand resting loosely on her hip, she rang the bell again.

"Fuck!" Kreesha said out loud. She cracked her bedroom window. "Who is it?"

The young lady looked up to where the voice was coming from. "Are you Kreesha?"

"Yeah," Kreesha answered with much skepticism. "And you are?" She blazed at her, even though she had an idea who this chick was.

"I'm Sparkle. Reign's wife?" she said more as a question than a statement. "Can I talk to you for a minute?" She was staring at Kreesha, daring her to say no.

"What do you need to talk to me for? Don't you think you need to be talking to Reign?"

"Oh, trust and believe I've already spoken to Reign. Now I need to talk to you. Can I just have a couple of minutes? We're both adults here."

Kreesha paused before slamming the window shut.

"Wifey!" she mumbled under her breath. "I knew it was coming but I am not up for this shit today!" She grabbed a robe and went into the bathroom to make herself more presentable. As she washed her face, brushed her teeth, and applied a little makeup, she griped, "This bitch is on my porch, on my time, so she is going to have to wait." She spoke into the mirror as she played in her hair. "Wifey," she mumbled again as if she didn't believe it and headed out of the bathroom. She grabbed the can of mace from her purse and slipped it inside her robe pocket.

When she got to the front door she paused before peering out the window to see if wifey was still out there waiting and to make sure she was alone. She wasn't about to get jumped inside of her own home. There was a white-on-white Acura Legend parked there, but no one was in it. "I can take this bitch," she concluded.

Kreesha opened the door and was ready to do battle. "How in the fuck you know where I live?"

"Bitch, please, I said I was wifey, it's my job to know!" Sparkle was staring at her all crazy.

"Ho, it's your job to say whatever the fuck it is you gots to say and get the fuck off my property! Bitch!" Kreesha was fingering her can of mace, itching to use it.

Sparkle held her ground, staring at Kreesha as if she couldn't believe what was before her eyes.

"I know you don't think I'ma invite you in for cookies and milk! Whatever you gots to say you can go ahead and say it!" Kreesha was trying her best not to pull out the mace.

"Whatever," Sparkle finally said. Seeing that her competition wasn't going to make this easy, she decided to get straight to the point. "Reign will be getting out in a few days. And as you know, we are married and have been for the last three years and obviously throughout his whole bid.

I told him that you was just an infatuation, something to do to help him pass his time while doin' his bid. But in a few days whatever business or fun you was having with my husband will be over. Oh, know this boo, once he gets out it's a wrap!" And she turned to walk away.

Not wasting any time with her comeback, Kreesha yelled, "Bitch, let me enlighten you a little! You can choose to believe that it's a wrap, but it's not. Obviously you don't even believe that shit since you took the chance of bringing yo' dusty ass over to my house talking some bullshit, half-ass, and inaccurate information. I mean, he may be married, but I can guarantee you that being infatuated is not in the equation."

"Oh, you don't think so?" Sparkle asked as she turned back around to face her. "What do you call hooking up with some nigga in prison on some pen-pal shit? And sneaking down to see him when you know that his wife is not going to be there? Face it, girlfriend, it's all an infatuation. You're just someone he's using to pass the time. Thanks for the car, bitch! But like I said, he's taken. The man is mines. It's over!" Sparkle turned and headed toward her car.

"Bitch, it ain't over until I say it's over! You'll see!" The next thing, Kreesha was running off of her porch in a rage when halfway down the stairs she stumbled and skidded the rest of the way kissing the ground. Full of embarrassment she peered up at Sparkle, whose gaze was dripping with disgust. When she got to the Legend, Sparkle had already locked the door and was starting the engine. "Nah, bitch, get the fuck out, bitch. You was bold enough to come over, get the fuck out." Kreesha was ready for war.

Sparkle cracked her window. "You dumb ass sucka for love! You ain't worth it. If you hadn't of bought me this car, I probably would have fucked your ass up. But I wanted to thank you personally for this and just on GP, I ain't gonna run yo' fat, stupid ass over!" She gassed the engine and pulled off.

Kreesha went back inside and slammed her front door so hard the iron fell off of the ironing board. She was pissed as she paced back and forth, not wanting to believe that the bitch had come to her house and was bragging on the car. She picked up her phone and pressed the memory button for her cousin Eboni. When the voice mail picked up, Kreesha paged her, then headed to swoop the iron up off the floor. Her phone rang, and she ran into the dining room to get it.

"Eboni?" she spat, completely out of breath.

"Yeah, what's up? And why you all outta breath? Never mind, don't answer that. I'm on my way to Wal–Mart."

"Can you stop over here? You'll never believe what bitch just left!"

"Since I won't believe it, then why the fuck should I guess. What bitch, Kreesha?" she snapped impatiently.

"Reign's wife. The bitch's name is Sparkle. The skank-ass ho had the nerve to come to my house. My fuckin' house, Eboni! Can you believe that shit?" she yelled into the phone. "That bitch! That motherfuckin' ugly-ass, high-yella bitch!" Kreesha was so heated she was foaming at the mouth.

Eboni held the phone away from her ear. "Look, Kree, you knew this day was coming. You also know if the shoe was on the other foot, you would have been at that ho's house your damn self! You fuckin' with a married man. You know what time it is. Fuck that bitch! I know you gonna keep doin' you. So why you sweatin' the dumb shit? As long as she ain't beat your ass, then who gives a fuck?" Eboni had to laugh at the thought of Kreesha getting her ass whupped.

"Oh, so now you got jokes? You know she ain't beat my

ass. It's just the principle of the whole thing. The bitch showed up at my front door telling me to leave her man, which is also my man, alone. And bragging about that corny-ass Legend. How the fuck she know where I live? You wait until that nigga calls!"

"Yeah, because that is who you should check. Because he's supposed to have her in check." Eboni was hoping to get off the phone without Kreesha again asking her to come over. "He'll be calling you soon."

"Whatever. I sure ain't gonna sit around waiting for that nigga. I am not in the right frame of mind. I might say something I'll regret later." Just then the other line clicked. "Be ready tomorrow. It's BBD day. I might call you tonight." She clicked Eboni off the line and checked her caller ID. It was Reign.

Chapter 2

"**Y**o, Eboni! It's time to rock and roll!" I yell into the cell phone at my cousin.

"I'll be on the porch," she yelled right back at my ass.

I know she's lyin'. I grab the keys to my rented Dodge something truck—I don't know what the fuck it is fo' real. I just know it's good enough for me to handle my business. Let me introduce you to the otha side of me, the business me. Oh, Reign? For dude, right about now, fuck him!

See, I'm that bitch when it comes to the weed in Memphis, Tennessee. That's all I serve, and I'm ballin' with the best of 'em. I leave the hard stuff to my boys because I like to be number one. The weed allows me to be just that, number one. If I was to get into the dope, then I would have to compete against fifty otha niggas, and I ain't tryna hear that. Excuse me. I'm pullin' up in front of Eboni's and this bitch said she was gonna be on the front porch! *Honk! Honk!* If I don't keep hittin' the horn, this ho will take even longer.

Anyhow, as I was saying, actually the weed business is fun as hell, and it being very profitable is a plus. My connect from Colombia delivers the real big shipments by truck and she . . . that's right, it's a she. My girl Express Mails pounds to addresses that I tell her to. I got a few suburbia neighborhoods on lock. While citizens Mr. and Mrs. John Doe is off at their corporate offices, unbeknownst to them their front porches are being used as receiving docks for my product. Me and my dawg, Eboni, cruise down the block, jump out the car, grab the boxes off the front porches, and we out. Express Mail has been real good to me. That's why me and my moms both own some of their stock. After we stuff the truck with all the Express Mail boxes, it's off to my uncle's garage where we BBD. That stands for Breakdown, Bag, and prepare for Delivery.

"I thought you said you was ready?" I snap on Eboni as she finally jumps her slow ass in the car. I toss her my cell phone and instruct her to call my uncle Roscoe and let him know we'll be there in fifteen. I do that to get on her nerves because she hates Roscoe. Why? I have yet to find out. She snatches the phone up and calls him. But not before giving me a look that is so sharp it could trim my eight-hundred-dollar luxurious weave.

When we pull up to my uncle's block, I can see the niggas waitin'. Why niggas gotta be so hardheaded? Is it because I'ma bitch? I tell them specifically not to come by until after five. Here it ain't even two-thirty and they're all posted up, attracting all this unnecessary attention to my uncle's house. My uncle is a working man. Been working third shift at the hospital for the last fourteen years. He smokes mad weed, though; just like my moms. I guess it runs in the family. One thing for sho', he makes sure he is up and ready when it's time to break it up, bag, and deliver.

So now I see that I gots to check these niggas. I put on my game face and jump outta the truck. I see Mace, Doobie, Alex, and that dyke bitch, Obie; she's family and works my last nerve. Me and Eboni are always strapped, even though we don't get into nothing. All the niggas in the game around these parts know we got all the big dawgs on our team.

"I told y'all niggas after five, not two-thirty. I ain't gonna run out," I say, looking them all up and down.

"C'mon, I got some runs to make. I would have to go all the way across town and back again," pleads Obie.

See what I mean? The family bitches always have an excuse. "That's not my problem. Y'all just can't be sitting out here in front of my uncle's house like this. It attracts attention. Come back around five."

Obie keeps talkin' shit, but I don't care. I simply tune her dyke ass out.

Eboni jumps in the driver's side of the truck. I wait until my faithful customers pull off, and I go inside to open the garage door. "What's up, Roscoe?" My uncle Roscoe reminds me of Fred Sanford. The only thing missing is that walk.

"You," he says, leading the way to his garage. "Corey is here to put in some work," he tells me.

"Good. The more, the merrier, and the quicker we can get done." Corey is his only son, and is the spittin' image of his father. He's just taller and darker.

Just that quick here comes another interruption to fuck up my day. Eboni's baby daddy has pulled up behind my truck, and he's yelling at her to get out of the truck and bring her ass home. I done told this ho that she can't be staying out all night, but she don't listen. Now this nigga Buck is six-foot-three and about two-hundred-sixty pounds. Me, I'm a buck sixty, five-foot-five, slanted eyes, toffee-colored, blemish-free skin. Eboni, she's five-foot-six and a buck seventy, light chocolate, long real hair, and bedroom eyes. Yeah. Us southern girls, we both got a lotta junk in our trunks. But us two together can't take his big ass. So I feel around for my piece and go over to the truck.

"What's up, Buck?" He's now banging on the window, yelling at her to get out. "Buck, this is a rental, so chill. All that bangin' ain't necessary. Eboni, get out!" I yell at her. This dumb bitch is ignoring us and is acting like she's talking on her cell phone. "Open the door, Eboni. Get out and talk to your man like civilized folks." I know some stupid shit is about to pop off. Hell, it always does with these two.

She cracks the window and screams, "I'll be there when I get there!"

I'm like, *Oh, hell, it's about to go down!*

"Naw, the fuck you ain't! You comin' home right now!" he screams back at her.

Now I gotta play mediator. "Buck, I'll bring her home in a few hours. We about to break down."

Now, this is a big nigga like I said before. But he's pussy whipped. She can't get rid of him if she wanted to. I told her one day she's gonna push this crazy-ass nigga too far and he's gonna kill her. But for now I gots to have her back.

"Buck, you know she was at my house last night. All you had to do was call over there. You know we had to get up early and handle this business." Why did I tell that fib? The nigga snapped.

"You a motherfuckin' lie!" He spits in my face. And I mean spit. I wipe my face with the back of my hand. "You a motherfuckin' lie!" he continues as if he forgot what he just said. "I was parked in front of your house until three this morning! You ain't right, Kreesha! You ain't right!" He's pointing his finger in my face. "You can't cover for her this time."

At this point, my uncle has closed the garage door and is coming over to where we are. "Buck, you gotta take all this racket elsewhere." He was attempting to calmly diffuse the situation.

"They ain't right, Roscoe, and you know it, man!" He turns back to Eboni. "Get the fuck out, Eboni! Now!" He tries to stick his big-ass hand through the crack of the window. Such a big dumb motherfucker! What's even more off-the-wall is she turns on the ignition and rolls the window up. Now he's screaming, I guess because his hand is hurting, but this only causes him to hit the window with his free hand, and it goes clear through to the inside. Glass starts to flyin'.

"Buck!" I holler his name. And now Eboni is screaming like she's being chased by an axe murderer and is trying to climb to the passenger side so that she can make a run for it.

I'm pissed off now and so is Uncle Roscoe. "Y'all niggas know we illegal as hell out here. If someone calls the police, we all goin' to jail, and I ain't goin' to jail for nobody." My uncle Roscoe pulls out his piece and puts it to Buck's head. "Nigga, you heard this ole man. Take this ruckus home where it belongs!"

"Uncle Roscoe, put that fuckin' gun away. You the one gonna make these folks call the police," I try to reason with him.

When Eboni gets out of the other side and runs for the house, crazy-ass Buck pays the gun pointed at his skull no mind and goes running after his sweet young thang. Before she can reach the steps Buck has her by the hair, and that bitch starts screaming like the bitch that she is. He's banging her head against the steps.

Now the neighbors are posted up on porches and in windows and shit, so I have to think fast. I run to Buck's car and move it out of the way because he had me blocked in. As soon as I jump into the truck, Corey is coming out the house swingin' a bat like he's Batman Joe. See, when it comes to family, we aim or strike first, then ask questions.

Poor Buck, he knows better than to fuck with Eboni. Especially on the family turf. I turn the ignition, tryna get ghost. I got enough weed on me to get the whole family, including Buck, who is gettin' the serious beatdown, at least twenty years. As I go to back outta the driveway, the Po Po is turning on our block. *Ain't this a bitch?*

Chapter 3

When Reign had called me the other day after his wife left, I didn't even accept any of his calls. I wasn't feelin' him. He's been blowin' up my line nonstop. But I am not ready to deal with him just yet. Yeah, I knew he was married, but I never had to deal with it or, shall I say, it never hit me until that ho showed up at my front door.

Let me tell y'all real quick how I hooked up with him. See, what happened was my cousin Tanisha had needed a ride to go see her man who was locked up. She asked me or more like begged me to take her down to the prison. I finally gave in. By the time we waited, got searched, patted down, talked to as if we were trash, I told her, "You better enjoy this visit because this is the last time you'll get me to bring you anywhere near this damn place!"

But damn, when I got inside the visiting hall, I instantly flipped the script. My anger was quickly forgotten and replaced with the sight of all of those fine brothas. Let me tell you, there was all shapes, sizes, and colors. I felt like a kid in a candy store or a fag in a boys' camp. I was dick watching and everythang.

"Dang, Kree! Pick your tongue up off the ground!" Tanisha's smart ass had the nerve to say. She was standing there hugging her man. They both started laughing but wasn't shit funny to me.

I was like, "Damn! Fuck the clubs! This is where all the niggas at!" So I was looking around and not even being discreet about the shit either. And then our eyes locked. I was checkin' him out and he was checkin' me out. His ass wasn't being discreet either. Because when the nigga stood up to stretch he didn't take his eyes off me. He wanted my ass to check him out. He was chocolate just like I like them. Looked about six-foot-two, waves, clean shaven, one-eighty/one-ninety pounds and had big muscular arms. The kind that I like to be swooped up in and tossed onto the bed. The icing on the cake was those pretty, pussy-sucking lips. Them bad boys were prettier than LL Cool J's. He met all of my criteria.

"Yo, Dwayne." I turned to Tanisha's man of the season. Well, I shouldn't say that because they've been on and off for the last three years. One thing for sho' is everytime the nigga goes to jail, she is always right there. "Dwayne. Who that nigga right there?"

"What nigga?"

"Him. Sitting next to the dude with the little boy on his lap." Whoever that was visiting him was bouncing a little boy who was giggling up and down on his knees.

"His name is Reign. Why?"

"Reign. Is he one of them homo-thugs? Is he gay?"

"Why? Do the nigga look gay?"

"You never can tell these days. Well, is he?"

"I don't know. Ask him."

"Nigga, you know. Ain't no secrets in the jailhouse!"

Dwayne started laughing. "Yeah, you right about that. But naw. I haven't known the nigga to get down like that."

"Damn, he is fine. Hold up. But what about that nigga sitting behind him? The one with the dreads?"

"What, do he look homo-thuggish as you like to call it?"

"I don't know. That's why I'm asking."

"Well, you don't want to fuck with him."

"Dayaam," me and Tanisha sang at the same time as we continued to stare at him. "What a waste!" we said together.

Dwayne leaned back and looked at Tanisha all crazylike. "What the fuck you talkin' about, what a waste?"

She rolled her eyes and gave that look that us sistas give. "I know I can make a comment." She sucked her teeth. "It is a waste. The nigga is cute. Why he gotta be gettin' fucked or fucking another nigga in the ass? That's all I was sayin'!" She was poppin' on her chewing gum.

"Well, you's a fine-ass bitch. Why you gotta be lickin' on another fine bitch's pussy?"

Oh, shit! I said to myself. *What have I just started?* My girl Tanisha was tongue tied.

"Yeah! That's what I thought!" Dwayne yelled as if his favorite All Star just shot the game-winning three pointer.

As we watched Tanisha jump up and storm off, I said, "Damn, Dwayne. Why you gotta call a sista out like that? And why you taking up for some faggot-ass nigga anyway? Let me find out!"

"Shit. Let you find out? I ain't takin' nothin' up the ass but a ho's tongue!"

"Yeah right, nigga! So hook this ho up."

"Hook you up?" he echoed.

"Yeah, nigga. Did I stutter? Hook a sista up and I'll tell Tanisha to put her tongue up your ass before we go," I joked.

"I'd rather have some pussy." He was staring at me. "Give me some pussy and I'll hook you up." The nigga had the nerve to be serious.

"Dwayne, don't even try it. I'm telling Tanisha when she comes back." I got serious right back at him.

"I'm only playin'. I'll hook you up."

That's what I thought. So hook us up he did. At first, me and chocolate-covered Reign started exchanging letters. Then he started calling. The nigga's tongue game was so nice I wanted to come see him. That was when he told me he had a wifey. And of course the slick-ass nigga said he was waiting to get home before he could say what their status was. For now she was sticking by him. But by this time I was feelin' this nigga so much I didn't give a fuck what the status was. She went to see him on Wednesday nights and Saturdays, and I had Sundays. She would never miss church.

So now I don't understand why I am so pissed that he has a wife, and I really don't understand why I won't accept his calls. It's not like I didn't know. For real? Since he's gettin' ready to hit the bricks, I'm trying to decide if I want to hang with this nigga or not. You know, do the otha woman thang. I don't want to get hurt. I'd rather get out before I let that happen. Niggas be real grimey once they hit the bricks and is quick to act like they can't remember yo' name.

Damn. Hearing myself say it shines a whole different light. I never thought I would be playin' second fiddle to a bitch for a nigga that I ain't never fucked, ain't never did shit for me and fo' real . . . I really don't know him.

Kreesha thought the situation over some more.

What the fuck am I talkin' about? I ain't never been a bitch to back down. And I damn sure ain't about to start now. So the fuck what! Call me home wrecker, triflin' ho, all of the above. I will be the last bitch standing. Reign is mines.

Chapter 4

"**C**hill, Kreesha. Chill," I tell myself as I hear the siren getting closer and as I roll the broken window all the way down to brush away the remaining glass pieces. I back out of the driveway, hoping to ease past the Po Po. If I get stopped, I gotta do too much shit. For starters, how about keep their attention off of the boxes of weed I got piled up in the back, coupled with giving the family enough time to straighten things out.

Here they come. "Fuck!" It's two white officers and they're coming fast, but then begin to slow down. I flash them a Colgate smile and wave at them. I can tell that this throws them, because they both turn beet red. My eyes dart to the side-view mirror as they pass by me.

"Whew!" My heart is thumpin', and my fingertips are turning white from gripping the steering wheel so hard. When I hit the corner I make a left and then I'm gone. Barely breathing I get three blocks over and pull into 7-Eleven. This is me and Eboni's meeting spot. I look around to make sure I'm not being followed, then pull out my cell phone to call Uncle Roscoe. Damn! No one's answering. I dial Eboni's celly. No answer. Now I'm sitting here bitin' my bottom lip and tapping my fingers on the steering wheel, hoping that everything's okay! I'm sweating bullets.

Finally, after about ten minutes, and me getting rid of all the glass, I convince myself that everything's cool. I got all the weed! Worst case scenario, Buck's ass is getting in trouble and so is Corey for beatin' a nigga with a baseball bat. But, still, why is no one answering their phone? And where is Eboni's dumb ass? She knows the drill. Whenever something goes down at Roscoe's, and if we get away, this is the meeting spot. Damn! Then it dawns on me: *If we get away!* Fuck! Something must have gone down. Shit!

I start up the truck and head for one of my runner's spots, Lil' Twist. I only get a block away from the 7–Eleven when I notice the flashing lights behind me. My heart is racing as I keep driving as if I don't see them. They ain't making no noise, and I need to get to a more crowded spot. You know you can't trust the men in blue. If they decide to Rodney King me, I need some witnesses.

Whoop! Whoop! Aaww shit! I pull over. It's a black officer and he's by himself. Okay. Maybe I can handle him. If he's a trick then it's on. If not, then I'm fucked. With that thought I slump back into the seat, trying my best to act cool.

I'm waitin' and waitin'. I know that he ran the tags about ten minutes ago. What the fuck could he be doing? I wait for what feels like another ten minutes. Oh, shit! Here comes another squad car. Dayaam! Dayaam! Dayaam! Why do I have to go out like this? And damn if I don't have a gun on me. The black officer steps out of his car, and so do the two new officers. One is black and the other one is white. They're all standing there talking and looking at me. The black officer who pulled me to a stop pimps over. My window is already down. I just look at him, cock my head to the side, and smile. "What's this, DWB?"

He doesn't see shit funny. "Can I see your license and registration please?" He's emotionless. So I hand it over, dropping the small talk. He takes it and goes back to his car. The other two are standing there still looking. I know I don't have any warrants. But if they decide to search me or this truck, I'm fucked. After about five more minutes, Mr. Emotionless gets out of the car, then goes and talks to the other two officers. Shit, here comes another cruiser. I watch as the first officer gets out, and I try to read the expression on his face. I'm straining my damn neck.

"Shit!" I say out loud. I can only lay my head back and close my eyes. I got a gun and about eighty pounds of weed all in my possession. Oh, shit! I didn't even see the dog in the latest squad car. He's running in circles like a maniac, barking and shit. Ain't this a bitch! Now the tears are falling. I get a flashback of all the dirt I've done and all of the times I said I was gonna clean up my act. The tears are falling not from fear, but anger. This shit that went down today was totally uncalled for. Thanks to Eboni, it's getting ready to go down. Here comes Officer Emotionless. I dry my eyes and slip on my shades.

"Oh, now you don't want to look at me?" Mr. Emotionless has the nerve to say in a flirtatious way. His remark and flirting catches me totally off guard, in a good way. He hands my paperwork back to me. The other officers are still standing there talking.

"No. It's not like that. I obviously look like shit because before you had no words for a sista," I flirt back.

"You just left Heard Avenue, right?"

Is this a trick question? "Yes, sir, I did."

"Why would you leave the scene of an accident? You know that's illegal, right?"

"Accident? I wouldn't call my cousin and her husband, who is drunk, acting the fool an accident. Would you? More of a domestic disturbance."

"No. But trying to convince my fellow officers that you

had nothing to do with it, now that is another story." He's letting me know on the DL that he's looking out for me. But at the same time I see that the boxes have just caught his attention.

I make an attempt to get his mind off of them and start to babble. "You have to understand that whenever my cousin decides she wants to stay out all night sucking a dick other than her husband's, you can rest assured there's gonna be some drama." He smiles. I think it's working. "Are you married?"

Damn. So much for flirting. He ignores the question, asks for my license again, and walks over to the other two cops. I'm trying to brace myself for what's getting ready to go down. They talk for a minute, and now they're on their way back over here. The white cop is coming up on the passenger side, and the other two are coming up on my side. The black cop with the dog stops dead in his tracks, listening to his walkie-talkie or whatever it's called, then breaks for his squad car. We all turn our attention on him as he gets on the radio, then immediately turns the siren on. The other two clowns must know what time it is because Officer Emotionless gives me back my license and then goes and jumps in his car. He, too, turns the siren on, and they burn rubber, leaving me sitting there in a dust cloud where I pass gas, a lot. I was so nervous that my stomach was full of air, doing somersaults, and I do piss on myself.

Later on that night it's business as usual. The only difference is instead of breakin' down, baggin', and servin' my clientele at my uncle's, I redirect everybody and everything to a spot that Lil' Twist has. I didn't want to take any more chances. So much for the scare I had earlier!

To sum up today's events, I thanked God for sparing me one more time. However, they took Corey and Buck downtown. They're both still down there as of this very minute. They wanted Eboni to come, but she refused as usual to press charges. That bitch knows she's guilty as hell. She said the Po Po had to pull Buck off of her ass and Corey up off of Buck. It was crazy. The nosy-ass neighbors were the ones who told the Po Po about the truck I was in. So the Po Po, wanting to be superheroes, took a chance on finding me. I believe they are superheroes, come to think of it, because they sure did find my ass. I was like a needle in a haystack.

Uncle Roscoe said now his house is hot and he knows they are going to be watching, so he's pissed. Some nerve. He ain't pissed when him and his young tricks is smoking up all the free weed they can smoke or when he's making all them extra dollars. But that's how we do. Me, Eboni, and Lil' Twist was stuck with all the work, and of course Eboni is still being Eboni. After we finished serving all of our people, she hit the streets, most likely for another all-nighter. You would think gettin' fucked up would be enough. But nooo, one day Eboni will learn.

Me? I took my black ass home. I'm dead tired and I've had enough excitement for one day.

Chapter 5

So here it is, two days later. Two days after wifey left my house and one day after that drama at my uncle's. I'm out here watering my garden in some hoochie momma shorts, a T-shirt with no bra on, and nothing on my feet. Watering my garden totally relaxes me. I suddenly hear bass and what sounds like Akon in the background. So I find myself scopin' at the black S Class Benz as it slows down and stops right in front of my house. The passenger window rolls down, and the music goes off.

"Damn, girl! Why you gotta be teasing a nigga this early in the morning? Lookin' like Ms. Parker from the movie *Friday*. Come here." It's this big dealer nigga named Doggy Mac.

My boy, Almighty, who is also in my clique and who used to be tight with my older brother before he got killed, jumps outta the car. "What's up, baby girl?" He comes over and gives me a hug. "I need to use your bathroom."

"You know where it is."

"Go holla at my man," he tells me as he jumps on the steps taking four at a time.

"Kreesha, come here," Doggy Mac orders.

Now, this nigga has been trying to get in my panties for the longest. But he has two strikes goin' against him. One, he's a red nigga and I don't do red niggas. Two, he has a crazy baby's momma. That ho will pull out a switchblade in a heartbeat over her man. And there is too much dick out there to be puttin' up with that shit. My face is too beautiful. But he's fine as shit and his money is long. I throw the water hose down and walk over to his side of the car. I'll flirt with him but that's about as far as it goes.

"Why you come through here this early waking up my neighbors? Y'all just gettin' back?"

"Yeah. And I do mean *just* gettin' back." He reaches over and squeezes my nipple while he kisses me on my cheek. He looks tired but he's still fine as hell.

"You don't want none of this," I tell him seductively.

"Who told you that? I want it, but somehow I can't seem to get it. You still go down and see that nigga?"

I laugh. "What nigga?" I'm thinking, *How does he know my business?*

"You know who I'm talking about." He massages my nipple and it's feelin' good as shit.

"Do you still go home to your wife?" Before he can come up with a good lie, Almighty jumps off of my porch.

"Aiight? Aiight? Break that shit up!" he says, guzzling down a soda.

"You told me to holla at your man; now you want me to break it up. Make up your mind. And stay outta my refrigerator!" I snap at him. Doggy Mac was still assaulting my nipple.

"Girl, please," he says, jumping back in the car. At the same time we notice that a taxi is slowing up the block. Almighty lights a spliff and leans the seat back to get comfortable.

"When are you gonna invite me over?" Doggy Mac is still focused on me and my tit.

Damn. My pussy's getting wet. He's working magic on

my left nipple. The taxi stops right next to us. I look, and I know my face turned an obvious pale. My knees turn to water; my throat goes dry as this nigga steps outta the taxi. Apparently Doggy Mac saw the look on my face, which told him who it is.

"Damn. I guess this delays my chance to get invited over."

I hear him vaguely, and see his lips moving, but I'm in shock. When I see that Reign has noticed Doggy Mac's hand on my breast, I roll my eyes at him and pretend to focus my attention on Doggy Mac, but I'm actually peepin' Reign out the corner of my eye. He throws his backpack over his shoulder, comes over, and stands behind me, wrapping his arms around my waist. I felt as if I was hyperventilating.

Chapter 6

"That nigga gonna get his ass killed messing with that married bitch," Seven said as he threw back his second shot of cognac. Seven was tall and was almost but not quite seven feet, yet still everyone called him that. All of the crew members who were sitting at the table were looking around to spot whom Seven was talking about. Almighty eyed their boy Freeze, who was all over Eboni.

"He been fuckin' with her for a while now, yo," Almighty told them.

"I know. But she married to that nigga who follows her everywhere she go and be doing all types of crazy shit to the niggas who fuck with her. He better watch his back; that's all I'm saying," Seven warned. "Or else we'll look up one day and find his dick stuffed in his mouth."

Everybody started laughing. "Shit. I hope Freeze got enough sense to do him before he gets done. Y'all feel me?" Tax added. They called him Tax because he was the collector. If someone owed their crew money, you definitely didn't want to fuck with Tax, a six-four, two-hundred-sixty-pound burly nigga. He had hands the size of catcher's mitts. If you came up short, he would Tax that ass.

Everyone was cracking jokes except for Tareek. Seven looked over at him and could see that he was pissed off.

Tareek and Freeze were always in competition, trying to out floss each other and fuck all the women they could. Last thing Seven heard, Tareek was the one fuckin' Eboni, and he was hoping that Tareek wasn't dumb enough to be catching feelings for some married broad. And to make shit worse, all of a sudden she's fuckin' with his man Freeze. "Bitches!" Seven said to himself.

"Naw. That nigga ain't smart enough," barked Tareek. "If that was my wife, I would have put my foot all up in her ass, and whatever nigga she was creepin' with."

"Nigga, she ain't your wife, so stop hatin'!" Seven teased.

By this time, Eboni, with her arm around Freeze's waist and his arm around her neck, was heading over to the table. Tareek's eyes were glued to Eboni's ass cheeks which were hanging out from under her Coogi dress as he reminisced about the last time they fucked and how her ass cheeks would jiggle. Eboni put you in the frame of mind of Delishis, Flavor Flav's love interest. She even had those deep dimples.

"I'm not hatin', especially over no ho. And she is definitely a ho. But I bet you I could get her to suck my dick before we bounce outta here tonight!" he challenged.

"How much, nigga?" Seven wanted to know, as he went to pulling out a roll of cash. Almighty and Tax went to digging in their pockets as well.

"Put me down," Almighty said.

"Me, too," Tax added.

"What up, y'all?" Freeze said as he and Eboni approached the table.

"You playa!" Seven answered. "What's up, Miss Lady?" He couldn't help but look at Eboni's nipples which were poking through her dress.

She just smiled as she held on tight to Freeze. She didn't want to look over at Tareek. So he decided he was gonna use this opportunity to fuck with her. "What's up, Eboni?" Tareek's tone was of somebody who knew a secret you didn't.

"Hey," she responded, still unable to look in his direction.

"Your husband takes the leash off for one night and you can't wait to fuck around on him." He was still using that tone.

"Actually, he's locked up. And you should know he don't, or no one for that matter will ever, have a leash on this." She smirked. "Freeze, baby, fill them in on what went down with Kreesha." Eboni wanted to get the spotlight off of her before things got outta hand.

"I thought you was going to tell them."

"I need to go to the ladies' room." She kissed him on the cheek and headed for the bathroom, but not before looking over her shoulder and giving Tareek a nasty look. She knew she was wrong for fuckin' with two niggas in the same crew. At first Tareek had been discreet, since he was married, but then he got bold and started calling the house and was wanting to get with her almost every day. That was pushin' it too close. He was also a nigga with a crazy wife which made him not worth the drama. Eboni was a free spirit and hated when niggas tried to smother her and get possessive. That was why her own husband was treated with a long-handled spoon. She was starting to catch feelings for Freeze and was liking his style. As far as she knew, Freeze didn't know about her and Tareek.

Freeze grabbed a chair and sat down at the table. "That big nigga Buck came over to Roscoe's and caused a scene. Eboni said they had just got in a shipment and hadn't even unloaded it when this nigga busted the car window, trying to drag Eboni out. Old man Roscoe pulled out his piece and everything." Everybody broke out into laughter.

"Oh, shit!" Almighty laughed.

"That ain't all. Dumb-ass Buck ignores the piece and still acts crazy. Corey had to come out swinging the baseball bat. He was beatin' his ass. And that's when the nosy-ass neighbors called the Po Po. Now, don't forget Kreesha got all that weed on her. She manages to get off the block, but they catch up with her after she leaves 7–Eleven. Now she got all that shit on her, but guess what?" He paused for dramatic effect. No one bit, so he finished the story. "They bring the dogs and prepare to check her out, but they get another call and jets! Is that luck or what?" Freeze was shaking his head in disbelief. "That shit would have never went down like that for me."

"Damn," Seven said. "You ain't never lied! Wouldn't have went that way for me either. I would have been under the jail by now."

Looking around, Freeze noticed all the money sitting out on the table.

"Tareek, make sure you let Kreesha know that she need to lay low or change up. If she ain't already flagged, she will be shortly. I'll check and see what I can find out. They just don't let niggas walk like that. Y'all feel me?" Seven was a little concerned.

"Somebody need to handle that nigga Buck. That shit was uncalled for. Especially over some pussy. He gone get everybody busted," Almighty said.

"Shit! His wife is the problem, not him!" Tax joked, looking over at Freeze. "I don't fuck with jealous husbands or married bitches. Couldn't be me. I'd have to fuck a bitch up."

"Fuck that! I like them married hos. Everything is out on the table, and they are very low maintenance when it comes to time." He emphasized the word time. Then he waved his hands. "Fuck that, nigga! Ain't nobody scared of him but your punk ass! He obviously ain't doing something right at home!" Freeze barked.

Tareek was sitting there pissed off at the entire conversation. He threw back a shot of Hennessey and Coke, wanting to beat Eboni's ass.

"Tareek, just make sure you let Kreesha know what time it is." Seven had interrupted Tareek's train of thought.

"Yeah. Speaking of Kreesha, that nigga she been going to see down at the prison is either home or on his way home," Almighty told them.

"What nigga?" Seven wanted to know because his radar shot up.

"Reign." Almighty noticed the confused look on Seven's face.

"You remember that nigga who shot Big Mo?"

"Oh!" Seven and Tax said at the same time.

"Yeah, I remember that nigga." Seven motioned for a waitress. "As long as he stays outta my way, I don't have a problem with him. That wasn't my beef."

"Aiight, man. Sleep if you want to. But I'm telling you, it's something about that nigga. I just can't put my finger on it," Almighty warned.

"Yeah. I have to agree," Tax cut in. "But like Seven said, as long as he stay out of our way, fuck him."

"I don't know how we gonna overlook him, since he's sniffing up the ass of our little sista." Tareek stood his short, stocky but muscular frame up and snatched up all the money off the table. "Let me go take y'all niggas' money!" Everyone laughed except for Freeze.

"What's so funny?" Freeze wanted to know.

No one bothered to answer as Tax and Almighty held their stomachs, laughing and pointing at Tareek as he walked away, waving the money he had in his hands.

"Y'all better tell me what the fuck y'all laughing at!" Freeze didn't see anything funny.

"You'll see in a minute!" Seven said through fits of laughter.

"Fuck y'all drunk-ass niggas. Laughing like y'all bitches and shit!" Freeze nixed them off. He looked around and yelled, "Where the fuck is that waitress at with my dranks!"

Eboni was standing in a circle talking to two of her associates, Nina and Rose, when Tareek eased up behind her, put his arm around her waist, and started to walk her to the back. "What are you doing, Tareek?" she asked as she tried to remove his arm.

"You need to be answering that question. You the one fuckin' my boy and all up in his face and shit. Where is the respect? Do he know we was fuckin'?" She didn't answer. "What you going to the highest bidder?" He was looking around for a dark corner. When he couldn't find one, he began leading her toward the bathroom.

"What are you doin'?" She wanted to know.

"What you doin'? You thought you was gonna be able to trick with us both? You a bold bitch! But you know what? You done fucked over the wrong nigga! What's gettin' me pissed is you ain't even trying to be discreet about the shit."

"Nigga, please! The last time I checked this was a free country. And you know me and you was just fuckin'. It was nothing serious. I don't know why you catchin' feelings." She noticed they were at the bathroom. "Why we stopping here?"

"We gonna talk." Tareek's ego was bruised at that last statement. It was on fo' real now. He had thought they had something or at least he thought that he was more than just a trick ass fuck.

"We already talked. I said all that I had to say. Freeze is going to come looking for me."

"Bitch, please!" Tareek laughed. "You just a fuck to the man. He's not concerned about your whereabouts."

Eboni was now getting nervous. "We can talk right here. Why we gotta go in the bathroom?"

" 'Cause you a ho. And I bet my crew that tonight you would be sucking my dick."

"Nigga, you done lost your mind!" She was trying to break away. "Freeze!" she screamed.

The bathroom door flew open, and a drunken couple came wobbling out. The female was fixing her clothes while her partner was leaning over her, trying to keep from falling. Tareek pushed Eboni into the bathroom, slammed the door shut, and locked it.

"Tareek, why is you trippin' like this?" Eboni was pissed because her gun was in her purse back at the table.

"I ain't trippin'. I just want my dick sucked, that's all. I want you to swallow, then go out there and kiss my man. Do that like the ho that you are." He was unzipping his pants.

"Nigga, you done lost your m—" POW! Tareek had punched her in the mouth before she could even finish that sentence. He yanked her by her hair. "Ooooww!" she squealed. Her neck and shoulders were still sore from when Buck beat her ass.

"I lost my what?" He watched in satisfaction as her tears fell down her cheeks, then said, "That's what I thought! Don't get it twisted! Now suck me off!" he ordered, grabbing her hair even tighter and pushing her down to her knees.

"Tareek, I don't want to," she pleaded, "you're hurting me."

"C'mon, girl. I ain't got all night." He slapped her again before placing his dick to her lips. "Don't fight it. Just suck me and get it over," he whispered as her tongue circled the head. He rammed his fist upside her head. "Suck harder! You know how I like it." She immediately began to suck harder. "You know you like this shit. Aaahh," he moaned as he watched her while still holding on to a fistful of her hair. "Bitch, suck a little harder! Shit, this feels good." He watched her work a few more minutes before making her stop. He motioned for her to stand up. "I may as well go ahead and get me some of this. Turn around. Let me get some for the road, since you want to fuck me and my man."

"Tareek, no," she begged as he was already pushing her so that she was bending over the sink and her cheek was smashed against the mirror. Before she knew it he was tearing off her thong and was pounding away inside of her pussy. "No, Tareek. Please."

"Ho, you done fucked over the wrong nigga." Humph! Humph! Humph! He pounded some more. "You tell anybody this happened, I'ma fuck you up so bad you're gonna wish you was dead, and then I'ma tell that country-ass husband of yours what a nasty ho you are." Humph! Humph! Humph! "Damn, this pussy is good. Who got the best dick?" Tareek was pissed off and felt that he wasn't dogging her enough, so he punched her in her head over and over.

Eboni was crying silently. She didn't even feel like opening her mouth. *How did I allow myself to get caught slippin'?* she asked herself. She felt relieved when he pulled out of her pussy, but screamed in agony when she felt him tearing her a new asshole. "Oh, God! Somebody help me!" she screamed out in searing pain. This wasn't the first time taking it in the ass but he was being savage with the shit. Tareek was now satisfied that he hurt this bitch.

"Who got the best dick? Answer me, bitch!" Humph! Humph! "Too late, bitch, I'm coming!" He trembled as he pulled out of her asshole and purposely came all over the back of her Coogi dress. Out of breath, he said, "Hurry up, turn around and suck me off. Make sure every last drop is gone." He pushed her to her knees once again. "Now answer me. Who got the best dick you ever had?" He slid his dick out of her mouth. "Answer me, bitch!"

"Damn. Where the fuck is Eboni? What the fuck, she go all the way home to use the bathroom?" Freeze looked around the club before standing up to go find her.

"Find Tareek and you most likely will find Eboni," Tax teased, but said it only for Seven and Almighty to hear. They all burst out laughing once again with Eboni being the brunt of the joke and all of them drunk as hell.

Something told Freeze to go check out the bathroom.

Chapter 7

"I'll get back at you," Doggy Mac says, looking up at Reign, smirking, and then pulling off.

"So that's the nigga who been keepin' you warm at night?" He wastes no time as he watches the Benz turn the corner.

"If he is, so what?" I push his arms from around me and say, "I suggest you worry about who's keeping your wife warm at night." I break for my front door with him on my heels.

Now keep in mind that I'm still in shock that this nigga showed up at my spot. My heart is pounding and my hands are sweaty. I've been waiting for this nigga and had planned it all the way down to how I would spoon feed him while serving him breakfast in bed. We talked about this day numerous times. But leave it to a nigga to pop up unexpectantly, catch me totally unprepared, and fuck everything up. This has been my number one fantasy for the last year. But now here he is in the flesh, and I am actually watching him close my front door and lock it.

"Can I get something to drink?" he asks as he throws his bag on the floor. I'm still speechless as I mechanically walk to the kitchen, open the refrigerator, and grab the liter of Sprite, and a glass, which I fill with crushed ice. When I walk back into the living room he's coming out of my dining room.

"You got some nice shit up in here." He grabs the glass out of my hand, brushes past me, and plops down on my white Italian leather sofa. I sit down across from my baby, but not before I slide the coaster in front of him. I do not play about my wrought-iron marble coffee table. He guzzles it down, and like a brotha with some home training, he places the glass on the coaster. He's staring at me. "So? That's the nigga you been allowing to keep you warm at night?"

I suck my teeth because I see he ain't gonna let that one ride. You know how niggas do. So I use this as an excuse to get up because him staring at me is making me nervous. It's weird because I feel like I know him, but then again I don't know him. I've never been around him other than inside of a visiting hall.

"Where you goin'? Come here." He pats the spot next to him. "I just asked a simple question. You fuckin' him or what?"

"Are you still gonna be fuckin' your wife?" Two can play this game. I sit back down but across from him. His long legs are stretched out as he leans back onto the couch, not taking his eyes off of me.

"Damn, girl. This shit is goin' down all wrong." He has the nerve to start smiling at a time when I don't see shit funny.

"What's so funny?" My defenses are all the way up at this point.

He throws both hands up in the air. "This whole scenario. Come over here. Why you sittin' way over there?" I slowly come over and sit next to him. He leans over and kisses my lips. "This wasn't supposed to go down like this."

He's looking all serious. "A nigga sits for years and fantasizes about how it's gonna go down when he steps in the crib." He closes his eyes as if he is visualizing it before he continues. "His woman is waiting for him with open arms, wearing a see-through negligee, got a bubble bath waiting, where she undresses him, bathes him, and feeds him strawberries while he's soaking in the tub. He then gets out the tub and gets his dick sucked until he comes and his woman swallows every drop. Then he licks her from head to toe, then eats her pussy until she comes and her body is twitchin' and jerkin'. Then you just fuck each other into a coma."

"Now that's what's up," I mumble under my breath as I cross my legs. This nigga has my pussy's full attention. That fantasy sounds damn good to me.

"You feel what I'm sayin', Kreesha?" He snaps me out of my stupor. But I don't say nothing. I just look at him. "Sometimes shit won't go as planned for a nigga. Instead of getting greeted with open arms, I step to the crib and my Shawdy all up in some other nigga's face, half naked, and he feeling all over her nipples and shit!"

Damn, so he did see that.

"I step inside the crib and got to ask for something to drink. I feel like a stranger. And my woman got the nerve to have a chip on her shoulder, like I did something wrong. Shit's crazy!" He puts a smirk on his face. Then again pops the question, "Are you fuckin' that nigga or what?"

"Pump yo' breaks because first of all it's none of your business. I'm not the married one here. You need to be worrying about fuckin' your wife or who in the hell she's fuckin', 'cause, newsflash, I ain't your wife!" Now I'm pissed. Hurt. Jealous. I feel used. Just unsure at this point. When I see the crazy look he's giving me, I get nervous and go ahead and confess. "No, I'm not fuckin' him and never have. He has a wife. A wife! Which brings me to ask myself, Why am I wasting my time with you?"

"Hold up. Hold up." He raises his voice at me, but at the same time he places his hand on my knee. "Let's start this shit over, aiight?" I just look at him. "Aiight? You knew I had a wife and I told you I don't know what's gonna be up with that until I got home. And you said cool. So why we even talkin' about her? My first stop was here. I'm at your crib, damn Shawdy."

We're just staring at each other, and it's so quiet all you can hear is the hum of the air conditioner.

Yeah. The nigga do have a point. I do have to give him some kool points for that one. However, I'm not gonna let him know it. "So, what? You think that you're just gonna run up in both of us? You want me to play the role? Be at your beck and call whenever you can get away from wifey?" I need to hear him say it, say that he's not gonna shit on me.

"C'mon, Kree. I'm here with you. It's you I want."

"So, what? Are you gonna divorce her? Yes or no, Reign?" I'm pissed and ridin' high on this emotional rollercoaster. I want him. I don't want to let him go. I want him to dump that ho that he calls a wife. I want this nigga all to my God-damned self. "Yes or no, Reign?" Damn it! I don't want him to see me break down. My eyes are filling up with tears. Fuck! I turn my head and wipe them off real quick before I turn to face him again. I want an answer. "Nigga, what?" I stand up, and I'm poking his forehead with my index finger. I'm so fuckin' gone over this nigga it ain't even funny.

He grabs my wrist and pulls me back down. "Why you sweatin' the dumb shit? You ready to fuck up what we have because you trippin' over shit that for real don't even matter!"

I see that I done pissed him off because he stands up. For real, I'm trying not to panic because I don't want him to go. But now I'm acting like a bitch. My breathing is sporadic, and those punk-ass tears are falling again. My pride still wants to hear him say it. Say it's gonna be me. Tell me I'll be the only one and he's divorcing the bitch, today. I'm looking up at him, thinking those thoughts, but the words won't come out. The only thing coming out is air from me gasping for more air. I must look pitiful because he grabs my wrist, pulls me up, and wraps his arms around me.

"Shawdy, don't cry. We gonna be aiight. I'm here with you and that's all that matters. Let me deal with my shit. I'll handle the divorce shit."

There! He almost said it! For now that is good enough. This unexpected homecoming has worn me out. My breathing is quickly returning back to normal, and I'm no longer crying. We're just standing there hugging.

"I thought you told me that you was gonna give me a big welcome home?" he whispers in my ear. I feel that magic stick gettin' hard as he squeezes my fat ass. "You not even glad to see a nigga." He tries to sound disappointed. This time he slaps my fat ass.

"I am glad to see you. But what about what you told me that you was gonna do to me as soon as you walked through the door?"

"Oh, it's like that?"

"It is what it is." I grab his ear the way that he likes me to grab it, and with that he begins to slowly undress me. Then he fires me up by kissing my face, neck, sucking my breasts, kissing the inside of my thighs, my knees, to my feet, back up to the insides of my thighs; then he starts fingering me.

I'm so wet I can hear my pussy moanin'. I look at his pretty, pussy-sucking lips and start praying. "Please, Lord, let this nigga know what he's doing because I really need to bust a nut. I'm sick and tired of doing myself."

He gets on his knees, and then I yell, "Oh, shit!" as the tip of his tongue is pressing against the tip of my clit. I grab that nigga's head with both hands and put it in a grip. "Now what, nigga?" I moan as I start to grind against his tongue. He's now lapping my pussy as if his freedom depends on it. Before I know what hit me I start to skeetin', and this nigga is not letting up. Now that's what I'm talkin' about. A nigga who swallows! If he can swallow, I can swallow. Now I'm sitting here spent, out of breath, and my pussy is twitchin' and jerkin'. I just busted a hella nut!

He stands up and starts to tear his clothes off as he's looking at me and says, "Now, bitch, what's up?"

Yeah, you got that, I'm thinking to myself. I'm so spent I can't even talk, only think. That shit was the bomb! Now he's standing here in front of me buck naked with his dick at attention. I can't talk, but I can suck some dick. Damn, and it's pretty, too . . . I get down, lean up, and start slurpin' his wand like it's a strawberry snow cone with extra strawberry syrup. Now, y'all know that shit is good. But just as I'm gettin' in the groove he grabs my head to stop me.

"I'm not ready to come yet."

Well, all right! You ain't said nothing but six magic words. I look at his dick, and it's long, hard, black, and pretty. He leans over, places his arms under my thighs, and lifts me up. Now that's what I'm talking about! A strong mandingo nigga that can handle a sista. I slide down on his dick and we both moan. He's holding me steady while I begin what I'm praying is a nice, long ride.

* * *

Meanwhile at wifey's

Brinng! Brinng! Sparkle groaned at the sound of the phone ringing. She took off today to prepare for Reign's homecoming party tomorrow. She was up all night scrubbing, dusting, washing, and redecorating. Today all she had to do was go grocery shopping and pick up Reign a couple more outfits. *Brinng! Brinng!*

"All right! All right! Damn!" She rolled over and snatched up the phone. "Hello."

"Hello! This is Jim Lowell. I need to speak with Mr. Reign Johnston."

Sparkle became alert and sat up, swinging her legs around on the side of the bed. "This is Mrs. Johnston. Who may I ask is calling?"

"I'm Jim Lowell from the U.S. Probation Office. I'm Mr. Johnston's PO and I need to reschedule our Friday appointment for today. He has until seven o'clock to get in my office."

"Mr. Lowell, how do you expect him to get into your office today when he doesn't get out until tomorrow?"

"Tomorrow? I thought . . . Hold on for me, Mrs. Johnston."

Sparkle was left alone to listen to elevator music. "This dumb cracker. Already harassing a brotha and he ain't even out yet. This is ridiculous," she said over the music.

"Mrs. Johnston. I'm looking at the paperwork in front of me. Your husband was released at seven o'clock this morning. Just make sure he finds his way into my office by seven tonight!" Mr. Lowell hung up without even saying goodbye.

Sparkle was sitting on the side of the bed still holding the phone as the tears flowed endlessly down her cheeks. The loud ear-banging beep the phone gives off when you leave it off the hook too long snapped Sparkle out of her trance. She hung the phone up, wiped her eyes, then picked the receiver back up.

Her best friend, Ameca, answered on the first ring. "Damn, was you waitin' by the phone for me or what?" Sparkle said through sniffles.

"What's up? I'm waiting on the job to call me back. What's the matter with you? Are those tears of joy I'm hearing?"

"Please. I wish. You ain't gonna believe this shit, but I'm just calling to make sure you have my extra set of house keys and everything else in case of an emergency. And whatever you do, don't give that nigga a set of keys."

"You know I have everything. What's up?"

"Reign came home today, and I'm on my way over to that bitch's house because that's where he is."

"What do you mean he came home today?"

"Just like I said. The nigga got out today, and instead of bringing his ass home to his wife, where he belongs"—her voice was getting louder with each syllable—"he goes straight to the bitch's house! Can you believe that shit?"

Ameca couldn't even respond at first. Even she didn't see this coming. She had told Sparkle several times to leave Reign's ass alone and to let his ass rot in that prison. "Damn! Yeah, I can believe it. That's some foul shit. But what did you expect? Niggas ain't shit! Bottom line. That's why I'm gettin' me a white man. Fuck all of them!"

Sparkle sucked her teeth. "I ain't going out like that. But God only knows what I'm going to do when I roll up over there and that nigga is posted up. If you don't hear from me, then you know what time it is."

"Naw. Fuck that! Swing by and pick me up. I'm going with you."

"Girl, please. You do not need to be there. Just handle

my business in case I get locked up." Sparkle hung up the phone. She turned to the mirror, looking at her puffy eyes, then snatched off the silk scarf she had wrapped around her head, threw on her sweats, and headed for the door. She stopped dead in her tracks when she realized she hadn't even brushed her teeth or washed her face. "Fuck!" she cursed, and ran upstairs to the bathroom. Before she knew it she was in the Legend driving like a bat outta hell over to the woman's house she had just visited two days ago.

Back at Kreesha's

I'm holding on for dear life, not being able to tell the difference who's hollering the loudest, me or Reign. Then bam! This nigga busts. When I'm sure that's what he did, I don't know whether to scratch his eyes out or beg him to keep pumpin'. I feel his dick shrink up, and it slips out as he eases me back down onto the sofa in slow motion. "You came?" I yell. "You came?" I push him away from me, causing him to fall back onto my marble table. He's looking at me as if I done lost my mind. "I waited a whole fuckin' year for this?" I scream. "That weak-ass fuck?"

"What the fuck is the matter with you?" Now he looks like he wants to slap me.

"Nigga, please!" I say in disgust as I'm looking around for my shorts. "Nigga, that was nothing but what? Three/ four minutes? You could've at least waited for me to get mines!" I'm livid as I'm jumping around on one foot, trying to squeeze my big ass into my tight-ass shorts.

"Girl, you got one off. I know I'm allowed to get me one!"

"Fuck you, Reign!" I'm pissed to the umpth degree. "What! You saving your energy for wifey?" I'm so mad I can't see straight. Our first argument at home is interrupted by the doorbell. "Who the fuck is it?" I scream as I'm putting on my shirt. Reign is standing there ass naked, and I don't give a fuck as I go and snatch the door open, almost tearing it off the hinges.

"I need to see Reign. I know he's here." It's wifey.

"Come in and get this nigga! You can have him!" She looks surprised that I say that. I guess she thought that I was gonna put up a fight. Normally, I would have. But that punk-ass move he made by coming so quick pissed me the fuck off. I step aside, motioning for her to come in, and then I slam the door shut. I cross my arms and wait to see how Prince Playa Playa is gonna get outta this one. Black-ass minute man!

Chapter 8

Tareek slapped Eboni across her face. "Who got the best dick, bitch?" Eboni peered up at him but didn't respond. "Ho, you gonna answer me!" He snatched her up by her hair. Blood was trickling down her nose.

"You got the best dick, Tareek." She stared at him with eyes that could cut through steel. She felt like shit. Her ass was sore, her head was pounding, and she felt cold.

"That's what I thought. Now fix yourself up and I suggest that you slow your roll." As he fixed his clothes, he said, "You fuckin' with the big dawgs. You can trick and mack them lil'-ass niggas all day. But I ain't one of them lil' punk-ass niggas. Baby, Tareek is a big dawg!" He slapped himself in the chest. "And big dawgs don't like to be tricked. I ain't no trick."

There was a knock at the door. Eboni breathed a sigh of relief. Her black knight was here to save her. "Yo, Eboni!" Freeze called out.

Tareek placed his hand on the doorknob. "I'm gettin' ready to teach you a very valuable lesson. I'ma show you what I mean about you rollin' with the big dawgs." He opened the door wide enough so that Freeze could see Eboni standing there. Freeze looked her over, then Tareek stepped out and shut the door behind him. Then he thought about it and left a crack in it. Eboni went to yank it open. "Bitch, you betta get off this fuckin' door!" he warned her. She turned it loose and stepped back.

"What's up?" Eboni heard Freeze ask.

"This ho thinks everybody is a trick. I'm teaching her that that ain't even the case. I don't know how she thought that she could fuck with two niggas in the same crew. Not this crew. Why you ain't tell her, man? I know you knew I was already fuckin' her."

"Tell her?" Freeze looked at Tareek as if he were crazy. "Tell her for what, pimp? You know how good she sucks a nigga off?" They both laughed.

When Eboni heard Freeze say that, she muffled her mouth so they couldn't hear her bawling like a baby. She couldn't believe that she was feelin' this nigga and he was just as grimey as they came.

"Hell yeah, I know she takes the skin off a dick. That's why I came back here so that she could do just that, suck me off!" They both started laughing harder and gave each other a pound.

"This ho thinks you really like her," Tareek told him on a serious note.

"Yeah. I do. I really like the way she sucks my dick." The burst of laughter cut Eboni to the core. "Man, on a serious tip, if she fuck around like she do on that chump-ass husband she got, what the fuck you think she gonna do to me? I ain't no fuckin' chump, but a ho is a ho in my book and I sho' ain't tryna turn one into a housewife." Freeze swore.

"Man, for real, though. I was feelin' her," Tareek confessed.

"That's because you's a chump-ass nigga," Freeze teased. "I just told you man, you can't turn a ho into a housewife! Only a chump-ass nigga like you wouldn't know that. Now

move outta my way so that I can get my knob slobbed."
Freeze grabbed for the doorknob.

"Hold up a minute." Tareek stopped him. When he
opened the door all of the way, Eboni backed into the corner. "Oh, you don't have to be scared; I'm done with you. I
told you I had a lesson to teach you," Tareek said as he
eased back into the bathroom, closing the door behind him,
leaving Freeze out there. "My man, he wants to holla at
you. But before he do that, I just wanted to tell you to get
yourself together. If you don't want to do that, then stop
playin' yourself tryna fuck with the big dawgs and go back
to trickin' with them lil' punk-ass niggas."

They heard Freeze yelling at somebody, telling them to
go use the other bathroom.

"Tareek, don't let him in here. Please don't let him in
here. I'ma get myself together," she begged, unable to stop
herself from crying.

"You wanted to talk shit earlier. Now you pleadin' for
mercy?"

"Tareek. Please don't do me like this." When he went to
reopen the door, she grabbed his shirt. He turned around
and mugged her face, causing her back to slam up against
the wall. He left, and Freeze went in and closed the door behind him.

Tareek made his way back to the table where his crew
was. He immediately snatched up the money on the table
and began waving the dollars around. "That ho can suck a
mean dick!" he boasted. "Y'alls' money was well spent, I
can tell you that much."

"Damn. It took you long enough. What you do, get
some pussy, too?" Freaky-ass Tax wanted to know.

"You know it, nigga! Now alls I need is a blunt and a
bottle of Dom P and it's a wrap!"

Meanwhile, Buck was just released and on his way home to an empty house.

Freeze pulled his pants up as he glared at Eboni. His heart was crushed.

"You finished?" she sobbed.

"Why? You ain't like it?" She shook her head no. "Bitch, I can't believe I was diggin' you. What? Why? Why you had to go and fuck my nigga? How you gonna fuck him but come to the club with me? I'm surprised that I didn't slit your throat."

"He made me come in here!" she screamed. "He raped me, Freeze."

"That's bullshit. You expect me to believe that shit?"

"It's true. You knew I was fuckin' him way before I started messin' with you and if he didn't rape me then why I look like this?" She pleaded.

"Rape, huh? Bitch, you got too much game with you." He shot her a look of disgust and left without saying another word.

By the time Eboni made her way from the bathroom, the club was crunk.

"Eboni!" Seven yelled out over the music. The attention of everyone at the table turned on her. "C'mere babygirl. You look like you been dragged in a cat fight."

She shot Tareek a look that said, "You ain't gettin' away with this."

Chapter 9

I peep the whole thing. Wifey takes about three steps before stopping dead in her tracks. It looks as if her legs are about to give out. I can feel her. I know that she can smell the sex that's permeating the air. This bitch then starts walking through my house as if she lives here. So now I'm beginning to follow behind her as if she's a crack head while making sure she's not trying to steal anything. After she found my dining room she—or rather we—head straight for the living room to where Reign is. This nigga has the audacity to be calm as shit as he's putting his pants on.

He looks at me and then turns back to her. "What are you doing here?"

"What am I doing here? Nigga, you have no idea what's running through my mind right now!" She is trying not to scream.

"Yeah, bitch! I know what's running through your mind. What? I told you it wasn't a wrap, boo. Your husband is straight outta the pen, and the dick ain't fresh no more. I busted his cherry. Instead of having his ass home with you he's at his other woman's house. What? You can't say shit now? You ready to kill somebody? That's what's running through your mind? Well, we face to face, bitch!"

"Reign, get this ho before I—"

"Kreesha, chill the fuck out!"

Sparkle shot Kreesha a look of triumph.

"Nigga, your PO called and said you need to get in to see him *today*."

I watch in anticipation as she storms over to where he stands and begins doing one of my numbers, poking him in the forehead with her middle finger.

"Reign, what in the hell is the matter with you? Has that little bit of time turned this brain into mush? I can't believe you would do something as gutter as this!"

"Gutter?" I had to laugh at that. "Bitch, if I'm gutter, yo' slow ass must be guttasnipe. And like I said, he stopped here first. I got the dick already." That bitch amused herself ignoring me and kept on poking him until he bent over to grab his shirt. He's unfazed while slowly putting the shirt on.

I'm watching this nigga's mouth like a hawk, waiting for some words to come out. But his slick ass don't say nothing! I can tell that she's just as anxious for him to speak as I am. I can also tell that this is really fucking her up. The bitch is totally humiliated. If I was her, shit, it would be on and poppin'. He's now fully dressed and still not talking as he walks out of the living room and leaves the two of us standing there. We both run behind him. Imagine that!

He's standing in the middle of the dining room looking himself up and down. "Shit!" he mumbles. "Where are all the mirrors?"

Oh no he didn't! We both look at him, our mouths hanging open. He looks at me, and when I don't answer, he says, "Fuck it! Don't you got something for me to wear?"

And before I know it, wifey is charging toward him, getting ready to fuck his ass up. He grabs her by both wrists and gives her that look that unmistakably says, "Bitch, you don't wanna go there!" Her body language says that she gets the message. She ain't as dumb as I thought. Then he says, "Let me change outta this prison shit. We'll talk in the car." You could have bought that bitch for a penny. "Aiight?" He steps close to her. "Chill for me, aiight?"

That ho is so mad she is trembling. But here I am getting jealous at the way he's talking to her. He got love for her and I don't like it.

"Go wait for me in the car while I change."

She snatches away from him. "I know you done lost your fuckin' mind if you think for one fuckin' minute I'ma go sit in some fuckin' car! Let's go now, Reign!" she orders.

"Who the fuck you raisin' your voice at?" I asked.

"Let me get outta this prison shit!" he fires at her. "Kree, get me something to wear." He has the nerve to sound agitated, as if I did something wrong.

"You got clothes at your home. The home where you should be!" wifey blurts out. Well damn, she doesn't give me a chance to say anything; he's talking to me, which means that she done fucked up. Because for real I wasn't gonna oblige the nigga, but since she wants to overstep her boundaries, in my house, two can play this game. The bitch oughta be glad I even let her ass in.

"You got clothes here, too." I am talking to him but looking at her.

He turns to wifey and says, "You can sit here or wait in the car, but like I said I'ma get outta this prison shit." And he starts for the stairs. She just stands there with her mouth open. I swear on my brother, it couldn't be me!

I follow him up the stairs. When he gets in the hallway he has to stop because the nigga don't know where the fuck he is going. I bump past him, walk straight to my bedroom, to my closet, and yank it open. "Pick out one outfit and leave the rest of my shit right where you see it." I sit down on my bed and cross my legs and then my arms across my chest. I was giving him major attitude.

"How is it your shit when you bought it for me?" All I can hear is the hangers sliding across the pole. I had this nigga a couple of suits, gators, Sean John, Vokal, FUBU, Ecko, Phat Farm, Enyce, you name it. This nigga can't help but be impressed. I see him smile as he holds up a white-and-blue RocaWear sweat suit. He lays it across the bed, then goes back and starts pulling out sneaker boxes. This nigga is like a kid in a candy store. Box tops are flying everywhere. I can't help but smile my damn self. He finally settles on a pair of white-on-white Air Force Ones. He starts undressing.

"You got me some underwear, right?"

I roll my eyes, then suck my teeth as I get up and go to the dresser that I have just for his things. I yank it open and then throw him a pack of boxers.

He snatches them outta the air. "Thanks."

I sit back on the bed.

After he's fully dressed, he checks himself out in the mirror. Once he's pleased with his appearance he comes over to the bed where I'm sitting, leans over, and places his palms facedown on the bed next to my thighs. He goes to kiss me on the cheek. With the quickness, I turn away from him.

"Oh, so it's like that?" he says real low and sexy.

"Yeah. It's like that from here on out. It's over between us."

He ignores what I just said and stares at me. I guess he knows I didn't mean it. "Don't think that I don't appreciate the time you did with me and all this shit here." He points his head over toward the closet. "I got you. A nigga appreciates shit like this."

I suck my teeth, trying to have mad attitude, but hearing him say that is breaking me down.

"When I come back over later tonight, you gonna let me in, right?"

Now this shocks the shit outta me. But I manage to play it off and give him that "*nigga,* please!" look.

"You gonna let me in? You know I gotta set the record straight. You think because of how it went down earlier a brotha can't bang your back out. You ain't even give a nigga a chance. No mercy on a brotha getting outta the pen a few hours ago and ain't had no pussy in years. Just because you don't bust three nuts, you get an attitude."

This time I let him kiss me on the lips. Only because he's making sense. I didn't look at the shit like that.

"Reign, don't insult my intelligence. You know you are not coming back tonight. Do not even play yourself, and I'm definitely not allowing you to play me anymore."

"Aiight. You'll see, I'ma come back and tear that ass up, watch. Can I have a kiss now?" I turn my head and he kisses me on the cheek. "Can I have a kiss? Please?" This time I turn to face him and he grazes my lips. "You know I got mad love for you, right?"

Damn it! I can't hold back the tears. He begins kissing them.

"Kree. Stop crying. I told you I got you." Then we kiss like we did on the visits; long, passionate, wet, and hard. We're in the zone. That is until wifey screams.

"Nigga, you got me fucked up!"

Damn! We forgot all about her. She's standing in the doorway looking crazy. I push Reign outta the way. "Bitch! How the fuck you gonna come up my stairs? This is my fuckin' house! I didn't invite you up my stairs!" We go charging for each other like two pit bulls. Then this bitch wants to play dirty. She pulls out a gun.

Reign yells, "Sparkle, no! What the fuck—" And that's the last thing I heard.

Three months later

"Damn!" I thought I was dead. I never got shot before. Last time I talked to y'all we were in my bedroom. That bitch had the nerve to shoot me in my arm, in my bedroom, in my own house! She is soooooo lucky it went in one side and out the other. I still thought I was dead. I nutted up like a bitch as soon as I felt the impact and burn of the bullet. What can I say? There's a first time for everything. But guess what? As soon as I was able, I pressed charges against that bitch. They locked her up and everything. I wish I could have been a fly on the wall when Reign went to see his PO and had to explain that his wife shot somebody on his first day out of prison, that she got locked up, *and* his lover pressed all types of charges. However, you know they are beggin' me to drop them. What? They must be outta their fuckin' minds! I want this bitch outta our lives. I want this bitch to go to prison. Pregnant and all. Yeah, you heard right . . . pregnant and all. Remember this is three months later.

On the relationship note, one that I don't like to sing too much, we are both pregnant. Yup! I'm six weeks and wifey is five weeks. You know she is pissed off royally that I'm pregnant. Shit, she's pregnant and I'm pissed off, too! He's my man just as much as he's hers. You feel me? One thing for sure, two for certain, he's in my bed every night. He may get up at two or three in the morning and go home to her, but that's something we both have to learn to deal with. I know I'm dealin'. And by the way, he did make good on his bedroom skills. No more complaints from me. My nigga is a real freak between the sheets. We lick each other's assholes and the whole nine yards.

On the business tip, shit is crazy! For some strange reason my weed business has almost doubled since Reign has been home. I'm not complaining but shit is just taxin'. Lots of times I'm tired as hell. But other than that I'm feelin' good and I like making money. I just wish my road dawg Eboni was able to roll with me. Let me give y'all the 411 on her. First of all, I don't know what happened with or what happened to her. Maybe she had a revelation from on high. I don't know. Alls I do know is that ole girl had locked herself in the house and was playing the ultimate goody-two-shoes housewife. That ho just flipped the script on me. She wouldn't go out or nothing. Buck was happy as shit. I had to find someone else to roll with whenever I wanted to get my party on. Reign don't even like to dance. However, and luckily for me the goody-two-shoes housewife charade lasted for about two whole months. Then she went back to being her true blue self. A ho! She dived right back into the same ole shit, staying out all night, totally disrespecting the fact that she had a husband at home. But this last time my girl stayed out one night too many. Buck caught her ass in the act. And this time he didn't even bother checkin' the nigga she was with. He beat Eboni until she was comatose, with a broken arm to match. She's now in a rehab center about forty miles from here. I'm on my way to pick her up.

When I get there this bitch is already packed and ready, sittin' in a wheelchair at the front door. I couldn't help but laugh at my roadie and partner in crime. She was looking like she just got her freedom papers. She's sittin' there with a sling on her arm, hair in braids, a pair of raggedy jeans, and a T-shirt.

"What's up, bitch?" I try to cheer her up. I figured she would be happy since she was going home. She gives me this fake smile as she slowly stands up.

"Ho, you're late," she snaps.

"I'm here ain't I?" I open the car door for her and then begin to load her few belongings into the trunk. "You know Buck is pissed off that you didn't let him come pick you up."

"He'll be all right."

"I swear, I don't understand how you got him so open," I tell her.

"It ain't for you to understand. Plus, I didn't want him to come because I got something I want to get off my chest."

This is the most serious I ever saw Eboni. "Really? What's up?"

"Finish packing up my shit and get in the car." She got in the front seat and I closed the door then I finished loading up her stuff.

Once we got situated and I had been driving for about half an hour, this bitch finally decides to talk.

"I called Big Dee and them and told them I had something for them."

"Bitch, what?" Big Dee and his crew were some grimey ass jack boys that my brother would holla at. Quiet as it was kept, only me, him, and Eboni knew about them. They were once my brother's secret weapon, but now they were me and Eboni's. "You know you were supposed to consult with me first, bitch. What, now you startin' to take shit into your own hands? You need money that bad? How much you need?" Shit, the last time we called on them fools, they wreaked major havoc and Seven and them was going crazy. Niggas was gettin' jacked left and right and at least four bodies turned up. Me and Eb had to act just like the next man, we ain't know what the fuck was goin' on. On top of that we barely got away with Seven finding out that we called them. Big Dee did slip up and get sloppy. "You jokin', right?" I looked over at her while trying to read her facial expression.

"No, Kreesha. I'm not joking."

"Well you better call and cancel. Shit is already hot and I can't think of shit that could be going on in your life that is so crucial. Is it Buck?"

"No, Kreesha. I want them to get Freeze and Tareek."

I damn near swerved off the road. "Freeze and Tareek?" I started laughing. "You tryna shut down your own crew members? Bitch, what kind of medication they had you on up in that rehab joint?" I looked over at her ready to crack some jokes and the bitch was sheddin' tears. "Eboni, what the fuck is the matter with you?"

"Kreesha, they raped me."

"They what?"

She turned away from me and covered up her face.

"Oh my God, Eboni."

"You believe me, right?" She was staring at me.

"When? Where? How?" I rattled off questions while trying to digest what she told me. "Oh my God," were the only words that I could manage to say.

"Well . . . do you?"

"Them muthafuckas! Of course I believe you! What kind of question is that?"

"I'ma get 'em, Kree. I put that on my granddaddy. I swear, I'ma get 'em. I'ma hit 'em where it hurts."

"You gonna kill 'em? Oh God. Don't answer that. Right now I don't want to know. Give me some time all right? I gotta digest this shit. But know that I got yo' back."

"Don't worry. You ain't got nothin' to do with this. This is between me and them."

I couldn't believe my ears.

* * *

On the other business tip, and it's the shit that tried to stress me out, what was I supposed to do when my man, my baby's daddy, said, "Look, baby, you know I ain't cut out for this job thang. I need some cash and I can't see me livin' off of you. I ain't built like that. I need you to put me on. I gots to do what I gots to do." What do y'all think I did? You damn right! I put my nigga on. Y'all know y'all would have done the same thing, so stop frontin'. I put him on to my Colombian connect who I've been dealin' with for years. My brother turned me on to these peoples.

Now peep this. After the very first meeting, she pulled me to the side and told me, "Kreesha, don't bring him here no more. I won't do business in front of him. Me don't trust him. Something about him. Me don't trust him. Bring Eboni. Me trust her. But no, not him."

I was like, "What the fuck! Bitch do you know this is my man?"

But that ain't the kicker. My boys, who are really like family and have been family since way before my brother got killed and when I was a shorty, they keep saying the same shit. Shit like they don't like him, why I'ma let him use me like that, I should have checked with them first, and I wouldn't like it if they hooked up one of their females to take food off my table. They said that they make sure the weed is all me and that I should have put him on to the heroin not the coke.

I am pissed off. I can't believe them. They really are acting like they're starving. And they all are super pissed off at me. They're just being greedy. It's not like them niggas just got this area on lock. They got outta-town cats and outta-state niggas coming to get served. I think they're just jealous 'cause my nigga is comin' up and he's comin' up fast. So at this point in time: Fuck them niggas and my connect! None of them ain't keeping me warm at night. Can't Kreesha have some happiness?

So now it's me and my nigga against the world. I'm moving my weed, and he's moving his powder. The crew is giving me the cold shoulder. Every chance they get, they stepping to me about puttin' Reign on. We are constantly beefin'.

Reign buys wifey a new house. Everything is as well as can be expected.

Chapter 10

Damn! My baby Kree was now movin' almost five hundred pounds every two weeks. If her Colombian connect wouldn't deliver to her personally, they would then do the Express Mail thing she told y'all about. This week, we ran out of product, so today we got a little something coming to tie us over. We got six boxes to pick up at six different houses.

Kree is handling this pregnant thing pretty well. Most of the time I forget that she's pregnant. Wifey, on the other hand, is another story. She's worried about this gun charge that Kree won't drop. She's sick all of the time, the doctor is always putting her on bed rest, and she can't even work anymore. They both are four and a half months. This is my first time being a father, so this pregnant shit is new to me. And here I am doing it twice. I'ma bad nigga!

I know y'all wondering, especially the playas, how I can hold it down like I am. Let me use this as an opportunity to teach y'all a little sumthin' sumthin'! Love and greed are two of the strongest emotions. Kreesha got a lot of love for a nigga while wifey is greedy as hell. I pretty much kept wifey in check while I was on lock by making her understand that those car notes on that Legend was being made because of Kreesha coming on the visits bringin' shit in.

Kreesha's down for whatever. Now, since I'm out, I make sure wifey understands that the nice house she was just blessed to move into and her having the luxury of being able to quit her nine-to-five is because of what "that bitch" as she likes to call Kree, brings to the table. So whenever she starts to get all slick at the mouth, I am quick to remind her to "Don't hate the playa, hate the game."

Anyway, after me and my boo Kree makes our rounds and pick up the six boxes, we head over to the Grand Marquis to break the shit down. We may as well do it in style. We get us a suite. We always make sure we have fun doin' this shit. Oh, and before I forget to mention it, just in case y'all wondering, Kree is also the shit between the sheets. Talkin' about curlin' a nigga's toes and havin' him whinin' like a bitch, she be doin' that, and I ain't even frontin' on tellin' y'all. You should always give a bitch her props if she deserves it. Now wifey is pretty much basic. I can pretty much fuck her how I want to and it's a wrap. But Kree, that's my freak. A nigga can get fucked fo' sho'! I'm talkin' about dick sucked, ass licked, she even takes it in the ass. What Parliament-Funkadelic used to sing? "Freak of the Week"? Well, that's what's up! That's why I gotta keep my eyes on her; I don't want no other nigga to get that.

At about one-thirty I gets a page from my boy Merkski, my Chinese nigga. He needs five pounds of weed and says that folks are sittin' around waitin'.

"Make that nigga wait, Reign. Don't leave me here to do all this shit by myself," Kree whines as she watches me dump one box out and then stuff five pounds inside.

"He needs it now, baby," I try to reason with her.

"I don't give a fuck! Are you listening to me?"

"Look, Kree. We can do this one of two ways. We leave all this shit here and you come with me, or let me make this run and I'll be back in not more than two hours tops. What do you want to do?" I don't give her time to answer. "You might as well get started so that we can get it done. The sooner we get done we can do us. Aiight?" Once again I don't give her a chance to answer. I just grab the box, go over and get me a kiss. The way she kisses me back lets me know it's all good. That's all I need to know. Because I really need to make this run by myself. Merk's sister is fine as hell, and the last time I served Merk, she was there and I could tell Shawdy wanted to holla at me.

"Reign, if you don't come back, I'ma fuck your ass up. You stood me up the other night, had me dressed and waiting, and didn't even pick up the phone to call me. I know you took that bitch out instead. Don't think I forgot." Kree snapped on me.

"It wasn't even like that. I didn't want to tell you this, but since you keep bringing that shit up, I'ma tell you what happened."

"Tell it then!"

"Your peoples got at me. They was interrogatin' me and shit. They don't want you fuckin' with me, Kree. They threatened me and they threatened you."

Kree started to say something, but changed her mind. She was looking stupid. "I'ma call them niggas up. Who are they to tell me who I can and cannot see?"

And sure enough, before I get out the door good, she is on the phone trying to catch up with Seven. I jet.

I jumps in my Z28, pop in my G-Unit CD, and I'm out. Forty minutes later I pull up to the meeting spot. It's an apartment building, and he said he'd be in apartment 4C. Merk came through the pen while I was in and that's how we hooked up. So I do trust him enough to roll up in this apartment building solo, even though it ain't feeling right. I run my hand over my piece just in case.

Boom! Boom! Boom! "What the fuck!" Two little boys

who don't look more than ten are wrestling, and they are all up on my freshly waxed ride. "Yo! Yo! Yo!" I yell as I jump out and run around to the other side to pull them off of my ride and yank them apart. "Damn, y'all, it can't be that serious!"

"He started it!" the smallest one yells. He's small but he was whipping ole boy's ass.

"No, I didn't!" The bigger one is trying to defend himself but swings and misses, and now they are holding on to each other, trying to get some punches in.

"Hold up! Hold up!" I have to break these lil' niggas up again. "I'll give both of y'all some money to go buy some ice cream if y'all will stick together instead of fighting." Neither of them hesitates to take me up on my offer, nodding their heads up and down while holding out their palms. I pull out some cash and give them five dollars each. I tell them they can make five more if they watch my car until I come back. It's a wrap. I get the Express Mail box outta the backseat, hit my alarm, and go inside the building. It's pretty decent and the elevator works. When I step off of the elevator, I get to 4C and I knock.

"Who is it?" a female asks. It sounds like Merk's sister; at least I'm hoping it's her. I don't even know her name.

"It's Black. Is Merk there?" Black is the name I use when I'm takin' care of business. I hear the dead bolts being taken off, and then the door opens. There she is. Damn . . . Shawdy is fine.

"Come in," she says, lookin' me up and down. "Did Merk tell you to come here?" She sounded ghetto, just like a sista.

"I wouldn't be here if he didn't. Plus, don't you think it's too late to be askin' that question? You already let me in. Even though I would like to be *in* somewhere else, but business first." Fuck that beatin' around the bush shit. I go for it.

I know she got what I was sayin', but she tries to play it off. "I don't know why he would do that when he's not here." She grabs the cell phone. "Let me call him and let him know you're here." She disappears in the back. Didn't even offer a nigga a seat. Damn, Shawdy got a nice ass, for a Chinese bitch.

"I didn't get your name," I say to Shawdy when she comes back into the living room. She was only gone for a hot minute.

"I didn't give it," she snaps. She then says something in Chinese over the phone before she hangs up.

"Damn, Shawdy."

"You can find Merk up at 7E." She comes over to the door and opens it.

"Can I get those digits before you throw me out?"

"Throw you out? I didn't invite you in. You came to see my brother, remember?" Her cell phone rings and she answers it. This time she spoke rapidly in her native tongue then she covers the mouthpiece and says, "But you can stop by on your way back."

"Bet." I'm trying not to show all 32s as I walk out and head for the elevator. I press the UP arrow and wait. Just as I turn to take the stairs, it opens up. I eye the cat already on before stepping in and pushing seven. As soon as the door closes this nigga pulls out his piece and puts it to my head.

"Set the box on the floor!" he orders, sounding like a cop.

Damn. This punk ain't waste no time. I knew I should have taken the steps, I kick myself. At the same time I'm glad that I only got five pounds of weed on me. I drop the box on the floor while praying that this nigga ain't trigga happy. I would hate to go out over a scrimpy five pounds and a little bit of powder.

"Place your hands behind your head," he orders.

"Are you a cop?" This nigga really reminds me of the Po Po. He doesn't answer. The elevator opens to the seventh floor. Fuck this shit! When he reaches down to grab the box I go to knock the gun out of his hand, but this nigga is not letting it go. The elevator door closes back as we go at it, causing the gun to fire off twice, the bullets hitting the wall the first time and the ceiling the next. When the gun drops to the ground, I go for mines, and this nigga punches me so hard in the mouth I hit the floor. I know he's coming after my piece, so I kicks him in the chest and he slams against the wall and makes this strange sound. Then he starts gagging and twitching while blood is bubbling out of his mouth.

"Shit!" I don't take my eyes off of him as I get my box and break outta the elevator as soon as the door opens. Just my luck, two young girls blowing bubble gum are standing there waiting to get on. I run past them and hit the stairs.

"Ooooohhh!" I hear them yell.

I don't know what floor I'm on. I'm just jumpin' steps, five and six at a time. When I finally get outside, the two little billy bad asses are still out there holdin' it down. They both got grins on their faces. I rush past them, knocking the little one down as I get my keys out, hit the alarm, and jump into my ride.

The big billy bad ass starts knocking on the window. "You said you was gonna pay us!" He has his whole mug pressed against my glass.

"Next time!" I pull off, and they start running behind me.

I grab my cell phone and dial Merk. Of course this faggot's voice mail kicks in. "Merk, nigga, I thought you was big-time! That's fucked up what you and your bitch-ass sister pulled. If you gonna rob a nigga, make sure the next time it's more than five pounds! You chump-ass nigga!" I toss the cell over onto the passenger seat. That little bullshit pissed me off. You call yourself lookin' out for a nigga and they turn around and rob you. You can't trust nobody. Now I may even have a fuckin' body on my hands, when I think back on ole boy gargling blood like that.

Shit! I'm zoned the fuck out and don't even realize it. I'm doing seventy in a thirty mph zone. I'm tryna to get the fuck outta Dodge. The only thing that slows my roll is a roadblock coming up at the next light.

"Ain't this a bitch?" I slow down, not believing that they all of a sudden, today, want to do a routine traffic stop or whatever the fuck it's called. Damn if I'm gonna stick around to ask them what they call it. I stop and put the car in reverse. I'm backing up, weaving in and out of traffic, pissing everybody off, when bam! I sideswipe somebody's ride. It looks like a narc vehicle. But like I just said, I'm not gonna stick around to ask what shit is. I keeps it movin'.

When I look again I see an arm placing the lights on top of that same vehicle. Fuck this shit! They're coming after me, and traffic is backed up. I stop the car and bail out running. I'm hoppin' over cars, dogs, fences, garbage cans, and was kickin' ass until a squad car swung around the corner coming up behind me. And then another pulls up in front of me. I slow down, out of breath, and come to a complete halt. They come rushing at me with their guns drawn.

"Lay down on the ground and place your hands behind your head!"

In the meantime, Big Dee, Raw Face, and Bobby rolled into town on the strength of Eboni. They had been trying to get a tail on Freeze and Tareek for almost three days. They finally caught up with Tareek as he came out of a gas station. They had been following him around for several hours. He pulled up in front of a condo and that's when they snatched him up and threw him into their car.

They took him to the room they had rented and pulled out a pair of handcuffs.

"What the fuck y'all want?" Tareek barked.

"Shut the fuck up, nigga," Big Dee snapped. "Cuff this fool. Where yo' partna Freeze at?"

"What y'all niggas want? Some money?"

"Where Freeze at?"

"He outta town. Look, I can take y'all to the money right now."

"When Freeze comin' back?"

"Tomorrow night," he lied. "I can take y'all to the money."

"Take us?" Big Dee pulled out a machete. "Give us the address. We can take our own damn selves." Tareek blurted out an address. "Y'all got that?" Big Dee looked over at his partnas in crime.

"I got it," Raw Face said. His face was burned off on one side.

"Bet. But nigga, I hate to bust yo' bubble. Naw, this ain't about the money. This personal, nigga. You like to rape women, huh?"

"Man, I ain't rape nobody. That's my girl." Tareek was pleading and now feared for his life.

"Bobby, what should I do with this nigga? Cut his dick off? His balls? I think that would hurt this pretty nigga more than anything."

"Naw, c'mon man. Just kill me, nigga. Fuck it! I done told y'all where the stash is," Tareek yelled.

Big Dee ignored him. "Bobby, you figured it out yet?"

Bobby smirked. That's all he could do. He hadn't spoken since he was eight years old. He walked over to where

Tareek was, grabbed him and made him get on his knees. He then stood in front of him, unzipped his jeans and pulled out his dick. Big Dee and Raw Face burst out laughing.

"Okay nigga, I see where this is going. With yo' nasty ass! My mans here want you to suck his dick," Big Dee remarked bluntly.

"Naw, naw." Tareek was shaking his head back and forth. "I don't get down like that."

"I don't neither. But obviously this nigga here wants to." Big Dee watched as Bobby snatched Tareek up by his neck, lifting him clean up off the floor and tossed him head first against the wall.

"Fuck!" Tareek grunted.

"Okay nigga. You either gonna get that dick of yours chopped off or you gonna suck my man off, right here."

Bobby yanked Tareek up again and put him back in position. His dick went back in front of Tareek's face. Bobby grabbed a hold of his dick and pressed the head to Tareek's lips, forcing them apart and slowly sliding his pipe in.

Tareek tried his best not to gag. The OG on his knees sucking another nigga's dick? He was wishing that he was dead. On top of that, the nigga's dick was smelling horrible. He heard Big Dee and Raw Face snickering in the background. Bobby's nasty dick was pushing up against the back of his throat. Just when he was about to bite this nigga's shit off, Bobby grunted. He then grabbed Tareek's head with both hands and bust his nut. He bust so hard that when he finished he was still holding on firm to Tareek's head. Big Dee and Raw Face were doubled over in laughter. Bobby finally pulled his shriveled dick out of Tareek's mouth and Tareek gagged and threw up, catching Bobby's Air Force Ones.

Bobby looked down at his sneakers, his eyes turned icy and he stomped Tareek in the nuts.

Everybody yelled, "Owwww."

Bobby pulled out his burner and cocked it, when the only door in the room came crashing in and bullets went to flying. *Blocka. Blocka. Blocka. Tatatatata.*

Tareek was shitting on himself.

When the smoke cleared, Freeze was standing against the door with a Magnum in one hand and a Derringer in the other.

"Reek!"

He looked around at the two unfamiliar bodies lying on the floor and the one on the bed and smiled. He couldn't help but to admire his handiwork.

"Nigga, get these cuffs off me. I saw the key on that table. And nigga, you was right behind me, fool. Why the fuck you just gettin' here?" Tareek was furious.

"Damn. You shit on yo'self, fool? What the fuck? You was that scared? What they do? Who are these niggas? And what's that? A nut on yo' mouth?" To Freeze that's exactly what it looked like.

"Fuck the questions. Just get these cuffs off, man. And what the fuck took you so long?" Tareek wanted to cry at the thought of him getting violated. Freeze finally uncuffed him.

"I lost y'all."

"That's all you got to say? What, you was clockin' some bitches? We got work in the car and you were s'posed to be watchin' my back, man." Tareek shoved him. Freeze fell back on to the bed right next to the bodies. And one of them was moving.

"You know how close I came to dying, nigga?" He looked around at the three bodies.

"C'mon. Let's get outta here. The Po Po will be here in a minute," Freeze warned him as he caught the body on the bed twitchin' again. "Nigga, who sent you?" Freeze yelled out, while standing over Big Dee.

"Fuck you. Eboni sends—" he mumbled, but was cut off by a bullet to his skull.

"I'ma kill her ass." Tareek vowed. "I should fuck you up, Freeze. I'm serious."

"Nigga, bring yo' shitty ass on. I saved yo' ass."

"No, you didn't," Tareek mumbled.

Chapter 11

I look at my watch, then over at my cousin Corey, who has his big-ass feet propped up on the coffee table. This nigga is chillin' like he's somebody rich and famous. He has a drink in one hand, joint and remote in the other, and is stretched all out. But I got news for his funky ass.

"It's check-out time. Corey, let's go!" My order falls on deaf ears. I should shoot his ass. I'm already pissed because Reign said he would be no more than two hours. Here it is almost four o'clock. I am glad I followed my gut and paged Corey to come and help me out or I would still be baggin' shit up. "Corey!" I scream as I toss one of the throw pillows at him. "Let's get this shit outta here."

"I thought we was waitin' on Black!"

"Fuck Black! He ain't here and I'm ready to go. And where the fuck you get *we* from? When did you become French? I called you to help me out, not lay around like some unwanted relative."

"You paid for the room for the whole night, didn't you?"

"Yeah, and?"

"Well, you can leave and give me the key. I'll wait here for Black."

"Oh, no, you won't! Both of our pagers are blowin' up. I need you to serve these niggas. They waitin'."

Corey sucks his teeth at me as he aims the remote at the TV and turns it off. Still not giving up, he says, "I'll handle everything, and then I'll come back here when I'm done. No need in wasting the room." I ignore him. "C'mon, Kree! The shit is paid for." He is now following me all around the room.

"Aiight, boy, damn!" I yell at him and start gathering up everything so we can roll out. "Let's just get the fuck outta here, please. When or should I say *if* Reign comes back, I want him to find my ass gone. He got me fucked up!"

"Girl, please. Why you gotta get all Carl Thomas on a nigga? The man is out taking care of business. Damn! Y'all be trippin' hard." Corey was sticking his nose where it didn't belong.

"Mind your business, Corey, before I bust you in your mouth."

"What?" He gets all up in my face.

"Nothin', boy." I push him out of my way. We pack up the weed that needs to be delivered ASAP in Corey's ride and the rest in mines. I reluctantly hold out the hotel key. "Don't fuck up the room, boy."

"Girl, shut up!" This punk snatches the key out of my hand and goes and jumps in his car. Before pulling off, he sticks his head out the window and yells, "Take your emotional ass home where you belong!"

I flip him both middle fingers, jump in my ride, and do just that; take my ass home. But not before I call Seven's ass again. I can't believe that nigga threatened me. I don't work for him and I have to once again let him know that. If my brother was here this shit would not be happening.

When I pull into my driveway, I grab my celly and check my voice mail. I got messages from everybody and they momma but no Reign. "I'ma kill him!" I page him once more before going into the house. Once inside, it's straight upstairs to put on some shorts and a T-shirt. I can't help myself. I page him again before heading for my refrigerator where I take out the milk, get me a bowl, and fill it up with some Apple Jacks. I go and flop down in front of my big screen. I turn on the news. I'm chowing down trying like hell to get my thoughts together. I keep thinking about Reign and wondering why the nigga couldn't call a bitch. It's shit like this that makes a ho put a nigga on a leash.

In the middle of me cussing him out and telling him what I think about him, I see a car that looks just like his on the screen. Now all of a sudden the news has my undivided attention. Five-O is everywhere. I'm reading the closed captioning, and it's only saying that they did a routine traffic check today. "If it's a routine traffic check, then why so many police?" I'm yelling out loud. The news anchor woman in the helicopter is just chillin'. "Oh, shit!" I jump up and go over to the big screen because what looks like an Express Mail box is sitting on the ground. Now I'm pacing back and forth trying to figure out what's happening. The news correspondent is focusing on the routine traffic stop and not my man's car. "Reign, baby, where are you? And what the fuck is going on?" I'm agitated as shit. My house phone rings, both cell phones go off, and my two way is bumpin'. Shit is going haywire. I'm now paranoid and scared to answer anything. I'm shittin' bricks, locking the doors, looking out the windows, flushing every little bit of weed I had in the house down the toilet. All the while wondering what in the hell Reign is up to? How is this nigga built?

But the damn phones won't stop ringing. "Shut the fuck up!" I scream, while standing in the middle of my living room floor. I snatch up the celly, ready to smash it into the TV when I notice Eboni's number on the caller ID.

"Hello."

"Bitch, why you ain't answerin' yo' phone? Turn on the six o'clock news! They probably gonna be showin' this shit all night."

"I'm already watchin' it."

"Well, I don't have to tell you then. You already know that nigga Reign is hot."

"No, the fuck he ain't!" I immediately defend him.

"Watch what I tell you," she snaps back.

"Oh, you gonna side with the rest of them niggas? I didn't side with Tareek and Freeze when you told me what they did. Fuck you, Eboni!" I hang up on her.

I'm pacing back and forth. "Reign, I need to hear from you!"

As if on cue my house phone rings and I run to pick it up. "Hello."

"Kreesha?"

I recognize my auntie Betty's voice. "Hi, Aunt Betty." She's my mother's oldest sister. Aunt Betty has been around. She sold dope, ran numbers, and even did some time for the Feds.

"Is that your car I saw on the news?"

She is also nosy as hell and don't miss nothing. "I think that was Reign's car."

"It's your car, baby. You paid for it, didn't you? Therefore, it's your car," she snaps.

I didn't say anything because it's no use in trying to justify or explain to her what the deal is. She thinks she knows everything. I'm beginning to think she's psychic.

"What's going on, baby?"

"I don't know, Auntie, but I'm not feeling good about this." That's all I could tell her and it was the truth.

"Baby, you know what kind of lifestyle you're living. I'm not gonna preach to you, not right now anyway. Plus, can't nobody tell you nothin'. You just like your momma and me.

But I do want you to be careful and remember that I'm here if you need me."

"Thanks, Aunt Betty." I hang up knowing that I need to call Seven outta respect to let him know that I may be facing a setback. I really don't feel like hearing his mouth, but it'll be worse if I don't call him now. After I take my bowl and set it in the dishwasher, I drag myself to the phone and dial his number.

"What up, my nigga?" I try to sound like everything is a-okay.

"What up, my lil' nigga? What's the special occasion? Who died?"

"Oh, so you got jokes now?"

"I'm not joking. You know damn well you never call a nigga no more, not even to check in and let me know that you aiight."

"That's what I'm doin' now."

"Oh, I see." He has the nerve to be sounding all skeptical and shit. "Well, what a pleasant surprise!" I could hear the smirk in his voice.

He's always been such a smart-ass. I am trying to bring myself to tell him, but the words won't come out. The line is quiet except for the sound of traffic in the background. He's obviously on the road.

"What, lil' nigga!" Seven yells, causing me to jump. "Let me find out you just called to breathe in my ear. Here. Breathe on Tareek."

"Seven, no!"

"I didn't know you was freaky like that," he teases but still passes Tareek the phone.

"Kree, what up? When can a brotha come over and get a home-cooked meal?"

"When a brotha can come over and cook it for himself. Just let me know when, so I can be there."

"Oh, Kree got jokes? I bet you don't tell that infiltrator Black you creepin' with no shit like that. Do you?"

"Hell naw. That's my nigga, what the fuck you think?"

"I think he's an infiltrator, that's what I think. Seven keep sayin' you got the enemy in your bed."

"Tell trick-ass Seven I said to mind his own damn business! Both of y'all need to be more concerned with those trick-ass hos y'all sleepin' with. Give him the phone back. I didn't ask to speak to you anyway!"

Tareek starts laughing and gives Seven the phone back.

"Lil' nigga, what's up?"

"What's up? Why you talking about me all behind my back? That's what's up."

"I never see you anymore to tell you the shit in your face! Why, what I say?"

"You know what you said. Telling peeps that I got the enemy in my bed."

"He is the enemy. And I've been saying that in your face. But being a female you allow your emotions to cloud your judgment. You're street smart but relationship dumb. I hope you peep that nigga before it's too late."

"You know what, Seven?" He is pissing me off. "I got this. Worry about yours. I am allowed to have somebody. And what the fuck is up with threatening me through Reign? If you got beef with me, bring it to me, not my nigga."

"Hold the fuck up! You think you Billy Bad Ass now? Who the fuck you think you talkin' too? I already told you what I had to say. And let me reiterate shit. If it go down it's gonna be you or him. Now the punk ass nigga lyin' on me. You betta watch that mutt you sleepin' with. If your brother was alive he wouldn't let you fuck with that nigga. Stop actin' like a love struck needy bitch."

I slam down the phone. It rings again and Seven's name comes up on the caller ID. I let it go to voice mail.

Ten-forty P.M. and still no Reign. "Fuck it!" I dial wifey. Obviously she's just as on edge as me because she picks it up on the first ring.

"Hello."

"This is Kreesha. Have you heard from Reign?"

She acts like she isn't gonna speak. Then she finally yells out, "Bitch, I know you are not calling my house looking for my husband? You must be smokin' that shit!"

No, this bitch didn't! I'm beginning to think she is crazy. I take a deep breath and calmly tell her, "Look, ho, now is not the time for all the drama. Reign left to make a run this afternoon, and I haven't heard from him since. Then I see his car on the news. I just need to know have you heard from him and if he's all right."

"I'm his wife, of course I heard from him." The crazy ho has the nerve to start laughing. Then the stanking bitch hangs up on me.

I call her right back. "Is he locked up?"

"Trick, you better stop calling my house!"

"You act like the nigga is there. I'm coming over since you can't talk like a ho whose husband is fucking another bitch that's putting food on your table! Bitch, you gonna show me some respect. I'm on my way!" And this time I slam the phone down, go change, and jump in my car.

Chapter 12

Reign

Here I am lying in a fuckin' jail cell for what feels like the hundredth time. Other than the one phone call, I've been by myself, having no contact with anyone. I called wifey and convinced her that everything is cool, and told her to call Kree and tell her that I'm locked up and to get me a lawyer. After I did that I regretted it. I should have called Kree first. At least I would have been sure the lawyer would've been handled. Wifey be catching ill feelings and will allow them to take over instead of taking care of business. I knew better, so it's my fault if the lawyer doesn't get taken care of. I wasted that one phone call.

Here it is almost eleven and no one is saying shit. Hell, I don't even hear other inmates. It's like I'm on the floor all by myself. Fuck it! I'll do a little more shadowboxing, a hundred more push-ups, and afterward I'm catchin' some z's.

The sound of keys jingling alerts me. I'm awake but I don't open my eyes. Somebody opens that noisy-ass slot in the door and yells, "Breakfast!" I hear the plastic food tray slam down. I don't smell food and it's fuckin' freezing in here. I'm not getting up for no slop, so I pull the blanket a little tighter and try to catch me some more z's. No sooner than I doze off, they are taking the tray back and slam the slot door so hard that if I wasn't awake, you best to believe I'm fully awake now. Damn! Now I'm lyin' here staring at the walls, thinking how I ain't been out a good seven months and here I am wakin' up in a jail cell. I promised myself that after that last bid I would never come back. I doze back off.

I almost jump out of my skin when some asshole starts kicking the door. Then the slot opens and the voice yells, "Johnston, get ready to shower. You have a visitor."

I turn over and holla, "Shower with what? Y'all ain't give me shit to shower with! I ain't even got no toilet paper!" I hop out the bed and go toward the door. I need to see this punk's face. But of course he slams the slot shut as soon as I bend down to peek out. "Hey!" I start banging on the slot. "I need some toilet paper and some soap to take a shower!" The punk is ghost. See what I mean? This prison shit is for suckas. I go over to take a piss, run some water over my face, and gargle with some tap water.

After about an hour I finally hear keys again, and this time they do open this big-ass steel door. I'm pissed off. "What happened to my shower, man?"

The cracked-out version of Ashton Kutcher says, "I just came on duty, man." He slams the door back. "What time did you get here?"

The motherfucker knows what time I got here. "I got here about four in the afternoon, man. I only had one phone call and I ain't have no toilet paper and nothing to take a shower with."

He feels my angry stare, and this fool is acting like he's concerned. But I know better. We walk in silence down the highly buffed hallway.

"Here we go," he says as we stop in front of what I guess is the visiting room for attorneys. He unlocks it. "Have a seat and someone will be with you."

"Who will be with me?"

"I guess your attorney," he says as he's closing the door. Then I hear him lock it. I look around and this is far from an attorney's visiting room. It looks like an interrogation room. It's even equipped with what I assume is the see-through one-sided glass window, and padded walls. "Damn. If they want to beat a nigga down, they can do so and they don't have to leave no bruises." I grab a chair and sit at the table when I hear keys. A door opens, but not the same one I came through. In comes a brotha and three white dudes. Brothaman reminds me of Michael Vick, and the three white cats look like a young version of Curly, Larry, and Mo of *The Three Stooges*. The only thing that stands out is one of them has a red curly fro.

"Reign Johnston, I'm Detective Kirkowitz, this is Reynolds, this is Hearns, and the big fella here to your right is Johnson." He was referring to Brothaman of course. Kirkowitz is Curly. Larry opens up a folder and passes it to Kirkowitz.

"Don't y'all think I need to have my attorney present?"

"Chill out, this will be very brief." He looks over at me and drops a bomb. "We have several witnesses who place you at the scene of a murder."

"Murder?" I stand up, knocking the chair over, and the two stooges along with Brothaman stand up with their hands glued to their pieces. "Murder? Y'all got me fucked up! I need a lawyer! Let me outta here!" I head for the door.

Kirkowitz is still sitting down. "I said this will be brief. You wanna go home, don't you?"

"What kind of question is that? Of course I wanna go home. Stop playin', man. You talkin' about fuckin' murder! I got in a little scuffle, and you tryna pin me with murder?"

"Well, that little scuffle is now first degree murder." He points to the glass. "Like I said, we have witnesses. So we have you on not only murder of a detective—and I might add, he was a rotten apple but nevertheless still a cop—but also possession with intent to distribute marijuana, five pounds, possession of a firearm, resisting arrest, and the nail that seals your coffin . . ." He pauses for effect, and that shit is working because my heart feels like it's gonna beat right outta my chest. He has this nasty smirk on his face. "You're a three-time loser." He holds up three fingers, then swings an imaginary bat. "This is the end of the road for ya. So you might as well sit down. You won't see the other side of that door for the rest of your years."

My head is spinning and I feel like I'm drowning. I grab a seat. Damn! How in the fuck did I get myself jammed up like this? I start reaching for a lifeline. "I thought you said I could go home?" My voice is almost squeaking.

"You can. But you gotta do something for us."

I'm looking at him like he's crazy. This time Brothaman pulls out a folder. He passes it to Kirkowitz, who slides it in front of me.

I look at it like it's poison. "I need my lawyer."

Kirkowitz ignores me and reaches over and opens it up. On top sits a mug shot of my baby, Kree. My stomach knots up. He then picks it up and holds it in my face. When I wipe my face with my hands, he then shows me pictures of her whole crew: Seven, Tareek, Tax, and Almighty. "We want them, Reign, and you're gonna get them for us."

"Man, you got me fucked up!" I get up and go to the door. "Let me the fuck outta here!" I start grabbing on the door.

"It's either you or them. The choice is yours," Kirkowitz says as he places his hands behind his head and leans back as if he doesn't have a care in the world. I saw myself kicking the chair and making him fall backwards, flat on his ass.

One of the twins places a set of handcuffs, a cell phone,

and a two-way pager on the table. "All you gotta do is give the girl the cell and pager. We'll take it from there. That's all you gotta do. You make the choice to walk outta here one of two ways. One is with the platinum bracelets. Y'all know how y'all like the platinum. Wear 'em and go back to that dingy-ass, dirty, cold cell. Or two, choose the phone and pager and you're on your way home to your pregnant wife or to your pregnant girlfriend and get you a nice hot shower, some pussy, and a nice hot meal. You make the call."

"Fuck you, man! I need my lawyer." I'm still at the door, trying to pull it open.

"Take the phone and pager and here's my card." He confidently reaches in his shirt pocket. "Have your attorney call me. This is your last chance. What's it gonna be? You play or you stay."

Chapter 13

As I'm cruising down Reign's block, I'm debating on whether to pull up in the driveway or just park out front. Fuck it! I put up the down payment for the shit, so I go ahead and pull up in the driveway. I grab my pepper spray and my piece. Just because she's pregnant, that don't mean shit! Hell, I'm pregnant, too! I'm walking up the steps thinking jealousy is a motherfucker! I ring the doorbell and then I knock. After about five minutes and nonstop ringing and banging, the witch finally comes to the door. This bitch swings it open so hard that I'm sure the doorknob put a hole in the wall. But I'm not the least bit intimidated, this is business. And I don't see why this bitch can't rise above the madness long enough to take care of the business at hand. So here we are standing face to face, belly to belly. It's like we're looking in the mirror. I break the silence.

"Look, I'm not here on no petty bullshit. I just need to know where is Reign and if he's all right?" This ho is looking at me like I have six heads.

"You mean to tell me that your pussy ain't good enough to warrant a phone call? Bitch, you need to wake up and smell the roses. When it all boils down, Reign is my husband, and no matter what you do for him or for us, and no matter what he tells you, he's still coming home to wifey."

I go to grab her throat, but she backs away from my grip.

"Yeah. He's coming home to wifey but not until he spends all night with me. But I didn't come over here to . . ." Oh, no, she didn't! The bitch slams the door in my face! I'm standing here ready to kick the door down and whip this ho's ass for real! As soon as I see Reign, I'ma smack him for even having such a dumb bitch on his team. He just lost mad kool points for that one. I swear I should kick in the door. I'm still standing here, and it takes me a few minutes to cool down and think with a level head. I go back to my car and check my voice mail. My gut tells me this nigga done got knocked. All of the signs are there. No sense in campin' out. I pull off and go on back to the crib. But that bitch can best believe I will be back!

Reign's side of the story

When I pull up in front of the crib it's almost ten-thirty the next morning. I'm still fucked up in the head over the turn of events that went down in the last twenty-four hours. I'm so fucked up that I don't see wifey standing in the doorway or Kreesha getting out her ride and creepin' up behind me.

"Nigga, put your hands up!" I feel something poking me in my back. "I said put 'em up!" I turn around, and Kree got her pistol out.

"Put that shit away, girl!"

"What happened, Reign? Where were you? You had me worried sick." She slides the steel in her pocket and gives me a hug, and I kiss her on the forehead. We look at my front door and wifey slams it shut. "You need to check that bitch. She's real silly." Then she pushes me. "Why the fuck you ain't call, Reign?" She pushes me again. "I ain't worth a fuckin' phone call?" She slaps me.

I grab her wrists. "They only gave me one call. I told Sparkle to call you and tell you that I needed a lawyer."

"Oh. So that's what's up?" She looked crushed. "That's what you fuckin' get! They should have let you rot in there! I called her and asked had she heard from you, and the bitch wouldn't even tell me. I had to drive all the way over here, and then the ho slams the door in my face." Kree is getting louder and louder. "You need to check that ho, Reign. Y'all niggas wanna wife them square bitches, but when it's time to get down and dirty, where they at? You know what? The more I talk, the more I'm wondering what the fuck am I doing? Fuck you and your wife! Y'all look good together." Kree turns and heads for her car.

I grab her and hug her from behind. "Baby, don't do this now. I need you. More than you can imagine. Don't worry about her, I got her as soon as I step foot in the house. When no lawyer didn't show I knew she didn't give you my message. Trust me, I'll handle her."

"Trust you. Yeah right! Just like you told me you would handle the divorce! Why are you still with her?" Kreesha was beginning to lose it.

"I told you I would handle it," I said, trying to assure her.

"Whatever, nigga. Like I said, y'all look good together." She tries to break away from me, but I hold on tight.

"I'ma talk to her, shower, change, and I'll be over."

"Whatever." She stops dead in her tracks and turns back around. "No! Fuck that! You check that bitch, but you shower and change at my house. You got me fucked up, Reign!"

I let her go and watch her as she gets into her car and drives off. "Fuck!" I kick somebody's tire causing the car alarm to go off, and head to my front door. I ring the bell before using my house key. When I get inside I can tell that wifey has been crying as she sits on the couch with her arms folded across her chest.

"How long do you think I'ma allow this shit to go on, Reign?" She jumps up and is all in my face. This shit is getting to be too much.

"Right now it is not about another bitch, Sparkle. Get your fuckin' priorities straight! I'm in the fuckin' jail needing a lawyer and you can't even make a fuckin' phone call!" I slap the shit outta her. I thought her neck was going to break. She is shocked as hell. She doesn't know what to do or say.

"You hit me?" she finally mumbles. "You hit me over another bitch!" she says in disbelief.

"This was about business, Sparkle. Not a fuckin' bitch!"

"What do you mean it ain't about another bitch? That's exactly what this is about! You're my husband, Reign. We are getting ready to have a baby. You creepin' with that bitch and it ain't even no secret. All my friends know about her."

"Fuck your friends!" We both are screaming at the top of our lungs. I grab this bitch by the throat, pregnant and all. "You married to your friends or me? Get your mind and emotions in check or get the fuck outta my house!" I turn her loose, pushing her back onto the sofa. "I can't believe you. I'm in fuckin' jail and you can't even deliver a damn message because you worried about those fake-ass church people you call your friends. What? You fuckin' them?" She's crying and shaking her head no. "You must be since you worried more about them than you are about me!" I turn around to leave.

"Where are you going?" She jumps up and grabs my arm. "Reign, don't leave. I'm sorry. Don't leave."

"You need to decide what you're gonna do. Get your shit together and help me or get the fuck away from me!" I slam the door behind me. I don't have time for the little shit. I gotta figure out how I'ma get Kree to use this cell phone and pager. Fuck!

Chapter 14

Kreesha's side of the story

Something told me to get my ass up that morning and go back to Reign's house. I sat in the car and patiently waited. What I really wanted to do was go and shoot that bitch of his. Before it's all over that's what I'ma end up doing. I can feel it. I had only been sitting in my car for about thirty minutes when he finally decided to pull up. Damn! He really was looking haggard. He was lucky he was looking like he had a bad night in someone's jail cell and not a good night fuckin' around in some other ho's bed. Still in all I was pissed off. That one phone call should have been to my fat ass. The bitch must have been waiting as well because when he pulled up, she was standing in the doorway. Fuck her! I grabbed my piece, got out of my car, and eased up behind Mr. Missing In Action. He was so lost in thought he didn't even hear me rollin' up on him. The bitch was watchin' everything, and was all up in my grill and I'm trying not to snap! "Can I help you, Sparkle?" I'm eyeing her to let her know to get the fuck out of my business.

She pushes the door open. "No, the fuck you can't."

"Look, both of y'all need to chill. I don't feel like hearing y'alls' bullshit. Take yo' ass home and I'll be over there."

I smacked my lips because his expression let me know to

shut the fuck up and do just like he said, take my ass home. So I did just that, but not before calling Sparkle a fake ass bitch.

About an hour after I got home, here he came. He didn't even say anything, he just went straight upstairs and I heard the shower come on.

"Awwwww, man!" It feels so good to take a nice hot shower. I haven't had a shower in twenty-four hours. I'm taking as long as I can because I gotta come up with something believable to tell Kree. Whatever it is, the shit gotta be good. Damn, this is fucked up. But I quickly put that in the back of my mind as the aroma of bacon, eggs, and grits assault my nostrils. Now that's what's up! I feel like I can eat a cow.

After I get out the shower, I throw on some sweats and a wife beater. Speaking of wife beater. I didn't want to hurt Sparkle by slapping her and grabbing her by the throat like that. But shit happens. And this morning wasn't the morning. I wasn't up for the usual bullshit.

When I get downstairs, Kree is at the stove. I creep up behind her, wrap my arms around her waist, and rub her belly. Damn, I hate to do this to her. "How's my baby doin'?"

"Your baby is fine, but it's me you need to be worried about. I'm waiting to hear what happened to you." She turns the fire off on the stove.

I turn her loose and go sit down at the table. She fixes two plates, sets, or should I say throws, one in front of me and places one in front of her. She's pissed.

"Can I get something to drink with this?" I ask. She rolls her eyes at me, pops up, grabs two glasses, and pulls the orange juice and her prenatal vitamins out of the refrigerator.

Those vitamins remind me once again that she is carrying my seed. "So how are you feeling?"

"Why you keep asking me that? What the fuck happened, Reign? Why are you beatin' around the freakin' bush?"

"Chill man. Everything cool." I go back to eating my food.

"Naw, shit ain't cool. You got popped with five pounds of weed on you, some powder *and* you on paper. You should still be in jail."

"Don't be fuckin' screamin' on me like that! I ain't yo' fuckin' child. I told you it was handled."

"Oh, it was that easy, huh? Just like that!" She snapped her fingers. I wanted to snap her neck. "Well, when do you go to court?"

"My uncle is a deputy sheriff, and he was able to help me out. Of course, it wasn't free. But it's handled. I'm just hoping that he keeps up his end of the bargain, because if my PO gets word, I'm fucked." There! I came up with a good enough story that I hope will put her at ease for the time being.

"You always talkin' about you got something handled. Just like your divorce. But that's a whole nother subject. *Will* your uncle or *won't* he keep up his end of the bargain?" She's staring at me intently.

"Damn, I told you I got it. Why you trippin'?"

"I'm trippin' because yo' ass was on the six o'clock news."

"How you know I was on the news?"

"I saw you, nigga."

"You saw me?"

Fuck, this is going to be harder than I thought, so I try and flip the script. "If you saw me, why in the fuck didn't you get me a lawyer? Why the fuck you waiting for me to call?" My voice is shaking the house. I abruptly stand up, knocking my chair back. Kree don't know what the fuck is my problem. "Ain't this a bitch?" I'm looking at her all crazy.

"Don't be screamin' on me."

"I'm fuckin' sittin' in jail when I could have been out! That's why I'm fuckin' screamin'!"

"That ain't my fault! Yo' own damn wife ain't call you a fuckin' lawyer. But I called my lawyer and he said you wasn't in the system. So now what?"

"What you tryna say, Kree?"

"Shit, tell a bitch something! I was worried about you. I don't want you to go back to prison."

I give off much attitude as I sit back down and pick over my food, pleased at my performance.

"I don't want you to go back to prison, Reign. Will your uncle cover for you? Will he hold up his end of the deal?"

"I hope he does. I'll know for sure by the end of next week." She's looking at me all crazy. "Kree, that's all I can tell you for right now. All we can do is wait and see. You know I don't want you to be worryin' about me. My unc said he'll be calling next week. Don't worry. I'm cool. I wish I would have called you first, but—"

"Spare me. I don't want to hear no lame ass excuses, Reign. You lost kool points for that one as well."

"Come over here and let me make it up to you. You know a nigga didn't get his nightly dose of Kree last night." I still gotta figure a way to put my plan in motion.

A week later

I finally got Kree to use the pager and cell phone. The Feds had been buggin' me nonstop. I let Kree go two days thinking that she lost her equipment. I took them both and dumped them. She was more than happy to accept the replacements that I gave her. She used her cell and pager to handle all of her business with the Colombians, her crew, and all of her customers. I was officially in. I was now an official bitch for the Feds.

Chapter 15

It's been almost a month since Reign got knocked. My belly is getting bigger and bigger. My family is getting happier and happier. This will be my mom's first grandchild, and Reign is treating me so good. I have no complaints. It seems like the bigger I get, the harder he's grindin'. He says he's tryin' to stash as much paper as possible. I ain't mad at him. I'm feelin' good, so I do the same thing, pregnant and all. Shit, being pregnant shouldn't stop no show.

My aunt Betty invited me over for dinner. She is a trip. She has just about all of her hair cut off and dyed it bright blond. She has three earrings in each ear, one in her nose, rings on every finger, and about ten gold chains around her neck. She had the audacity to sit me down and tell me that the day Reign got knocked, it was the Feds who took him into custody. She said he made a deal with the Feds that he would give them my Colombian connect, Seven, and the rest of the crew in exchange for me and him walking.

I asked her what was she smokin' and why she wanna go there with me? She had the nerve to tell me I'm very street smart but when it came to dealin' with the niggas I'm as dumb as a donkey. I said, "So are you!" Why I said that is beyond me because she smacked the shit outta me. I was shocked as hell. I told her I was tellin' my momma and outta respect I was leaving instead of jumping all in her shit. She had the nerve to tell me to "Bring it on and if you're feelin' froggy, then jump!" I figured that this ole lady done lost her mind. I told her, "You lucky you my aunt." I then asked her where was she getting all this info from. She told me that I must have forgotten that she's been in and out of the game all her life. And that it didn't matter where she got it from. The streets are always talking. She said, "You're running fast down the same road I took. I did eight years for a sorry-ass, punk-ass nigga. Don't do like I did. And don't say that I didn't warn you. A hard head always makes a soft ass."

That evening I sat and thought about how Reign's case mysteriously just went away. I dismissed what my aunt was saying and told myself not to pay her any attention because she was making me paranoid. I told Reign everything my aunt said and he told me not to worry about the haters. That we was gonna pack up and move to another state as soon as it was okay for the baby to travel. Then he left for Western Union. I needed him to wire some funds to my Colombian connect.

Three and a half months later

Eboni and me was back at. She was back at home and workin' with me. Reign and I had a beautiful baby girl named Reigna Shameeka. She looks exactly like me except for those eyes. She has his eyes and eyebrows. As soon as she turned a month old I was back on the grind. Oh, the witch had a girl, too. She name the baby Tamia. I don't re-member the middle name. But Tamia came out looking just like Reign. She only has the mother's complexion. He wouldn't be able to deny her if he wanted to. He had the nerve to bring the baby over to my house. But y'all know me. I know how to act like an adult. However, I made sure his ass took my baby over to hers.

The tripped-out thing is my moms and my aunt Betty really thinks that my baby belongs to them. It comes in handy for the most part because I don't have to worry about a babysitter. But lots of times I have to put them outta my house or either go over to theirs and literally take my baby from them. What part of the game is this? But Reign? That nigga could have gotten Father of the Year. He changed diapers, made bottles, the whole nine. Exactly . . . fucked me up too. He took so many pictures of his daughters it was ridiculous. Talkin' about he was going to need them. He was actin' straight up as if he would never see them again. Now that shit was real crazy to me.

Today Reigna is two months old and I already dropped off the baby at my aunt Betty's house and it's only eight-thirty in the morning. Reign will be here around nine tonight to pick me up. I can't wait! We are going to a hotel to get our freak on for the first time in two months.

But in the meantime, my girl Mari is coming up from Mexico. She's bringing me five hundred pounds of weed. The streets are waitin'! She says she has some other shit to do, so I guess she's killing two birds with one stone. Even though she actually lives in Cali, she also has an apartment in Memphis that she uses when she slides into town. Whenever she comes to bring me some work, she rolls dolo, and her drivers would roll dolo and carry the merchandise. Usually me and her would kick it, but I told her not tonight. I got other plans.

She checked in with me about eleven o'clock to let me know that she had made it into town. As soon as I hung up, I rented a car because it was time to take care of business:

breakdown, bag, and deliver. Then I could go and get my freak on.

Later on that day

"Damn! It's one-thirty. Where is Mari?" I was ready to bounce.

"Probably gettin' some dick. You know she ain't come all this way just to serve your black ass! I know you ain't mad at her!" That was Eboni's smart ass. Even though she probably was right, I wanted her to shut the fuck up. She's been runnin' her mouth all fuckin' morning.

"Where the fuck is she?"

"Just keep blowin' up her cell and pager. She'll eventually call you back as soon as she can get off the dick. Plus, what she gonna do with a truck load of weed?"

"You finally said something that makes some sense."

"Bitch, please! I always make sense. You just don't listen."

I was glad she was being herself again. Ever since the hit men she hired to take out Tareek and Freeze got hit, shes on pins and needles.

Two more hours have passed. It's three-thirty. Still no Mari, and it's no way we are going to be done by nine o'clock. Something ain't right. I can feel it. I call my cousin Corey.

"Corey, what's up?"

"Chillin' while waitin' on you. I wish y'all would hurry up. Where the fuck y'all at?" Corey asked, while looking out the window.

"Me and Eboni are over Treecy's. What kind of cars are cruisin' the block?"

"What?"

"Just check, nigga! Let me know what's ridin' around out there!"

Corey, while on his cordless, follows orders and goes outside to sit on the front porch.

After about five minutes of checking things out, he finally tells me, "It's a couple of Intrepids with tinted windows."

"Fuck!" I knew it. That's dem boys. "Handle your business," I tell him, then I hang up. "Something is going down, Eboni." My stomach had been churning all day. My gut tells me to dial Eboni's house, and just like I thought, on the first ring someone picks it up.

"Hello," says the voice of a white man. I slam down the phone.

"Eboni, they're at your house."

"What? Who's at my house?" She grabs the phone and starts dialing.

"The Feds. That's who and what."

"Hello." I guess she wants to hear them for herself. "Who is this?" Eboni asks, then obviously not liking what she hears, hangs up. "Damn, Kreesha. We busted? Are we busted?"

"Apparently so." My voice and hands are trembling as I call Corey again to let him know that they're at Eboni's.

"Hello." The white male's voice booms over the speaker. I slam the phone down.

"Damn, Eboni. They at Corey's, too!"

"I don't want to go to jail, Kreesha."

"I don't either," is all I can say at this moment. I get up the nerve to dial my house phone. Them bastards answer on the first ring. I'm trying hard to hear what they're doing or saying in the background.

Then this cracker interrupts me, "Kreesha, we know this is you. Turn yourself in." I gently hang up the phone.

"C'mon, Eboni." I grab my bag and keys, and we go cruisin' the hood checkin' on all my spots. Fed trucks and cars are everywhere. Luckily we are in a rental and they aren't stopping cars. My heart drops when I see them on my aunt Betty's block. She has the baby. I now begin to feel like I'm smothering.

We head on back to Treecy's to lay low and focus so that I can figure out my next move. That's when I wonder, Where in the hell is Reign? I grab my cell phone to call him. Then it hits me like a ton of bricks. "It's this damn phone!" I throw it against the wall. I feel like I'm going to throw up.

"What the fuck?" Eboni asks with her mouth as Treecy asks with her eyes and they're lookin' at me like I done lost my mind. I'm too embarrassed to tell them that my man gave me a fuckin' Fed phone. I use Treecy's house phone to page Reign, and ten minutes later he calls back.

"Who is this?" he says instead of hello.

"Baby, it's me, please come and get me. The Feds are everywhere. They're around Aunt Betty's, Mommy's, Corey's, Eboni's, and my house. Where are you?"

"What?" This punk-ass nigga is tryna play me. My brotha always taught me to keep my enemies close.

"You heard me! Where the fuck are you?" Fuck it. I don't give him a chance to answer.

"Just hurry and come and get me. I'm at Treecy's." The phone felt like it weighed one hundred pounds. "Eboni, you got your burner?"

"Of course."

I didn't know what I was going to do. I was hurt and confused. How could Reign do this? I still didn't want to believe it.

He got there in almost an hour to be exact. I gave Eboni the rental, and me and Reign went and hid out at a hotel. Here I am thinking I'm hiding out, but in all actuality, I'm hiding with the police. I was totally shook. He finally got me to relax a little, well, enough for me to give him some, and I must say he wore the pussy out. How we ended up fucking is beyond me. He was acting relieved, but I couldn't figure out why. Shit, I too needed something to ease my mind. After the fuck and a fifth of Hen dog, I was lit. For a minute I had forgot that the Feds was lookin' for me. I can honestly say that the two years we had been together, this day's lovin' was the shit!

Reign

I had both of my baby girls. I had shot them over to the mall to get their pictures taken. Everyone oohed and aahed over how cute my babies were. I couldn't have been more proud. I had them dipped in Baby Phat matching jackets and skirts with some crisp white K-Swiss sneakers. I even combed their hair. Naw, I'm jokin', I put one pink barrette on their curly little fros. Both of their ears was adorned with diamonds and they had little gold bangles on their wrists. They were definitely commercial ready . . . my pretty babies.

On top of that the hos was jockin' a playa. "Oh, your daughters are so beautiful." And "Isn't that sweet!" I was hearing that shit all day long. And all day long the honeys was tryna step to me. I decided that I would have to do this more often.

When I got back to the crib, Sparkle was being her usual bitchy, hatin' self. But I didn't give a fuck what she thought because my daughters were going to grow up close. Hell, they're sisters! Nothing or nobody could change that.

"Ain't it time for you to take *her* home, Reign?"

See what I mean? This bitch is tryin' me already. "Her?

She got a name, it's Princess Reigna." I purposely stressed the s at the end of 'princess.'

"No, her mother named her Reigna. I know her name very *well*."

"*Well*, act like it. And you need to check your attitude."

"I ain't got to check shit. Fuck you, that baby, and that bitch! I don't have to be okay with you bringing your bitch's baby over to my house."

"Bitch, you showing out now. But don't think I won't slap the shit out of yo' ass in front of both of my daughters. This is my house and it's my baby." Reigna started crying. I turned my back to Sparkle to attend to my precious daughter. "Do something with yourself, go make her a bottle."

"You make me fuckin' sick," Sparkle snapped.

"The feeling's mutual." I picked up my crying daughter. "It's okay, boo boo. Daddy got you. Shhh. Shhh." I did what any father would do. I began to rock my baby. "Damn, what is takin' yo' evil ass so long?" I yelled toward the kitchen.

Sparkle reappeared with an attitude, of course. "Here, give her this," she said with a smirk on her face.

I snatched the bottle from her ass and stuck it in my baby's mouth. Immediately, Reigna started guzzling down the bottle. "That's what was wrong with my baby. You was just hungry," I cooed, as she finished the bottle. I burped her, picked her up, and took her home.

Kreesha

My baby has been running a fever and screaming at the top of her lungs for the last three hours. When she started throwing up, I started freaking out and called my moms who called Aunt Betty.

Reign was constantly putting damp, cool towels across

her forehead. "Fuck this shit, Kree, we about to take her to the muthafuckin' doctor. She feels like she is on fire."

"Something ain't right. My baby has never been sick." Kree hung up the phone in a panic.

"Do you know how stupid you sound? Babies get sick all of the time. Their first two years are the most crucial. Even I know that."

"Okay, Dr. Spock. Are you going to come with me to the ER or sit here looking stupid?"

"Look, my daughter is sick, ain't no time for us to be arguing." My head was hurting from Reigna screaming at the top of her lungs. And now Kree was fuckin' with me.

We finally made it to the emergency room and there was no change in Reigna's condition. After they admitted her, I left my baby and Kree to go find a vending machine. I grabbed a soda and some chips. What I really needed was a blunt and some Hen dog. I found the first couch I saw and chilled. Next thing you know, I had dozed off.

I was awakened by a family of six or seven Mexicans that were loud as fuck. I looked at my watch. Damn. What's taking them so long? It's been almost two hours. I get up to see what was going on. Just as I'm questioning the receptionist at the front desk, Kree comes bursting out of the doors of the ER like a bat out of hell.

"Reign, what the fuck did you feed my baby?" she yelled, pointing her finger at me with tears streaming down her cheeks.

"Get your damn finger out of my face. What's wrong with you?"

"She's in ICU. My baby's blood pressure is so fuckin' high, that it's damn near stroke level for an adult. She's severely dehydrated and in the past couple of hours she's had two seizures. The doctors asked me for a bottle to see what was in it and they said it had an astronomical amount of salt. So now, they're calling Social Services and the police because they think I put this shit in her fuckin' bottle . . . and they told me I had to leave."

I stood there stunned. I didn't know what to say. I was lost in thought. Before catching myself, I gritted, "Fuckin' Sparkle."

"What did you just say?" Kree damn near screamed at the top of her lungs. "Did you let that bitch of yours make my baby's bottle?" She was breathing like a pit bull.

"Y-yeah," I stuttered. Kree began screaming and crying. "Wait a minute! Calm down! Sparkle wouldn't do no crazy shit like that." At least I was hoping she wouldn't.

"Oh, yes the fuck she would. She did that to my baby! How could you, Reign? Fuck this! I'll be back."

Almost instantly, her tears stopped flowing and she was lookin' crazy. "Where are you going?" I asked her.

"Don't worry about it. You stay here with your daughter and you better pray to whatever God it is you serve that my baby gets better and does not turn out mentally retarded. I'm about to go do some shit I should have done a long time ago."

I watched as Kree stormed through the double doors. I knew exactly where she was going. What was I to do, call Sparkle and warn her? Hell naw, maybe after Kree gets finished I might still choke the shit out of her ass. Shit is getting out of hand, poisoning my baby and shit.

Kreesha

I pulled up to that bitch Sparkle's house in no time. But not before I stopped and gave the doctor, the Po Po, and Social Services her address. I sped all the way to her house, thinking hard on all the shit I wanted to do to that bitch. I wanted to get her for the old and the new. I didn't even tell

Reign about her putting sugar in my gas tank. But, oh, this bitch is getting ready to pay. Fuckin' with my baby?

I banged on the door, damn near tearing it down. As soon as the bitch swung it open, I saw black. I hit that bitch so hard in the mouth that she flew backwards then fell forward. That's when I turned that bitch over, dragged her ass outside on the porch and attacked. After that, I don't remember much of anything, except for the police putting the handcuffs on me and watching the EMS haul her ass into the back of the van. A smile crept slowly across my face. Luckily for me, a warrant was already issued for Sparkle's arrest for child endangerment and I think attempted murder. That's what brought the police to her house. When they found me, I was pounding on her motionless body. It took three officers to get me off of her.

One of the officers, who was a woman, told me she didn't blame me. She then wrote me a ticket for public disturbance, whatever the fuck that means. I was expecting and prepared to go to jail and I didn't care because when I ran across Sparkle's ass again I was going to fuck her up . . . again. The officer must have read the surprised look on my face.

"Go ahead and get out of here. Your baby needs you," she said.

My punk ass was trying not to cry. My voice squeaked, "Thank you so much."

"Ma'am?"

I stopped and turned around hoping she hadn't changed her mind. "Yes?"

"You might want to go home and get cleaned up first."

I breathed a sigh of relief as I looked down at my clothes and my hands. They were covered with blood. I can only imagine what the rest of me looked like.

"Yeah, you're right. And thanks again."

I got in my car and drove off feeling a little better. I

would have killed the bitch if I thought I could have gotten away with it. Maybe next time.

Reign

I can honestly say that I know firsthand what it means to be worried to death. My daughter is laying in ICU and I can't do shit to help her. I feel helpless. I keep callin' Kree but she won't answer her phone. Sparkle's dumb ass ain't answering either. What the fuck is going on? An ass whupping shouldn't take this long. I called Sparkle's girl, Ameca, and she wants to know when is someone coming to pick up Tamia. She said she went to drop the baby off but Sparkle wasn't home. Now I know for sure that shit ain't right.

An hour later Kree shows up with her mother, Aunt Betty, and some fake ass looking attorney trailing behind her as if she's a fuckin' celebrity.

"What's going on? Where the fuck you been?" I snap, not givin' a fuck about her fake-ass entourage.

"Handlin' mine. You better go check on yo' bitch. She's down there in the ER." She smirks.

"I've been calling you for three hours straight. What did you do to her?"

"Don't worry about that."

"What happened to your face?" I'm just noticing the many scratches. "Aww shit, Kree, don't tell me—"

"Look, I don't have time to answer your twenty-one questions. I have to check on my baby."

No, this bitch didn't. "You mean our baby."

"Naw, nigga that's why I brought my lawyer. So he can issue a restraining order against you."

"What? Bitch, you ain't in Hollywood."

"Nigga, don't be callin' my daughter no bitch!" Her moms gets all up in my grill.

I put my hand up in her moms' face, letting her know now is not the time. "Kree, what kind of shit you on? This fake ass lawyer ain't gonna issue me shit."

"I didn't want to do it but–"

"But you let your phony ass entourage talk you into it."

"No, Reign, you can't be trusted. You took my baby around that sick bitch."

"Come on, Kree, you can't blame me for what happened. This is my daughter as much as yours. You know I wouldn't do shit to hurt her."

"Naw, I don't blame you. I—"

"Yes, the fuck you do!"

"I don't trust you, Reign. You got a baby by the bitch. You are a good father and I know you want your daughters to grow up together, but fuck that! I don't want my baby nowhere near either one of you. And you won't be able to be alone with my daughter anymore."

"This is bullshit! You can't keep me away from my baby."

"Oh, I can and I will. Because of that bitch, my baby is on the brink of death and it happened while she was in your care."

"Girl, you crazy as hell."

"No, Sparkle is crazy. What kind of sick person would take salt and put it in the bottle of a four-month old? You can say what you want, but don't come over, don't call, don't do shit."

"Whatever. Let me get out of here before I do something to you."

"Yes, go ahead and leave please."

"Yeah all right, you got that shit off in front of yo' funky little entourage." I walked away wanting to put my foot all up in her ass. Aunt Betty, her moms, and the fake ass lawyer was grittin' on me hard. Wait till I catch that bitch by her-self.

Before I left, I stopped by the desk to inquire about Sparkle. They gave me her room number. When I approached her room there was a doctor and a nurse coming out.

"Excuse me, can you tell me how Mrs. Johnston is doing?"

They both stopped in front of me. "And you are?" the doctor asked.

"I'm her husband, Reign Johnston."

"Your wife has been severely beaten. She suffered a ruptured spleen, two cracked ribs, and a broken jaw."

My mouth dropped open.

"I've seen a lot worse." He assured me.

"Can I see her?"

"Yes, go right ahead. Because of the pain, she is pretty well sedated but not totally out of it."

When I entered the room, no one could have ever prepared me for what I saw. Sparkle looked like someone who had been in a car crash. She was fucked up. Her jaw looked like she had two socks stuffed in it. Her eyes were swollen shut as if she were asleep. She couldn't open them even if she wanted to.

Kree really did a job on her. If I wouldn't have known what happened, ain't no way in hell I would have believed that Kree did this shit. I would have asked, "You and what army?" It was just that bad. They say don't fuck with a woman's kids. I guess Sparkle had to learn the hard way. Well, there's nothing I can do here. I left to go ask the nurse or doctor a few more questions and to see what things I needed to bring back up to the hospital for my wife.

Chapter 16

Two whole months had passed from the day the Feds did that sweep and since my baby came home from the hospital. Thank God Seven and the crew wasn't included. Reign was still on the grind. Me? Fuck that! I wasn't doin' shit but taking care of my baby all the while praying that she wasn't mentally retarded.

I'm staying away from Reign's hot ass. That nigga tried to play like I was crazy. If it wasn't for my daughter, I would have been killed by him.

Shit had been real quiet, but like Beanie Sigel said, "I can feel it in the air." And plus, the Feds was actin' like I was off the hook. No undercover cars cruisin' the block, no phone calls, not even to my attorney. So, I wasn't gonna rock the boat. I guess they was calling themselves puttin' me to sleep.

I still haven't heard from Mari. But sources told me that the Feds had stopped her drivers while they were en route with all of that weed. All of their phones had been intercepted. The Feds quickly made a deal with her drivers to take them straight to Mari's house. They promised to let them walk if they did.

For real, I was walking on egg shells. Seven and the rest of the crew were keeping their distance, and because of that I was beginning to fear for my life. Aunt Betty would just look at me and shake her head. All of that mixed with paranoia and the fact that the Feds didn't come back around had me feeling like the shit was about to blow. And about a week later, sure enough, the Feds came knocking at my door. It was exactly five A.M.

"FBI! Open up!" I hear a couple of voices yell out and then three loud booms as the door flies off its hinges.

"Give me a minute, let me throw something on!" I scream at them as I turn to run upstairs.

"FBI! FBI!" they scream out.

"Okay! Okay!" I run back downstairs wearing a nightgown only. I have no bra underneath or panties. "My baby is upstairs sleeping." They throw me to the floor and handcuff me. While my ass is hangin' out, I look at the female federalie with pleading eyes. "Please get my sweatpants lying on the chair in my bedroom." The punk-ass male Feds lift me up, then push me outside. Damn! My eyes get large as I see that they are rollin' what looks like fifty deep. It's only me and a baby. What they think I'ma do? Pull a Scarface on 'em?

A few minutes later the female federalie comes back with the sweatpants and helps me put them on. "Your mother Sandra is on her way over to get the baby," she tells me.

"Is she still asleep?"

"For now, yeah."

They push me toward the sheriff's car. I know they are in there fuckin' up my crib! Dirty bastards! Jealous hatin' asses. "Can't I sit in the house until my mother comes to pick up my baby?" These clowns don't even answer. They just open the door and shove me in the backseat. I start to panic, but relax a little when I see my moms pull up on the lawn like a bat outta hell with Aunt Betty ridin' shotgun. They both run straight into the house. I'm surprised nobody stopped them. They must have called her as soon as they hit the block.

The sheriff has his radio on. I'm listening to the reports as they are coming over the speakers. I hear them say that they are at Eboni's and had arrested her. I hear them say that they got Tax and he had a weapon and sixty thousand cash. My mom comes back out with the baby and two diaper bags. All the while I'm thinking that this shit is all my fault.

The sheriff jumps in his ride and takes me downtown to the precinct. They got two vans full of niggas. This smart-ass shows me who's inside of both vans. I see my uncle Roscoe, Corey, Tareek, Treecy, Tax, Almighty, Eboni, all crammed in one van. Just as I was thinking that's everybody, here comes another van with all of my main customers who bought anywhere from forty to one hundred pounds every time I copped. I see Mace, Doobie, Alex, Obie, Lil' Twist. Seven had a bodyguard who kept his money. She was a body building chick named Mikki. She was in the second van also. They had filled up two vans. *Damn.* Where is Seven?

Everyone is accounted for except for Reign. Oh yeah, that's right. That nigga is the police. An unmarked cruiser finally pulls up carrying Seven. Freeze isn't here, but we knew that he was out of town. I'm sure he'll be staying right where he is. I do a double take when I see Matt, my boy in the wheelchair. He's paralyzed from the waist down. The Feds just don't give a fuck! They'll lock up the crippled, young, old, lame, deaf, dumb, blind, innocent, and guilty. And crammed next to him is Tone, the nigga I would creep with every now and then. I know he wants to fuck me up, personally. Shit, all of them looking at me like I told on them and this shit is all my fault.

We all were hauled downtown to the Federal Building where they hold bond hearings and get booked and processed.

When we got outta the vans, it was media frenzy. The press was having a field day. TV cameras and microphones were everywhere. This was big news for Memphis.

Come to find out Reign had turned himself in. He was given a bond. My boy Matt in the wheelchair, Eboni, and Uncle Roscoe also got bonds. Everybody else was denied for various reasons. Seven because he was a flight risk, Corey missed court too many times, and I don't know about the rest of them cats. Me, they didn't even give me a hearing when they gave everyone else theirs. But one thing I did get: a message from Seven ordering me to do Reign or get done. When I heard that shit I was too through. I couldn't believe my family would turn on me like that. I just broke down, wishing that my brother was living. During my next few days of being on lock, I spoke to my moms about twice. Her, Aunt Betty, and the baby was fine. I needed a plan. Reign got me fucked up.

On the fourth day they finally gave me a bond hearing. My mom and Aunt Betty was there and so was Reign.

At the hearing the prosecutor leaned over and tells my lawyer to ask me if I remembered the Channel 24 news. He was talking to my attorney as if I wasn't sitting right there in front of him. But I wasn't gonna trip. I guess that's how they do in the courtroom. It's cutthroat. The prosecutors are out to win it by any means necessary. So I joined in on his little game and spoke to my attorney as if the prosecutor wasn't there. I told my attorney that I couldn't watch TV in the county jail. After I thought about what he said for a few minutes, I couldn't figure out what he was trying to say, so I just nixed it off.

Finally I made bond! Reign was there when they let me out. He gave me this weak-ass hug. I started to cuss his ass out, but I was so glad to be free, I said, "Fuck it. Take me to go get my baby. I miss her very much." On my way over there I mentioned to Reign that the prosecutor asked me if I remembered the Channel 24 news. I asked, "Did something else happen while I was locked up?"

His response was, "Not that I know of."

Chapter 17

Two days later I had an appointment to see my lawyer. I took Reign with me but had him wait out in the lobby, since his ass insisted on coming with me.

The first thing my lawyer hit me with as soon as I stepped into his office was, "Young lady, I normally don't recommend that you talk to the prosecutor; that's what I'm getting paid for. But in your case, I advise that we go talk to him. You can listen but my advice is not say a word. Do you understand?"

I'm like, What the fuck? So I asked, "Is this what you're advising me to do? Why would I talk to the prosecutor?"

"In your case, I'm not advising you to talk. I'm advising you to listen."

Reign was pacing back and forth out in the lobby when I finally came out. I immediately told him that my lawyer suggested that I talk to the prosecutor. Then I asked him, "What do you think I should do?"

Before I could get the words out of my mouth good, he answered, "If I was you, I wouldn't talk to them."

My knees got weak as more and more signs were pointing to him being the police. Right then it took everything I had within me not to blow. "My lawyer said I should at least listen to what they have to say, so that's what I'm going to do."

The nigga is already dark. Well, he just turned three shades darker. "Then why in the fuck you asked for my opinion? You got your mind made up! Fuck it!" He looked at me, trying to avoid eye contact, then said, "Do you! I'm going to get something to eat. I'll be here when you get back."

I went back into the lawyer's office and said, "Let's do it!" He was already ready. He grabbed his briefcase, and we jumped onto the elevator. As we walked around the corner to the Federal Building, I was feeling like I was walking to the gas chamber or some shit like that. We weren't even there yet and I felt doomed.

We arrived at the Federal Building and took the elevator to the eighth floor. Obviously they were expecting us because when we walked into the conference room, already seated around the table in little chairs were the prosecutor, whose name was Pete, Ms. Lynch the IRS representative, and FBI agents Reynolds, Hearns, and Johnson.

The prosecutor said, "I want you to sit in the big chair, Ms. Henderson." He pointed to a big, cushiony, leather reclining chair. After I sat down, he said, "I gotta give it to you, Ms. Henderson, you were a smart girl, considering all of the other kingpins you are associated with." He named Seven, Tax, Freeze, Tareek, and Almighty.

"Don't label me with them motherfuckers! Those niggas are big-time!" I blurted out.

My lawyer jumped up and came over by my side and grabbed my shoulders. "Just listen, okay." He put his finger up to his lips, motioning for me to keep mine the fuck closed.

The prosecutor continued, "Yeah, just listen, Ms. Henderson. You don't have to say anything. You were smart and you cost the government a shit load of money, but you weren't smart enough. You know the cell phone Reign Johnston gave you?"

"Who?"

My lawyer jumped up again. "Just listen."

This bastard had the nerve to repeat himself. "You know the cell phone that Reign Johnston gave you?"

"Who is Reign?" The room began spinning at the sound of his name. The prosecutor was now sounding just like Charlie Brown's schoolteacher. It was like I had just taken some acid or some shit like that.

"Your boyfriend, Reign Johnston. That phone that he gave you." He pointed over to agent Hearns, who raised his hand.

"That was my phone," he said. "Every time you got a call, I got a call." Agent Hearns had a huge grin on his face.

Then the prosecutor said, "You know that pager Reign gave you?"

Agent Reynolds hollered, "That was my pager! Every time you got a page, I got a page."

I broke down and cried. My lawyer came over and gave me some tissue.

The prosecutor said, "Don't cry, now, you're a big girl. However, I do want you to know that Reign Johnston sold you out, and the baby, for his freedom. At least he hopes so. But it actually started with the five pounds. Don't you remember when you were on the phone talking to your aunt about seeing his car on the Channel 24 news? We were already listening to your aunt's calls. So"—he paused, obviously satisfied at his handiwork—"Reign started working for me on that day. From that day on he was our property. Ms. Henderson, I had the pleasure of listening to all of your phone calls. You had all the right answers, but you were too in love to accept that he was the police. You had the enemy right there in your bed. Because of him, you are now facing anywhere between five to twenty-five years. You can join Mr. Johnston and cooperate, or don't."

"Give us time to consult," my lawyer jumped in before I could open up my big mouth.

The prosecutor continued, "Several people have already issued their statements against you. The only thing you could do is tell us what we want to hear to help yourself out. You got that daughter to raise. We know a lot. I know you put fifteen thousand down on Reign's house and it was a non-qualifying loan. I know that you put eighteen thousand down on yours. I know everything in your house is all paid for. I know that you have never worked a day in your life. I know about the shipment of three-to-five hundred pounds of marijuana that would sell out in two, three days. I know about the cocaine and the Express Mail boxes delivered to unsuspecting residents while they are hard at work. Mr. Johnston, your boyfriend, spilled his guts. We were already conducting an investigation on the kingpins, and you got handed to us when you placed a call to Seven, aka Mr. Kevin McKnight. You were a big bonus! But you were in the process of moving and always on the go, so we couldn't get you on tape. So that's where Mr. Reign Johnston came in. You were a bonus that connected the dots to all of the kingpins."

The entire room was silent except for my sniffling.

My lawyer said, "Give us a couple of days."

I looked at him as if he lost his mind. A couple of days? I needed time to pack and leave the fuckin' country! I was so sick I couldn't even talk. My lawyer helped me to my feet and practically carried me out.

Chapter 18

"C'mon, Kreesha, get yourself together." My little-ass lawyer was calling himself, picking me up off the floor. I don't know what he was thinking. I outweighed his ass by at least fifty pounds. I wasn't lying on the floor, I was sitting down, and I did have my back up against the wall. He was turning red because of all the attention I was attracting. He handed me his handkerchief. "Stop crying. Dry your eyes. Get it together."

"What do you mean don't cry?" I yelled. "My life is over. How could they do this? How can the Feds get away with settin' people up like this? How could Reign do this to me?" I was bawlin' like a two-year-old who just got his bottle snatched out of his mouth.

My lawyer was finally able to get me up and into the bathroom. I eventually got myself together, and we headed on back to his office. On our walk over my lawyer was constantly flappin' his gums. I screamed, "Shut up! I can't think and listen to you at the same time." He shut up. A few minutes later I told him, "He's probably still at your office."

"Who?"

"Reign. My boyfriend who set me up, my daughter's father."

"Damn it, Kreesha! How are you going to play this off?

How are you going to ride back with him? Look at you! You look devastated! You can't let him know, not yet." We stopped in front of his office building. "Kreesha, this is serious. You can't let him know that you know. Do you understand me?" Spit was flying outta his mouth.

"I got you, Mark. I got this." He looked at me all skeptical and shit. "I said I got this."

"Okay. But I need you to think about what you want to do and be in my office first thing in the morning."

"What do you mean what I want to do?"

"Kreesha. They've got you. That, that, that guy up there gave you to the Feds on a silver platter! Weren't you listening to them? They've got you. It's a no-win situation."

"Look, I'll call you in the morning."

"I said be here in the morning, not call."

I walked away, leaving him standing outside, and went up to get Reign, while wondering if he was gonna be there.

This motherfucker was sittin' where I left him and was thumbing through a magazine, like he didn't have a care in the world. He was really playin' his role. "C'mon, Reign. I'm through here." He got up, and we walked silently all the way to his car. The tension in the air was mad thick.

No sooner than we got seated in the car, he asked, "What they say? What they say?"

I was so sick I couldn't even talk. This nigga shut the car off. *Oh, shit!* I thought to myself. *He's getting ready to kill me!* But fuck that! Not before I kill him.

He banged on the dashboard and screamed, "What the fuck did they say?"

I burst out crying. At this point there was no doubt in my mind that he knew that I knew that he set me up.

I looked at him. "When I got with you, you ain't have shit! Your punk ass was barely makin' commissary! I was your star team player. I even carried your seed, put you on, and now your wife, her family, all of y'all is eatin' real good, because of me. How could you give me a phone and beeper for the police? Where is your fuckin' spine? How could you do this to me? Fuck me, what about your daughter? I'm about to go to prison, nigga. I did everything. And you would play me like this? You snake-ass faggot!" With the look he had on his face, you could have bought him for half a penny. I had never, ever seen that look on his face. I can't even describe it.

"Kreesha, listen to me. They tricked me. They said they only wanted the Colombian connect. I gave them the Colombian connect so that me and you could walk. Even my uncle, the deputy sheriff, cosigned for the Feds. They all tricked me, Kree. You gotta believe me. You know I would never get that gutter with you."

"Nigga, you busted and you still lying! What am I supposed to do now? I got a fuckin' contract hangin' over my head. Everyone is pissed at me. No one wants to be bothered with me. They talkin' five to twenty-five years, Reign. You fuckin' asshole!" I slapped him. "What about the baby? And the fucked up part about it is the Feds had no problem putting you on blast. What? You thought I wouldn't find out? Not! It's over for you 'cause as soon as them Colombians and Seven get wind of this, yo' ass is grass." I'm crying a river fo' real now.

He took my hand and whispered, "Let's leave the country."

I looked at him like he was crazy. "Do what?"

"Fuck these Feds! Let's leave the country. Go home, gather up your loot, pack a few things, and when I get there we'll go pick up the baby and we jet." I stared at him, and this nigga was dead serious.

"Just like a coward you want to run. You should have thought of that before you gave me them hot ass phones. How are we gonna do that? What about your wife?"

"I'll handle her."

There he goes again with that I'll handle her shit. Does it ever end? I thought. I should take that as a sign.

"Let's go, Kree. Aiight?" I just looked at him. "Kreesha, let's go, aiight?" I nodded my head yes. He started the car up and looked at his watch. "It's almost four. I'll drop you off, and then I'll be back around ten for you and the baby. Aiight?" He leaned over and kissed me before pulling off.

Everything was gonna be all right.

Reign

Whew! I didn't know how I was going to get Kreesha to roll with me but I did it. That bitch gotta be dick whipped. I need to bronze my johnson and put him in the Hall of Fame. I mean damn.

On my way over to the crib, I'm trying to figure out how to get over this next hurdle. I gotta talk wifey into letting Kree roll with us. It's only temporary. We just gotta add Kree to our itinerary and get her passport.

When I get into the house the first thing I see is Sparkle lying on the floor, her hands and feet tied together and her mouth duct taped.

"C'mon in, nigga." Tax is sittin' on my living room couch with *my* fuckin' .387 resting on his lap.

On impulse I turn to run, but I'm met with a Louisville slugger in my stomach that folds me over. I grunt and roll back and forth on the floor as my stomach feels like it's going to split open. And then I feel a foot coming down on my neck. I can barely breathe.

"Snitches get stitches, boy." Seven nonchalantly pulled out his two-way and looked at it. "Just like a ho ass nigga. Instead of trying to help his wife he tries to run." Seven sighed as he put his two-way back in his pocket. "Make sure Kree puts her snitchin' bitch to sleep."

He tossed the bat onto the couch, kicked me in my stomach and disappeared out the door.

Tax tied me up and then swooped up a limp Sparkle and took her upstairs.

Kreesha

"Shit." I am on edge and paranoid as hell. I'm thinking to myself my phone is tapped and they are probably watching my house. But then again probably not. If you work for them, the government lets you get away with all types of shit. Look at Reign. He was working for them and still grindin'. Didn't even change up his routine. The system is fucked up. The Feds are some grimey muthafuckers! I'm running around the house trying to fill up three bags. One with cash, one with my stuff, and one for the baby. At 9:48 I hear a faint knock. I know this nigga still has the key. Why isn't he using it? I run to the door and swing it open, and yell, "I'm almost ready!"

"Ready for what?" In comes Freeze. I'm kinda shocked and confused. I know he's on the lam, but here he is standing there, and he's looking very serious. "Why you lookin' at me like that? You look like you seen a ghost." He steps inside and closes the door.

"I thought you was Reign." I go and give him a hug. "You okay?"

"I'm free, so for the time being I'm okay. You cook tonight? Me and Reign is hungry. He told me to tell you to bring him a plate."

I didn't cook. Now I'm really stuck on stupid. "Bring him a plate? Where is he?"

"He's at one of the spots. We tryna put our heads together to decide what we're gonna do. We're in a fucked-up situation. We need you in on this meeting. C'mon and ride with me, he can bring you back home."

We jump in his ride, and all kinds of thoughts are running through my mind. But then I really start to freak when it looks like we are going to Reign's house. "Where we goin', Freeze?" He must have sensed that I'm in panic mode.

"Chill, Kree, we goin' to your man's house. I said one of our spots." He started laughing. "I know you stalked the nigga there a time or two, so don't act like your ass ain't been there before. Plus you brought the muthafucka right?"

"Isn't his wife home?"

"So? Fuck her. This is business. Business always comes first."

"Was that business when y'all raped Eboni?" I had to get that off.

He smirked at me and then he smiled. "Actually, it was."

"And how do you figure that?"

"Let her explain it to you." He left it at that, letting me know that was a dead issue as far as he was concerned.

We rode in silence the rest of the way to Reign's block.

"I never have been inside of his damn place," I said, as I'm looking at the porch where I beat Sparkle's ass.

"Well, you bought it. Don't you think you're entitled?" I just sit looking stupid as he turns the car off. "Come on. I ain't got all night."

We get out, and as I'm trudging up the steps, why does it feel like I'm walkin' to my doom? He taps on the door, and finally it opens. But guess who opens it? Tax. Now, when I see this nigga, I know for sho' something ain't right.

"Tax." I weakly say his name.

"What up, baby?"

"You're free."

"Well, you know they can't keep the good niggas down."

"I hear you," I half-heartedly say as I peek around, eyeing my surroundings.

We all walk into the living room. "Oh my God!" I scream, and I run over to Reign and try to untie him. They got him bound like a pig. His nose is busted, lips bleeding, eyes swollen, and he has a knot on his head. "Why y'all do this to him?" I'm screaming at Freeze and Tax. I get up and go find the kitchen, grab a dish towel, and wet it.

"If you don't do him we gonna have to do you. And that didn't come from me, that came from Seven. And I know this guttersnipe ain't more important than you and your daughter." Tax shoved Reign's gun into my hand.

"I can't do it," I say weakly.

Tax then holds up what looks like some IDs and says, "Kree, why you so gone over this snitch-ass nigga?" He throws the IDs at me, and they scatter on the floor. I pick them up. This nigga has passports for him and his wife. He has birth certificates, social security cards, the works. I look over at Reign. Of course, this nigga has me speechless once again.

"Yeah, you seein' right. Ole boy was on his way outta here. But guess what? You wasn't invited!" Tax said in a sing-songy voice. Him and Freeze burst into laughter. Tax holds out his gun. "Do this nigga right now, Kree. Don't let this nigga play you like a sucka!"

"I was comin' for you, Kree. Tell 'em." Reign is trying his best to talk through a mouthful of blood and loose teeth.

I was seeing fire. "How could you do this to me? What did I ever do to you?" Once again this nigga had me crying a river, but this was the *last* time.

"Girl." Freeze had lost all patience. He picks up the Louisville slugger and slams it into Reign's head. I swear I heard his skull crack. "I told you I ain't got all night!"

"Shut up, Freeze!" I scream. "Where's the bitch? If I ain't going, she ain't either." I run up the steps.

I hear Tax saying, "What the fuck is the matter with her? Kree is a dumb bitch!" But I don't care. I grab the first door that I see, and they got wifey tied up, mouth gagged, and she's lying on the bed. I look around, and her shit is packed and ready to roll. I don't know where the baby is. She looks at me, her eyes get big, and she is trying to say something. I'm in a zone. "I know you tried to kill my baby. I told you I was going to get you." I don't even hesitate. I go over, put the gun to her temple, and squeeze two times. That shit felt good. I smile as I wipe a splash of blood off my cheek. My adrenaline is flowing. I run back down the steps and stand in front of Reign. He starts begging.

"Kree, I always loved you. A nigga made a mistake."

"Well, you was my mistake. But I'ma show you how to handle it!" I pull the trigger. Once, aiming at his head, then again, at his heart. His bloody body lay limp on the couch.

"Don't you feel better now?" Freeze asks me.

Tax comes over and takes the gun outta my hand. "You did good, sis, for what it's worth. But Seven told me to tell you that you violated our code. You let the enemy in."

He is now aiming the gun at me, and you know what? I don't even give a fuck!

I slowly fall to my knees. Freeze starts laughing. "Damn, yo! This look like some New Jack City shit! Am I my brother's keeper?" he yells. "Am I my brother's keeper? Kree, you really playin' this shit out." They both fall into a laughing fit.

When the first bullet hits me, it feels like I just swallowed a ball of fire. I hear my aunt Betty saying, "You gotta be careful of who you sleep with." Then I hear Tareek say, "We gotta do the same thing to Eboni, she's waiting on us." When he fires the next bullet, the Grim Reaper picks me up.

As Freeze and Tax were leaving the house Tax said, "She was soft just like her brother. I told you that a soft heart and emotions is what would bring her down. Bitches ain't built for the game, I don't give a fuck what nobody say."

"Plus, people was tryna tell her. But she wouldn't heed them warnings. You gotta heed them warnings." Freeze ended this chapter with those words of wisdom . . .

Acknowledgments

All praise is forever due to the Creator, the Beneficent, the Most Merciful. To my King: Thank You for your unwavering support and patience with a sista that can't slow down. Thank you for allowing me to think that I'm running the show. The Bulletproof Love just gets thicker. Kisha, you know I appreciate all of your sacrifices, every day. I know you hate when the mail man comes with envelopes from me stuffed with things to do. Do you want to sometimes press 7 when I call? You better not, sista! Hang in there. I'ma be Oprah, you're Gayle. I pray that I'll be there shortly.

To all of the other sisters who sacrifice their time to help make me to be that force to be reckoned with: Hijrah, who is always willing to do whatever, whenever, and never complains. Shakira, thanks for all of the copies and copies and more copies. Samataha, please don't get carpal tunnel from all of the typing. We appreciate it. Aisha, a/k/a Roz: I love you. My dawg from way back when. Thanks for doing whatever you can. Hasana & Wahida, stay focused and do what I told y'all to do so that y'all will be ready for me. Your moms will be there shortly. Jabaar, Amin, Hussein, Samaad, Al-Nisa, Birdie, and Hafida and all of the brothas. I appreciate you all. Especially those out there beatin' the streets with my books.

Ron-Ron. You inspired me to write this story. This goes to you. I miss you. Keep your head up and stay on the right track. Malika, I didn't forget you. Keep making me proud. Get that college degree. You go, girl!

Nikki Turner. To the sista who don't like to drive. You said it all when you made the trip down to see me. Hold fast. You put the "T" in Thorough! Thanks for everything. *Felon* mag, thanks for the interview. And Jaheim, where you at? Call Uncle Charlie or Earl, I got a project for you! Holla!

To my readers who always give me feedback. KK Wall, Sandy Moore and Red and Keisha. Thanks a mill. Jeracha, we gettin' ready to do big things!

To my agents—thanks for everything you have done and will do. And Adina, I thank you for your help while you were at BlackPrint. One Love Ma!

To all the authors who send me books, mail, and shout outs—Al-Saadiq Banks, Darren Coleman, Marvin Ellison, Darrin Lowery Smith, Brenda L. Thomas, Tiffany Womble, K'wan, Kwame Teaque. I appreciate the love. To the bookstores and street vendors. I got y'all.

Last but not least. To my readers. Y'all are the fuel to my fire. I love y'all. And thanks sooooo much for the support!

I'm out! One!

P.S. *Enemy in My Bed* and its acknowledgments were written back in '04.

Keeping My Enemies Close

Kiki Swinson

Chapter 1

Men aren't worth shit

"**H**e better be gone when I get home. I put up with a lot of his shit, and this was the last straw," I mumbled out loud as I waited for the traffic light to turn green. The woman in the next car probably thought I was losing my mind. I was so preoccupied with my ongoing conversation I could not have cared less what she thought. And as soon as the light turned green, I left her in the dust and was immediately reminded that I was less than two blocks away from my apartment.

A huge knot formed in the pit of my stomach the instant I pulled into my apartment complex. The thick summer air smacked me in the face the moment I opened up my car door. As we all know, the summer brings out the freaks, so the parking lot behind my apartment building was crawling with people. Right after I locked my car door and began to walk toward my building, all the so-called hustlers lined up alongside their vehicles and started whistling at me, but I couldn't be bothered. *Been there done that, got the T-shirt and the hat. I'd rather work for mine. It's time for me to rise to the top and stand on my own two feet,* I reminded myself. One guy in particular kept making comments about how he would love to take me out to dinner and get to know me better. When I continued to ignore him, his true colors came out.

"Oh, bitch, you ain't all that just because you're pretty with long hair and a fat ass. I fuck with hos that look better than you!" he screamed.

But again, I refused to entertain any of their bullshit. Every last one of those lame-ass niggas had at least three baby mommas, drove a pimped-out Chevy or an Oldsmobile with twenty-inch rims, and had an IQ of 105. They were immature as hell, and as soon as they ran across a half-Indian and black chick with a college degree and some class such as myself, they got all intimidated and started showing their asses. So the way I handled them was by ignoring them and keeping it moving. I sure wish I would have done the same thing with the nigga I spent damn near four years with.

When I met Todd, my so-called man, I thought that he could change the world. Yes, I knew he was a hustler from Young's Park, but what did I care; he gave the money and excitement I was looking for. Not to mention he was F-I-N-E. He had a body to die for, which I later found out came from having nothing to do but work out during a five-year bid in Indian Creek State Penitentiary.

At first, blinded by Gucci bags and Jimmy Choo shoes, I overlooked his blatant infidelity. But after six trips to my primary care physician for antibiotics to cure my dripping pussy, I had had enough. The last time he cheated, I warned him that I would not take it anymore, but what did this motherfucker do? He pushed the envelope, tested the waters, and started fucking with a nineteen-year-old chick named Rema that lived right around the block from me. And to make matters worse, I heard the bitch was three months pregnant. Now what kind of shit was that? But you know what? It's okay. She can have his grimey ass because I am done with his bullshit once and for all.

Now, as soon as I stepped into my apartment, I immediately knew something was amiss. I was overwhelmed by a strong odor; it smelled like Clorox mixed with ammonia. I began coughing and gagging. "What the hell?" I said out loud as I continued down the short hallway toward my bedroom. The smell got stronger the farther I went. And when I entered my bedroom, I found that my closet door was gaping wide open. Upon further review, I noticed that every stitch of my clothes were gone. "Wait, now I know this nigga didn't steal all my damn clothes," I said to myself, confused. By now I had my hands covering my mouth and nose because the fumes were so strong. I closed the closet door, noticing that the sheets were missing from my bed, and the mattress had been sliced and diced, with cotton spilling out of it like a gutted animal. I began to get nervous. I ran into the bathroom, which was adjacent to the bedroom. There I noticed that my medicine cabinet hung open and was empty; the cabinet under the sink was also empty of my toiletries and smell-good essentials. The mirror on the medicine cabinet was smashed, and the glass lay in the small sink below it. Even my cushioned toilet seat had been sliced up, which would have made taking a shit impossible at that moment, although the nervous knot in my stomach was forcing me to feel the urge. Nevertheless, nothing prepared me for what I found next. Amidst all of the coughing, gagging, and eye tearing, I managed to pull back the shower curtain. "OH NO THE FUCK HE DIDN'T!" I screamed, incensed.

Todd had filled the tub with water, bleach, ammonia, Mr. Clean, laundry detergent, and any other household cleaner he could find, and put everything I owned—my clothes, toiletries, shoes, boots, expensive handbags, my mink jacket, contact lenses, bed sheets, towels, and face cloths—in the solution. All of my shit was ruined; there was no saving it. The bleach and ammonia together could make a bomb, so by mixing it, it had eaten away most of the material that comprised my belongings. Smoke was rising from the bathtub, and I was scared that if I touched anything, it would explode. I left the bathroom in shock, I ran into the kitchen to survey if he had done any other damage, and yes, he'd struck again. I found all my dishes broken and in the sink. The glasses were broken into shards so small it appeared that he must have taken his time with a spoon or a hammer to smash them. I could not even get the glass out of the drain; that's just how small the pieces were. By this time, I was hysterical. I walked into the living room expecting disaster, and once again Todd didn't disappoint me. He had sliced up the leather sofa and the love seat. The DVD player and Sony surround sound system lay in shambles. I pressed the power button on the television, and sparks started flying out of the back. Seeing this sent me running. The TV didn't explode, but I later found out that he had poured water into the back of it. I stood outside the front door of my apartment and fumbled through my handbag for my cell phone. When I finally found it through all the junk I had scattered inside, I grabbed it and immediately dialed my best friend Tenisha's number.

"Hello," she answered with a hoarse voice, pretending to be asleep.

"You sleep?" I asked, my voice quivering.

"Yeah," Tenisha breathed into the receiver.

"Well, get up! You ain't gonna believe what this nigga did to me!" I screamed.

"Mmmmm," she moaned, hoping that if she sounded like she was out of it, I would tell her I'd call her later.

"Come on, Tee, I know that fake sleep act. Now, get up and stop being selfish all of your life! I need to talk to you!" I yelled, on the brink of tears.

"Okay . . . what happened now?" she asked reluctantly. I knew she was tired of all my Todd stories, especially after all I'd been through with him and always managed to give him the benefit of the doubt and go running back to him with open arms. But this time it was different—he was gone for good this time. So I needed her shoulder to lean on.

"Girl, he destroyed everything I owned. He put all my shit in the tub and poured bleach, ammonia, and whatever else he could find in it." I began to cry. Then ten seconds later, I broke down.

"Why did he do that?" she asked nonchalantly.

"Because I told his ass to get out."

"Well, this ain't the first time you told him to get out, so there must be something you're not telling me."

"I just found out that bitch Rema is pregnant."

"You mean that young chick he was fucking around with?"

"Yes, and she's parading around here telling everybody, too."

"Oh, now *that's* serious."

"I know. And that's why I couldn't let that one slide."

"You did right by putting his no-good ass out. But I think I would've done it a different way, like change the locks or something so he would not have gotten in to mess your shit up."

"Well, it's too late for that," I replied between sobs.

"So, what are you going to do now?"

"I don't know. But I can't stay here while the place is like this."

"Wait there, I'm gonna come by and see you," she said.

"Okay, I'll be standing outside waiting for you," I told her, and then we hung up.

Tenisha arrived at my apartment building in no time. She found me sitting outside on the hood of my candy apple red 2006 Acura TL with eighteen-inch chrome rims.

"Come on, take me in the house and show me what that bastard did," she said as she grabbed a hold of my arm. She literally had to drag me upstairs to my apartment. That's just how weak I had become. My whole body had become numb after it hit me that everything I owned was gone. Tenisha had the same reaction when she entered the apartment.

"Oh my God! I cannot believe that motherfucker did this to you when he was the one out cheating! The nerve of that bastard!" She cursed, surveying the damages for herself. "I know one thing, you need to get on the phone and call your cousin Marlo so he can get his crew together so they can go out and look for that sorry-ass nigga and whip his ass!" she continued.

I stood a few feet away from her and watched her make a lot of facial expressions and hand gestures as she spoke her mind. I guess she thought that I was exaggerating over the phone.

I shook my head. "Nah, I'd rather not, because if Marlo saw this shit, he'd probably kill him," I told her. And it was true. My cousin Marlo would do just that. He and I were first cousins on my mother's side. We practically grew up together and slept in the same bed, so he's more like a brother in a sense. I'm one year older than he is, but he still acts like he's the oldest, which is why he's so protective of me. I love him to death, so I refuse to bring him into my drama with Todd. Not only that, if Marlo got wind of what was going on, his sister Kamryn was going to definitely find out. She's got a big-ass mouth. She heads up the gossip mill of the family, and when she finds out dirt she lets everybody know. God forbid if my mother found out what was going on with me and Todd. She'd probably have a stroke. And I can't have that. So, I had to handle this matter on my own.

"Let's go. You're staying at my house tonight," she told me, helping me toward the front door. I could barely walk. All I could think about was everything that I owned in the world was destroyed. I didn't have shit but the clothes on my back, a little over eleven hundred dollars in my bank account, and the Gucci bag on my shoulder. So I was in bad shape. I've got to use six hundred of it on my car payment and my insurance that's due. I just hope and pray something comes my way.

I ended up following Tenisha to her apartment which was less than three miles from my place. She lived in Dockside apartments off South Military Highway, not too far from Military Circle Mall. My apartment was near the mall, too. As a matter of fact, it was off Popular Hall Drive. So it only took us a hop, skip, and a jump to get back to her place. And once we got to her house, I could hear her telephone ringing inside while we were standing outside her front door, so she quickly fished around in her bag for her keys.

"Shit, that's the phone call I'd been waiting for," she cursed, rushing to unlock and open the door. The way she ran to the phone, I thought it was a job calling. Tenisha had not worked since we left high school. But she stay fly. She had all the latest handbags, shoes, clothes, coats, beautiful jewelry, and she had a nice car. Her mother was one of the worst crack heads in Norfolk, so she wasn't getting shit from her. Tenisha was a man hustler. Whereas I wanted a man to settle down with and fall in love, Tenisha's favorite men were dead presidents, Franklin, Grant, Jackson, and Lincoln. She was all about her paper.

I watched her as she yanked the cordless phone from the base. "Hello. Yes. I'll accept the charges," she said into the receiver, out of breath. "Hey, you. No. I had to run out the house for a minute," I heard her say. I went into the living room and lay on the sofa. My head was pounding. Tenisha stayed on the phone a few more minutes before calling me.

"Larissa, can you come here a minute? I want you to speak to somebody," Tenisha yelled from the kitchen.

I got up from the sofa and dragged myself back into the kitchen. "Who is it?" I wondered aloud, my face screwed up.

Tee muffled the receiver with the palm of her hand. "I want you to say hello to my man's cellmate."

"I don't feel like talking to your man's cellmate," I grumbled and turned around to leave.

Tenisha came stomping down behind me, with her hand still covering the mouthpiece of the receiver. "Girl, get your ass on this phone and talk to this man," she whispered, shoving the phone in my face.

"For what? What can he do for me locked up behind bars?" I snapped.

"Well, for starters he can put a few dollars in your bank account if you'd just get on the phone and say hello."

"Girl, please, that nigga ain't got no money." I pushed the phone away from me.

"Larissa," Tee said, grinding her teeth, trying to prevent from cursing me out, "if you'd stop jumping to conclusions and just get on the damn phone, you'd find yourself in better shape. Believe me, the nigga I'm trying to get you to holler at got plenty of money. Now won't you stop acting stupid and say hello?"

I couldn't respond to her after the comment she made. I just stood there and looked dumbfounded. Meanwhile she put the phone up to my ear. "Hello," I said in a low whisper.

"How you doing?" I heard the smooth baritone voice say. I couldn't front. If this cat looked anything like the voice sounded, then I knew he was fine.

"Who is this?" I asked nonchalantly.

"My name is Sean. But everybody calls me Supreme."

"Nice to know," I replied casually.

"What yours?"

"Larissa." I sighed heavily.

"Are you all right?" He changed his tone.

"Yes, I'm fine." I tried to sound a little livelier.

"So, what's good? Got a man?"

"Not anymore."

"Well, can we be friends?"

"I'm sorry, but I am not in the mood to be making new friends," I growled, screwing my face up at Tenisha. I'd become really irritated by his advancements because he doesn't know me from the next chick. All he wants is some companionship. He probably could not care less about what I look like just as long as he can get a couple of collect calls through. And besides, what in the hell can he do for me? Nothing but try to get me to write him, go visit him, and ask me to send him money for commissary, and I can't do it. I can't afford any handouts right now. Shit, I'm the one who needs one, so in other words he's barking up the wrong tree.

Tenisha nudged me in my arm. "Stop being so damn mean and give him a chance, will you?" she whispered.

"Well, that's cool. But if you change your mind, hop in the ride with your homegirl the next time she comes this way."

"All right," I told him, and handed the phone back to Tenisha.

She abruptly snatched the receiver out of my hands, but it didn't bother me. I turned right back around and headed into the living room.

Tenisha was able to utter a few more words to her friend Jay before the timer on the call ran out. And before I knew it, she was dead on my heels. "Why you had to be so cold?" she didn't hesitate to ask.

"Look, Tee, I just got out of a crazy-ass relationship. So I am not trying to get in another one, especially when I don't even know him. I mean, he could be some kind of rapist or crazed maniac or something."

"Girl, Supreme isn't a rapist. He used to be the biggest crack dealer in the Tidewater area. That nigga was paid out the ying yang when he was on the streets, and all the hos used to sweat the hell out of him, too."

"Okay, all that sounds good, but what in the hell can he do for me while he's on lock?" I asked incredulously. Tenisha must be out of her fucking mind.

"Do you know that that nigga still has dough?"

"How long has he been locked up?"

"I think he's been locked up since '97. But Jay told me he's on his way home, so he's looking for a chick that'll ride with him for the rest of his bid. And believe me, if you get with him, he's going to make sure you are all right."

"Okay, and what is he going to get out of all this?"

"Look, all I know is that he's looking for a fly-ass chick to come home to, that's it. You fit that bill, so act like you got some sense and get with the program."

I shook my head. "Tee, I don't know about this."

"Girl, just look at it like this: if you get with Supreme, you aren't gonna have to worry about money problems or wonder if he's lying in another ho's bed," she said pointedly.

"I don't know, Tee. I am so tired of trifling-ass men," I

whined, putting my head down on the arm of the sofa. I was really frustrated with the opposite sex.

"Wait, before you say another word, I have a picture of him and Jay together," she said as she started toward her bedroom to get the photo. *This bitch is really serious,* I said to myself. Looking down at my feet and the only pair of shoes I had, I reminded myself that things didn't look too good for me financially.

"Girl, if I wasn't fucking with Jay, I would've snatched Supreme up a long time ago," she announced as soon as she came walking back into the living room, holding several Polaroid pictures. She flopped down next to me. "This one right here is Supreme," she said, pointing to one of the two guys in the picture. I snatched the photo from her hand and held it up close to my face. The two guys were bending down, giving each other a five with their hands locked—the typical jailhouse pose. The guy on the left was the one Tenisha said was Supreme. He was definitely handsome. And from that wife beater he was sporting, I could tell he was bench pressing at least two hundred pounds of steel a day. He also had on a fresh pair of sparkling white Nike Air Force Ones, which looked really neat on his feet. The gray sweatpants he wore didn't look half bad either.

"He's all right," I finally said, throwing the picture back on Tenisha's lap. But quiet as kept, homeboy looked real good. He kind of put me in the mind of that actor Idris Elba from Tyler Perry's movie *Daddy's Little Girls*. He had that actor's chiseled features and his height, his build, and his dark skin complexion. He was definitely my type.

"Oh, you're so phony because that nigga looks real good," she said as she took another look at the photo. "I told you if I wasn't fucking with Jay, I would be all over Supreme," she continued, and I believed her. Tenisha was light-skinned but with squinty eyes and a head full of weave. She was a very beautiful woman. And she had the body to complement her beauty. My ass was much bigger than hers, but she's a much bigger freak, so men find themselves gravitating to her more so than me. It's been like this since we became best friends in high school, so I don't think it's going to change anytime soon.

Instead of responding to her comment, I closed my eyes and pretended not to hear her. So she slapped me on my knee to get my attention. "I am going up there to see them tomorrow, so let me know what you're gonna do," she said, irritated, and then she walked out of the room.

Chapter 2

How I got my groove back

At the last minute I decided to take the ride with Tee up to the penitentiary to see this Supreme cat. I did it only because she badgered the hell out of me. I heard her on the phone with Jay last night, so he probably had something to do with it, I'm sure. Tenisha lent me her fuchsia-colored Roberto Cavalli wraparound dress since I had nothing to wear of my own. I slid on my Gucci sandals, combed my hair down from my wrap, and called it a day.

"Damn, you look better in that dress than I do," Tee commented.

"That's just because I've got more ass than you."

"So I've noticed," she replied sarcastically, giving me the *so what look,* and then she turned around and headed toward the front door.

"Are you driving your car?" I asked.

"Yes, we are," she told me, and then she made her exit. "Make sure you lock the bottom lock," she continued, her voice fading out.

"All right," I said, and met her in the car a few moments later.

* * *

It had been a minute since I had to visit a nigga in prison, so to go through all that searching shit was beginning to become a little nerve-wracking. I sucked it up since this wasn't going to be an everyday occurrence. Of course, the visiting room was packed to the rim. Baby mommas and their kids were all over the place, so me and Tenisha scooted out their way and found a seat near the vending machines. On our way through the crowd we got a few stares, but that shit didn't flatter us at all. I could not have cared less about these damn jailbirds staring at me. I can't say that for their women, though. If looks could kill, me and Tee would be laid out on this floor. But since we were alive and still breathing, I refused to be worried about how they were hating on us. As long as they kept their distance from us, then everything was going to be all right on my end.

Now, about twenty seconds after we took a seat at the table, Tenisha noticed that Jay and Supreme was looking around the visiting room for us. "We're over here." She stood up and waved.

When Tee got their attention, they started walking toward us. "You know we're gonna have to sit at separate tables, right?" she mentioned to me.

"I'm not sitting with him by myself," I protested.

"Well, you're gonna have to. That's rules. And besides, even if the prison did allow Jay and Supreme to sit together, I wouldn't want y'all all over top of me while my boo and I talk dirty to each other," she replied flatly, and then she moved forward to greet Jay.

Right after they embraced each other and kissed, they took the seat at the table just a couple of feet away from me. Jay did manage to speak to me before Tenisha abruptly ushered him away. I spoke back and immediately shifted my focus to Supreme.

"Hi," I said in a low whisper. Mesmerized by his entire being, I couldn't take my eyes off this man. Pictures did him no justice. Supreme was a handsome man. From the low-cut waves that danced around his head to the full and well-trimmed beard that caressed his smooth face. His nose was the perfect size, his eyes were deep set, interesting, and his shoulders were prominent . . . like an athlete's.

"Hello." He smiled, and took a seat next to me.

The moment his body shifted, the scent of his cologne hit me like a ton of bricks. The fragrance was nice and light, and it did him some justice. I was literally about to wet my panties. "I know you are surprised to see me," I said.

"No, not really." He smiled.

Stunned by his comment, I said, "What do you mean by that?"

"Let's just say that I am the type of man who believes in the powers of destiny."

"Yeah, okay," I responded nonchalantly, and then I glanced over toward Tenisha and Jay.

"So tell me about yourself," he said, licking his LL Cool J lips. He was making me weak as hell.

I hesitated a moment to gather my thoughts. "Well, I am twenty-eight. I work for a law firm as a paralegal. As of yesterday, I am now single. I don't have any children and that's pretty much that," I rambled, summing up my boring life in a few seconds.

"No man, huh? I can't believe that," he said, raising his perfectly shaped, fuzzy eyebrows.

"Believe it. I'm sure you heard about my little ordeal. I've given up on the relationship scene," I replied, not bothering to hold eye contact with him.

"Ahhh, come on, ma . . . you can't let one bad apple spoil the whole bunch. Do me a favor . . . Don't give up on love just yet," he said, placing his smooth hands on top of mine. The heat from his palms warmed something inside of me. Although he was in prison, and it seemed like his future was bleak, I felt a connection to Supreme. It was a connection that prompted me to come back to see him that following Saturday.

Chapter 3

Addicted

It was a month into our relationship and a handful of visits later that things with Supreme and me changed. The day was breezy, and I'd decided to wear a black-and-gold Juicy Couture skirt with the blouse that matched perfectly to my visit with Supreme. Tenisha was kind of quiet on the drive up there that day. Things with her and Jay were going south because she found out that Jay's baby momma had been sneaking up there to see him. When she questioned him about it, he played it off like it was nothing, even though Tenisha strongly felt differently. Nevertheless, it didn't stress her out to the point that she stopped going to see him. Evidently, she was holding on to the mere possibility that if she did her part, he'd leave his baby's mother alone because she continued to visit him. And according to her, the other reason she kept going up to the prison was because he was lacing her pockets with cash, so she was going to ride that horse until his legs broke.

Now looking back on me, I was sort of quiet that trip as well because I was thinking about my last visit with Supreme and how close we got to actually fucking right there in that crowded-ass visiting room. I was thinking that today we'd probably go all the way. There was a CO that was cool with Supreme and would let us go in the bathroom alone, so this time around I was even more nervous. I was nervous to the point of perspiring underneath my armpits.

But that, of course, didn't stop my pussy from getting wet as he placed his warm, juicy lips on top of mine and tongued me down. As smooth as he was, he slipped his pointer and middle fingers inside my throbbing, wet pussy and had me screaming silently for him to push his meat right up in me.

But then I thought about it. "Wait, you got a condom?" I asked.

"Ma, I'm in prison, so how am I going to have access to rubbers. And anyway, I ain't fucking nobody else, so you ain't got to worry about catching anything. Trust me, we straight," he moaned into my ear, while at the same time he slid all nine inches of his rock-hard dick inside me. As soon as the head of his penis made the connection to my g-spot, I almost went into a state of shock. This man was literally ripping me apart, but he was doing it in a gentle way. He held my body up in the air the entire time while I wrapped my legs around his waist for leverage. So I was getting every ounce of his dick, and boy was I enjoying it.

"Oh, shit," he moaned, which was a clear indication that he was about to come but I wasn't ready. I guess the awkward position we were in—standing up against the wall—made the pressure between my clit and his dick rubbing against each other create the sparks that were flying around. "Mmmm," I cried out, grabbing on to his neck tightly.

"Damn, you got some good pussy!" he wolfed, and then in the next three seconds he clutched my waist and abruptly drove his dick and my pussy tightly together and held me as close as he could.

"Wait," I whispered. Then I bit down on my bottom lip.

"This shit is so good, I can't hold back," he warned me, his body trembling, and then it happened. All his warm juices squirted inside me without another moment's notice. And when he released every ounce of come he had built up in him, he damn near collapsed and almost dropped my ass into the bathroom sink.

"Damn," I said when he finally let me down to the floor.

"What's wrong?"

"I wasn't ready for you to come yet. I didn't want you to stop. I felt like I could've rode you forever."

"I'm sorry, baby, but I couldn't help it. Your pussy was driving me crazy!"

I smiled at his comment, even though I didn't get my chance to climax. I figured what the hell, I get to come all the time, and besides, I'd get another crack at him.

Now after he and I took a quick washup at the sink, he walked out of the bathroom first. I followed about two minutes later. When we took a seat back at our table, he grabbed both of my hands into his and assured me that he would take care of me the next time around. That was the beginning of my obsession with Supreme. I had honestly fallen in lust and in love right in a fucking prison bathroom. Not only that, I had no idea what the next phase of the plan was going to be.

Chapter 4

An indecent proposal

I watched as Supreme's mouth moved, but I couldn't believe what I was hearing. "Did he just ask me to bring drugs into the prison?" I said to myself. I was really in shock. Just the night before, over the phone, Supreme had promised me that he would protect and take care of me. He had sent me to his boy uptown for a few dollars to get some clothes, and he always asked me if I was all right financially. What had changed? I had no idea. But here he was telling me that shit was tight on the street and he had a new hustle inside the walls. The catch was this hustle involved me risking my freedom. Let Supreme tell it, the risks involved were slim to none. He already had an arrangement with the same CO that let us fuck in the bathroom. The CO would make sure I was safe bringing the shit in and getting it to Supreme. I tried not to show my disappointment when I looked up at Supreme.

"I can't believe you would put me at risk," I said.

"Ma, this is for you. I can get any bitch to do this, but I know you struggling and shit. I feel like you my shorty and you deserve to be put on," Supreme explained, using his own logic.

"I have to think about it," I said, a little annoyed.

"Don't think too long, ma, I got chicks lined up wanting to do this. Let me know when I call you tonight," Supreme said with stern warning underlining his tone.

I thought about Supreme's words and his proposal all the way home. As soon as we got back to the apartment and got settled, I decided to see what Tenisha thought and I'd make my decision from there. I sat down on the living room sofa next to her and said, "Let me ask you a question."

"What's up?" she asked, taking her attention off the television.

"If you were me and Supreme asked you to bring something illegal into the prison for him, would you do it?"

"What does he want you to bring?"

"Some weed."

"Yeah, I would do it because that would be easy to hide."

I was shocked by Tenisha's response. "Are you serious?"

"You damn right I am serious! If Supreme asked me to rob a bank, I would do it in a heartbeat!"

"So you mean to tell me you would put your freedom on the line to bring some weed into a prison?" I asked her straight up.

"Girl, I've been doing that for niggas for years. How you think I've been making my paper?"

"And you mean to tell me that you never get cold feet?"

"The first couple of times I did it I was really scared. But after that the trips just became so easy."

"I don't know," I began to say, shaking my head.

"Come on, Larissa, stop acting high-and-mighty. That nigga is gonna hit you off real lovely. Trust me, he's gonna have you back on top of your game in no time, and then you'll be able to get your own spot again," she preached. She made things seem like a win-win situation.

"I still don't know," I said apprehensively.

"You can fuck around and lose Supreme if you want to. You'd be a dumb-ass, and I'm your best friend so I'ma tell you the truth. Take that little bit of weed, stuff it in your pussy, let that nigga lick it out, and walk out of that fucking prison with your pockets heavy," Tenisha replied, walking off like she usually did after she gave me a life lecture. I felt happy to have her as a friend. Since she was so street smart, she always simplified things for me. I was going to do the favor for Supreme . . . but just once. Then just once turned into dozens of times. It became our normal routine, and after the first couple of times, I was addicted to the money.

Chapter 5

Wrestling with the devil

Tenisha was in her bedroom when her telephone rang, and I was in her guest room getting dressed. The excitement in her voice indicated that it was Jay calling, so when I heard her say that she would accept the charges, I smiled and thought to myself that once again I was right. But when I heard her say, *"Supreme, what happened?"* I knew right then and there that it wasn't Jay. It was Supreme she was talking to, so something was wrong. I rushed out of the bedroom half dressed, and when I arrived in her room, she was sitting on the edge of her bed with her mouth wide open. She looked like she was in shock, so I walked over to where she was and asked her what was the matter.

She muffled the receiver of the telephone and said, "Supreme just said that Jay got sent to the hole."

"For what?" I wondered aloud.

"Supreme said the COs had a shakedown, and when they went in Jay's room he had a shank hidden inside of his mattress."

"Oh, shit, so how long is he gonna have to be in there?"

"He's not sure," Tenisha replied, and then she went back to talking to Supreme.

I stood alongside of her and watched how she was making conversation with Supreme. Her mannerisms were different this time. I mean, at one time she acted like he made her mad with certain comments she made, but then she would switch it up and act like they were really cool. So I didn't say anything. I let it ride because she knew him longer than me; plus, she was the one who introduced us, so I figured what would be the beef.

She ended up handing me the phone about five minutes before the timer ran out, and I didn't start a beef about that either. I basically made the best out of what little time we had left. He was able to tell me that he couldn't wait to see me tomorrow and that he loved me, so I was happy about that. We ended our conversation with a lot of kisses, and from the expression I got from Tenisha through my peripheral vision, she seemed like she was hating on me. I started to ask her what her problem was, but I figured what's the use, she would only lie about it.

Later on that day I headed out to the store so I could pick up a few things. Tenisha wanted to bake a chicken pot pie, but we were lacking a lot of ingredients, so I made a list and hopped right into my car. On my way there I ran into my cousin Kamryn. She was standing on the block talking to this kid that works for her brother Marlo. I pulled over by the curb and hollered at her for a minute.

"What's up, boss lady?" I yelled.

She turned around to see who had just said something, and when she saw that it was me, I heard her ask the guy to excuse her and then she walked over toward my car.

"What's up?" She smiled.

"Nothing much. What's up with you?" I wondered aloud.

"Girl, I am just standing out here trying to handle Marlo's business."

"Where is he?"

"He's out of town with some new bitch he met a couple days ago. You know how he is; he loves to play big dawg with these skeezers!"

I laughed because she was right. Marlo is a cool guy, but he has always been a sucker for new pussy. I don't care how scandalous a bitch looks, if she has a small waist line and a fat ass, he is going to take her ass to the nearest resort so he can fuck her for at least three days. Trust me, that nigga loves to trick up his money. And the women knows it, too. That's why they are always on his dick.

"When is he coming back?" I asked.

"I don't know, but he'd better be back tomorrow and take care of this mess he left on me."

"What's wrong?"

"You see that asshole over there," she said, pointing at the guy standing on the corner. "He doesn't know how to hustle one bit. You should've seen that nigga running down behind every car he sees, trying to get motherfuckers to cop product from him. I mean, how stupid can he be? I asked him if he was trying to go to jail. And he said, nah. But I can't tell. Because the next car he runs down behind might be the fucking police, and then who is he going to call? Not me and definitely not Marlo, because he ain't gonna answer his phone. So his best bet is to lay his stupid ass back and wait for the fiends to come to him."

I started to comment on the subject about the young boy, but I got sidetracked by this other nigga who appeared on the scene. He was walking hand in hand with his chicken head. And when Kamryn saw how my attention was diverted to the couple behind her, she turned around to see who I was looking at.

"Oh, shit," she said, "is that your man Todd with another bitch?"

"We aren't together anymore."

"Since when?"

"Since like a month ago."

"For real? What happened?" she asked.

"You see that pregnant bitch with him?"

"Yeah."

"Well, that's why," I told her.

"Oh, so that's his baby?"

"That's what she said," I replied, and before I could say another word, Kamryn stepped away from my car and approached Todd and the chick. I sat there in amazement because I knew she was about to let him and that bitch Rema have it. And guess what, I was right.

"Now I know you ain't coming around here flaunting your bitch!" I heard her say.

Todd was shocked like hell to see Kamryn approach him like that. But he was a belligerent nigga, so I knew he wasn't going to stand there and take her disrespecting him, especially in front of his new baby momma.

"Who the fuck you think you talking to?" he roared.

"Yeah, who you think you talking to, 'cause I ain't no bitch!" the chick said.

"Shut up ho, because you are a bitch! And anyway, I wasn't talking to you. I'm talking to that bitch-ass nigga you walking with," she roared back at him, as she walked a little closer to him.

"A yo Kam, if you know like I know, you would step the fuck back before I knock your ass out."

"Nigga, now I know you didn't just threaten me. Do you know my motherfuckin' brother will kill a nigga behind me?"

"So what, you think he's the only nigga with a pistol?"

"I know he's not. But he is the only nigga around here that has more clout than you, so if you threaten me again, he'll have your ass got by the A.M.," she warned him.

"So what, you think I'm scared?"

I got out of the car to try and defuse this situation because this little argument between Kamryn and Todd was
about to get really ugly. And I know from experience that
Todd isn't gonna back down and Kamryn isn't either.

"Come on, Kam, this nigga ain't even worth it," I said.

"Yeah, Kam, listen to your cousin. She ain't gonna tell
you nothing wrong."

"Shut the fuck up, Todd! Because whether you know it
or not, I'm really looking out for your dumb-ass!"

"Bitch, you ain't doing shit for me. You better look out for
your own ass before I put something tough on you again."

"You really think you did something by fucking up all
my shit at my crib, huh? Well, you didn't. Because right
after you left, I got my next man to buy me every single
thing you fucked up. And believe me, the shit I got now is
better quality," I replied sarcastically, and then I smiled.

"I don't give a fuck about that shit! I'm glad you got another man. Now I ain't got to worry about you running
down behind and begging me to take you back."

"Todd, I ain't never run down behind you and your dripping dick! Nigga, you were always running back to me
every time I put your ass out."

"My dick was only dripping because of your stinking
ass!"

"Nah, nigga it was that ho you're with!"

"Bitch, I ain't never had VD, so you got me mixed up
with the next chick," Rema said.

"Well, you may not have had it, but if you keep fucking
with this nigga, you're gonna get it sooner than later," I
warned her, and then I laughed.

"Yep, you better listen to her," Kamryn interjected, "because that nigga you standing next to is as grimey as they
come. And as soon as you think shit is good, that's when
he's going to turn your world upside down."

"Come on, baby, don't listen to these hos!" Todd said to Rema and grabbed her by her arm. "These bitches want to be in your shoes so bad it's killing them."

"Trust me, we don't," I tried to assure her. But I know that my words went in one ear and right out the next. But who cares? He's her headache now, so she will soon feel all the pain I went through.

After Todd's dumb ass left, all the shit he put on me fell right off my shoulders. It felt like a load was lifted off of me, and for the first time since he and I had been together, I finally felt free. Not only that, I had some closure, so now I know I am going to be fine.

Chapter 6

A reality check

For the past three weeks Tenisha hasn't been able to ride out to the prison with me so she could have her visit with Jay. According to Supreme he is still in the hold, and he will be there for another four months. So after I made my trip up to see my baby today, I came straight back so Tee and I could hang out a bit. We decided to catch a movie and get something to eat afterward. MacArthur Mall was the location we picked since the movie theater was connected to it and there were a lot of nice restaurants sectioned on the first floor.

Tee and I had about thirty minutes before the movie started, so we took a stroll around the mall to do a little window shopping. On our way out of Aldo's shoe store, we ran into my cousin Marlo's big Shaquille O'Neal-looking ass dressed down in a crisp white tee, a pair of True Religion jeans, and some fresh white Nike Uptowns. He had some red, pretty, fly chick on his arm carrying a slew of shopping bags. From the labels I could tell that he'd taken her to the bebe store, Banana Republic, Zie Spot, the Coach store, Cache', Nine West, and Man Alive. Homegirl hit his pockets real hard, and I wasn't mad at her either, because I knew whatever he spent on her didn't put a dent in his stash at all. Marlo was a paid nigga. He had a few spots in Norfolk on lock, and everybody respected the hell out of him for it. As long as we've been adults, I can't remember nobody ever trying to fuck him over. He was the type that wouldn't take any shit off niggas, which was why Tenisha suggested that I get him on Todd for fucking up all my shit in my apartment in the first place. Knowing Marlo and the people he's got on his payroll, I was certain that Todd would have ended up floating in the water underneath the Berkeley Bridge. And since I couldn't have that shit on my conscience, I elected not to approach Marlo with it. So maybe one of these days Todd will come around and thank me.

"Looks like you've been spending a lot of dough." I smiled.

"Yep, it sure does," Tenisha added.

Marlo smiled back. "You know how I do."

"I sure do. So you think I can hold a few dollars," I asked, holding my hands out.

"Come on, dawg, you know you can," he assured me as he handed me about fifteen twenty-dollar bills.

"Think I can get some, too?" Tenisha wanted to know.

"I'm kind of tapped out right now. So call that nigga Jake and tell him to hit you off," he told her and swiftly shifted his attention right back on me.

I laughed on the inside because I knew what that was all about, and so did Tenisha, but it went right over Marlo's new girlfriend's head. Though, I'm sure she would have wanted to know that Marlo used to fuck around with Tenisha. They probably dated for about a year, but when Marlo found out that Tenisha was taking his money and sending it to a nigga named Jake, he cut her off. Now I know that sounds really crazy, but it was true. She tried to deny it, but the cat she was sending Marlo's dough to told some cats he knew about how Tenisha was taking care of him while he was on lock, and when that shit got back to Marlo, he made Tee's ass suffer. I mean, he stripped her of all the shit she had. Come to think about it, she lost everything. But the way he did it didn't come close to the way Todd played me. Marlo just simply had a few of his people come up in her crib and pack all her shit up; simple and plain. Now, she went off a bit, but she did more crying and begging than anything. Marlo didn't feed into her bullshit, which is why he doesn't fuck with her today. Quiet as kept, I am the main reason he didn't whip her ass. I literally begged him not to put his hands on her because I knew he would have killed her for sure. He had a lot of anger and rage in his eyes when he kicked down her apartment door, so I'm really surprised that he didn't cuss her ass out just now when she opened up her mouth and asked him for some money, too. I guess he doesn't want his new chick to see him in rare form.

"How long have you been in the mall?" I asked, taking the attention off of Tenisha.

"About two hours now. But we're getting ready to head out this joint because I've got some business to take care of," he told me.

"What's your friend's name?" I asked.

"Oh, shit, I'm sorry. This is Adrienne," he said, smiling. "And Adrienne, this is my cousin Larissa and her friend."

"Nice to meet you." Adrienne smiled.

"Well, the friend has a name," Tenisha interjected sarcastically.

"I'm sure she does, but that's not important right now," he replied, and then he put his hands around my shoulders and pulled me into his direction. "Let me holler at you for a minute," he continued, ushering me a couple feet away from Tenisha and Adrienne both.

"What's going on with you and that nigga Todd?" he didn't hesitate to ask me.

"Nothing's going on," I replied, giving him a weird expression.

"Well, what's this shit I'm hearing about him trashing your apartment a few weeks back?"

I hesitated, hoping my mind would think of a quick lie before Marlo realized that was what I was doing. It was too late; he had already figured it out. "Come on, Larissa, don't lie for that nigga."

"I'm not," I finally said.

"So what's up, then? Why am I hearing that nigga talk shit about you on the streets?"

"Marlo, you know how whack that nigga is. I don't know why you even let him bother you with the shit he does."

"The shit only bothers me when I hear that he's out there popping shit about you."

"Just ignore him."

"I ain't gonna ignore shit! The next time I hear that nigga mentioned your name, I am going to kill him myself," he warned me.

"Please don't let that moron be the cause of you getting the death penalty, because he is truly not worth it."

"Do you think I give a fuck about that shit!" Marlo began to get agitated. "That nigga is very disrespectful, and I didn't like how he used to carry you. I mean, this nigga used to fuck the same bitches I was fucking. Now, how gutter is it to see a nigga my cousin is fucking sneaking out the back door of the bitch's house I'm fucking?"

I shook my head when Marlo ran down the scenario concerning Todd. And for the first time I saw exactly what he had seen. Todd was a disrespecting asshole, and he made it known to everybody in the neighborhood that he didn't give a fuck about me. So he did me a favor by carrying his no-good ass. I just wish he would've done it a long time ago.

"Look," I finally said, "I honestly don't have a comment for that. I'm just glad the nigga is gone and I am out of that apartment."

"How is it over there where you at now?"

"Who, Tee's house?"

"Yeah."

"Oh, it's all right. I mean, it ain't bad. But there's nothing like having your own spot."

"Well, go look for a place and let me know what you gon' need to move in there."

"Nah, Marlo, I can't have you doing that. I'll be all right."

"Yo, let me explain something to you," he began to say, "you are my cousin. My favorite cousin at that, so I got to look out for you."

I smiled at Marlo because I felt the love he had for me. After we said a few more words to each other he told me he was giving me a couple days to call him and let him know where I found a place so he could set me up in it. I said okay; we kissed and departed ways.

Marlo and his female companion disappeared down the other end of the mall. They were headed in the direction of the parking garage, so I know their shopping spree was over. Meanwhile, Tenisha had her ass on her back. She talked me to death about how Marlo played her silly ass to the left. I ignored most of the shit she was saying because it truly wasn't relevant. Thank God, a call came through on her cellular phone to take her mind off Marlo, because he definitely upset her world. I guess what they say is true. *What goes around comes around.*

Chapter 7

The set up

"**L**et me cater to you . . . baby, this is your day . . . any-thing for you, my man . . . you blow me away. I got your slippers, your dinner, your dessert, and so much more . . . let me cater to you," I sang along loudly with Destiny's Child. The rhythm of the music and the words had me ex-cited. Yes, I wanted to cater to my man. As I drove toward our meeting place, my pussy got excited. I couldn't wait to see Supreme. It had been two weeks since our last meeting, and I needed a Supreme fix. He was like a drug, and his sex was my high. I was a fiend.

I parked my ride and looked at myself in the mirror. I was good, as usual, I looked good. "Mmmm, I can't wait to feel that nine inches," I whispered, licking my lips in the mirror. That was practice for how I was going to seduce my man. Yeah, our situation was a little different than usual, but that was fine with me because the sex was to die for. I wasn't going nowhere, and whatever Supreme wants . . . Supreme gets.

"Next!" the CO shouted, ushering me and several other women down the line. As I received my cursory search—

mouth, around my bra straps, shoes, pocketbook, and my walk through the metal detector—I began to feel sick. My stomach churned, and I suddenly felt the urge to hurl. Swallowing hard, I willed myself to be calm. "Pass!" the CO instructed, sending me through. I had made it. Phew! I inhaled deeply and continued through the processing room. I was finally done signing in and being treated like a prisoner.

My legs were unsteady as I marched through the doorway of the visitors' room. It was a combination of being excited to see Supreme and being purely nervous because of what I was about to do. Although I had taken this same walk for the past five months, today was different. I was unusually nervous, and I told myself this would be the last time. My heart pounded against my chest, and fine beads of sweat appeared at my hairline.

Why the fuck do I feel like this? Bitch, be calm . . . don't get spooked now you about to get some good dick and good money, I instructed myself. It seemed like all eyes were on me today, and maybe they were. I had on a dress . . . as usual. All girlfriends of prisoners knew it didn't pay to go on a visit with pants on. Today I had taken special care in getting ready. Thanks to my newfound income, I was able to buy some nice things. I strutted in a pair of beige Christian Louboutin heels, an off white Michael Kors baby doll dress, and topped that off with a cream-colored Isabella Fiore bag. My nails were freshly manicured, and my perfect auburn curls danced around my face. Yes, I was doing it.

I approached the table and locked eyes with my man. *Damn, he looks so fucking good,* I said to myself. Sean "Supreme" Miller was all man. His deep-set chestnut brown eyes, smooth mocha-colored skin, and perfect teeth could make my pussy wet from a distance. I couldn't deny this man shit. If he would've asked me to kill the president, I probably would have considered it.

"Hey, you," I cooed, flashing a smile as I pulled out my chair and sat down.

"Damn, you look good as hell. What's up, ma?" Supreme responded, grabbing my hand and kissing it.

"You're such a gentleman. I missed you," I said, smiling brightly and trying hard to calm my previously unchained nerves. I must admit, I felt slightly better once I sat down. Something still wasn't sitting right with me, though. I looked around for CO Coefield, and he was in his usual spot by the vending machines. Good! I said to myself. "So what's new?" I asked Supreme, licking my well lip glossed lips.

"Yo. It's the same as usual, ma, you looking fucking too good to be true," he replied.

"What am I supposed to do?" I whispered nervously. Supreme gave me a disapproving glare. He knew it was unusual for me to act so shook. But it was also unusual for me to have as much stuff on me as I had. Four squirrel packs was the most we've ever tried out. I pushed the limit this time because Supreme told me that each pack could make four or five fat joints, which he could sell inside for one hundred dollars or more each. That meant more money for him and more for me. I was still fucked up in the head about how much shit was involved.

"So, ma, what kind of food you eating that's making you looks so sweet?" he asked, trying to sound chipper to calm me down. I knew what he was asking me in code.

"I had stuffed baked chicken today," I answered, letting him know the deal.

Supreme reached out for my hand and squeezed it. I guess that was his way of saying he'd take care of it. His touch comforted me for a second. I looked around again, and Coefield gave us the signal. I also noticed a lot of new COs around today. I ignored my feelings and went along with the plan.

"I'll be right back," Supreme said, breaking my concentration and motioning to Coefield. *What!* I screamed in my head. *I usually go to the bathroom first!* I bit into my cheek to keep the vomit that sat at the back of my throat from spewing out of my mouth. Coefield came over to the table, and he and Supreme walked toward the bathroom. A few minutes later I nonchalantly got up from the table and walked to the bathrooms. Looking over my shoulder several times, I was sure nobody had seen me.

Coefield was right in front of the door. I handed him what he was due, and I stepped inside. Supreme was in the third stall . . . our stall. He already had his dick out and hard. I walked in, and my heart started racing. My pussy was so wet that it moistened the insides of my thighs, making it hard for me to keep the package up there.

"Damn, you about to make me lose the package," I complained playfully.

"Well, come here, let me get that for you," Supreme said, grabbing me around the waist. He hoisted my skirt, pushed me against the wall, and dived headfirst into my coochie. His packages slipped right out with no problem. Supreme sniffed them, inhaling deeply, and put them down his pants; he then proceeded to please me. He stuck his head right back down by my moneymaker and began to tease my clit with the tip of his tongue. "Oh," I moaned softly, trying to keep my leg up in the small stall.

"Mmmm," Supreme cooed as he forcefully inserted his tongue in and out . . . in and out.

"Give me that dick," I whispered. I knew our time was running out, and I didn't want to miss out. Supreme stood up and wrapped his muscular arms around me. He hoisted me up on the wall and mounted me from the front. "Ugh," I let out a groan as his fat member penetrated me. I rolled my eyes, and Supreme got into a perfect rhythm, grinding his hips into mine. My back ran up and down the cold steel of the stall, but it was all good; the pussy pounding I was taking made up for the burns I was getting on my back.

"Yo, ma . . . this is the best pussy I ever had," Supreme wolfed breathlessly.

"Yeah, daddy . . . this dick is so good to me," I whispered back.

The next thing I heard was a loud, calamitous noise coming from behind me.

"What the fu—?" Supreme started to say, but before he could get the words out of his mouth, a swarm of men in riot gear, complete with body shields, came stomping into the bathroom. *STOMP! STOMP! STOMP!* It sounded like a herd of elephants running from danger. I jumped down from Supreme's grasp.

Shit, my life is over, I thought right before the door was forced open.

"Don't move!" one of the men in riot gear boomed. *Is he talking to me?* I asked myself, confused and in a daze. He was surely looking directly at me, but he couldn't be talking to me.

The next few minutes moved in Matrix-like slow motion. Those minutes felt like hours. Several hands grabbed on to my slender arms, yanking me toward the cold concrete floor. I landed with a thud on my stomach.

"What's going on? What is this all about?" I screamed, barely able to breathe, with my heart threatening to crash through my breastbone. A hot feeling invaded my entire body, and my arms and legs went numb. I'd never felt so many hands all over my body at once. I had a knee in my back as I was handcuffed like a fucking mass murderer. I couldn't think straight. Tears flowed out of my eyes like Niagara Falls. "What did I do? What did I do?" I cried out.

"Ma'am, you are under arrest. You have the right to remain silent . . ." The words crashed down on me like a ton of bricks. As I was lifted off the floor like a little rag doll, I looked up and noticed Supreme being escorted out in handcuffs as well. *Oh my God, what did I do wrong this time?* I said to myself. My life as I knew it was over. I knew that what I had done could send me away for a long time.

Chapter 8

A certified jailbird

I sat in a small, rank, and dirty crowded holding cell in Chesapeake jail. The women in the cell were just fucking trifling—mostly ugly crackhead-ass prostitutes. There were a few boosters thrown in there, but those bitches were ghetto and busted, too. I held my head in my hands, thinking about where I went wrong. Larissa Taylor wasn't a jailbird, and I damn sure didn't deserve to be in a stinking-ass jail cell.

My first concern was Supreme. I know that sounds stupid, but in the few months we were seeing each other, he had treated me like a rare diamond. His phone calls were always reassuring—he would tell me how beautiful I was and what he was going to do for me when he got home. His letters were real love letters; in fact, he was the first man to tell me he loved me before I said it to him, and the adventure of having secret voyeuristic sex during our visits had sent me over the top. I was really in love with Supreme. Seeing him in those handcuffs had broken my heart, especially because I felt responsible. I knew he would probably be re-arrested and sent to the hole. I felt like shit knowing that he was almost at the end of his bid and because of me he would probably have more time tacked on. Supreme had just gotten transferred to Indian Creek from Haynesville State Penitentiary, and he only had two months left. Now, because of me, he might get sent back up the river. Tears rolled into my hands as I sat there thinking about my man and my life.

After the COs took me into custody, I was questioned about where I had the drugs and the weapon hidden. "Weapon! I don't have no fucking weapon!" I screamed at them. Of course they didn't believe me. Two COs from Gang Intelligence interrogated me for over two hours. I told them over and over that I didn't have a fucking weapon. *Where would they even get an idea like that?* I thought to myself. Two female COs searched me and I was made to sit on the body cavity chair—which helped them find the weed. I had four squirrel packs of the best weed in Norfolk stuffed inside my pussy. It was the most I'd ever brought into the jail. I knew it was a bad call. I had reservations about it from day one. Supreme had begged me to do this one last favor for him and he wouldn't ask me anymore.

My best friend Tenisha had warned me as well, saying, "Girl, what you won't do another woman will. Shit, you know how many bitches want to be with Supreme." I listened to her. I was afraid to lose Supreme, so I ignored my initial gut feeling, and with apprehension, I caved and decided to do it. Now I was in deep shit.

The Chesapeake city police picked me up from the prison and escorted me downtown to their domain and immediately threw me in their nasty-ass cell. And after sitting around for about three hours, a short, fat female deputy finally came over and told me that I could make a phone call. I ran to the locked cell door and waited for her to open it. My phone call was very important. The lady led me to a bank of pay phones. I didn't have a quarter to my name, and there were no free phones in central booking.

"Shit!" I cursed. I immediately had the collect operator call Tenisha's house. I wasn't sure about calling a cell phone number collect. *RING! RING! RING!* The phone just rang and rang. With each unanswered ring my heart sank deeper. I needed Tenisha right now. After about fifteen unanswered rings, I put the phone down. The CO asked me if I wanted to make one more call. I thought about her question.

Now, I contemplated calling my parents, but I thought that would be a huge mistake. My father would be so disappointed in me, and with the condition of his heart, I couldn't risk him being upset. My mother was a different story. She would probably hang up the phone on me once I told her where I was. She never hid the fact that she couldn't stand me—her only daughter. From the time I could remember, she never treated me like I was a part of her. My father was what kept me going all these years. He gave me what I needed and loved me unconditionally. When my mother convinced him to leave Virginia and go back to South Carolina, I was devastated. I knew she was doing it to spite me. She knew I didn't want to leave all of my friends behind; besides, I had just started college at Norfolk State University. Nonetheless, I came home from school one Friday and the moving truck was there. I promised my father that I would continue school and visit him every chance I got. I kept my parents' condo, and for a little while I did go to school. School was short-lived for me. Working to pay them rent and trying to keep up with the latest fashion led me down a path of destruction. I quit school and started looking for love—someone to take care of me like my father had for so long.

With no family in Virginia, besides my cousins Kamryn

and Marlo, I had my best friend Tenisha to fall back on. We'd been friends since ninth grade. We did practically everything together because she lived less than two blocks from me. Tenisha always had my back and I always had hers. Having her back was how I got the three-inch scar on the left side of my face.

We were in tenth grade when it happened. Tenisha had told me that six girls were going to try to jump her after school and she needed my help. "Of course I'm there," I had told her. I remember she was supposed to meet me at the south gate behind the school so we could gear up—put on our Vaseline, change into our fighting sneakers, tie our hair up, and get our blades ready. When I got to the south gate after my last class, Tenisha wasn't there. Panic struck me. I immediately thought something had happened to her. The next thing I knew, I was surrounded by about fifteen girls. They started talking shit, and I wasn't backing down. I knew Tenisha would be there any minute. I didn't have a chance.

"Oh, so you talking shit about us, saying we look like bums. You think you all that 'cause you light skinned," one girl barked, getting up in my face.

"I don't even know your ugly ass," I snapped. That was all I remember saying. The next thing I felt was a burning pain in my face, head, and neck. I remember falling and grabbing the side of my face while trying to shield myself from kicks and stomps. Blood was everywhere. I touched my face and looked at my blood-soaked hand and passed out.

"Taylor! What you gonna do?" the deputy screamed, breaking up my thoughts.

"Can I try one more time?" I asked, desperately hoping Tenisha would pick up her phone. I thought about asking the deputy for a quarter; then I looked down at my feet, and as if it were an act of God . . . there was a shiny quarter up against the wall under the phone bank. I picked it up with the quickness and slid it into the phone slot. My fingers shook as I dialed Tenisha's cell phone. Again, no answer. "Tee, it's Larissa, I need you right now. Come down to Chesapeake jail, I got arrested. I'm getting ready to see the magistrate in a minute, so I'm gonna need some bail money." I left the desperate message on Tenisha's voice mail. *This bitch must be laid up with a nigga somewhere*, I thought, growing angrier by the minute. I was led back to the crowded-ass cell. Now I had to wait to see the magistrate.

Chapter 9

Left behind bars

After the prejudice-ass magistrate denied my bond, I was sent upstairs to the fifth-floor housing unit for women to rest up because I was going to pay the judge a visit in less than twelve hours. As soon as I was put inside the block, I rushed to the pay phone and tried to get Tenisha on the line again, but conveniently enough she was still not at home, so I hung up the phone and headed into my cell. My mattress was hard as a brick, and the jail-issued wool blanket wasn't that much better. It was thinner than a sheet of paper, so I damn near froze to death overnight. The next morning couldn't come quick enough, but it came.

Around five-thirty in the morning a young, black female deputy called me and two other chicks' names and told us to stand at the gate so we could head out to court. I didn't hesitate one bit to get to that gate because I wanted to get the hell out of there. I also knew that after I paid the judge a visit this morning, I would be granted a bond, and then I would be getting out of this place, so I was feeling kind of good.

"Ladies, please stand clear," she instructed us. Then she

turned toward the control booth and yelled, "Open gate six-B."

The gate slid back, and we stepped outside of the cell block. "All clear," she yelled once again, and then the gate closed back up.

The courtroom was packed. Throngs of family members and friends of the defendants stood along the walls in the back. I was led to the first row of hard benches. Sweat drenched my entire body. I looked around; there were so many people waiting to see the judge. It was like an assembly line. I turned toward the back and scanned the crowd. There was no sign of Tenisha. *She probably didn't check her messages,* I rationalized.

"Please rise. The Honorable Judge Martin Lohan presiding," the court officer said perfunctorily as the judge took his seat.

"Order, let's come to order and begin," he said, banging his gavel twice.

A sickening hush came over the room. I watched as one by one, people—men and women—were read their charges. I observed each one standing shackled behind the defense table. My heart immediately began pounding, and pangs of nervousness flitted through my stomach.

"In the matter of the State versus Larissa Taylor," the judge said. I was led to the defense table. A short, bald-headed white man stood up next to me. This was the first time I had seen him.

"Your Honor, I have not had the opportunity to meet and discuss the matter with my client, therefore, we enter a plea of not guilty," the short man said. He was sweating like he had just hiked up Mount Everest. I was confused as hell as I looked down at the soaking-wet munchkin that I guess was my court-appointed attorney.

"Good. Your client is being charged with possession with intent to distribute a controlled substance in an institution, and disruption and disorderly conduct in an institution," the judge said.

"What?" I asked, looking up at the judge.

"Shhh," my lawyer warned. "Your Honor, our plea stands," the lawyer replied.

"Your client is remanded to the Chesapeake city jail. Bail is set at twenty-five thousand dollars. Discuss with your client the plea deal options. Court will resume for your client in thirty days," the judge said with finality as he banged his gavel for the next case.

My knees buckled as the judge's words settled in my ears—*twenty-five thousand dollars, thirty days, plea deal.* What had I done to myself? Looking for love and acceptance from a man had gotten me here. As I was led to processing, where I would finally have to shed my street clothes for the jail jumpsuit, tears streamed down my face, and all I could think about was how this had all started.

The words "*Girl, you better get with that nigga!*" kept playing over and over in my head. I honestly wanted to scream because I then realized that I really did it this time, and again it was all behind a fucking man. But the worst part about it was that there was no way I would be able to fix it. *What the hell am I going to do now?*

Chapter 10

Changing the game

The very next day I finally got in touch with Tenisha. She answered the phone on the second ring.

"Larissa, girl, I am so sorry. I just got your message last night. What's going on?" she asked, sounding a bit apologetic.

"Somebody set me and Supreme up, and now I'm in jail and these fucking people ain't trying to let me go."

"What did the judge say?"

"He told me I was staying in jail until my trial date."

"When is that?"

"A month from now."

Tenisha screamed at the top of her voice. "What kind of shit is that? They are acting like you killed somebody."

"I know," I said, sounding down, "but what can I do?"

"Did they give you an attorney?"

"Yeah, I had one of those fake-ass court-appointed attorneys, but he acted like he was working for them instead of me."

"That's how they do," Tenisha said. "So when is your visiting days?"

"I'm not sure, but look, I'm gonna need you to put me on three-way with my parents."

"Are you sure you want to do that?"

"What other choices do I have? I'm not getting out anytime soon, so I've got to call them."

"Girl, your mother is going to have a heart attack."

"I know, but it's better that she have it now than later," I expressed.

"Have you tried calling your cousin Marlo?"

"No. I haven't tried to call him or Kamryn. You know how she is with her mouth. Everybody in her neighborhood would know about my business, so I wasn't trying to go there."

"Have you heard anything from Supreme?"

"How can I? Did you forget where I was?"

"I'm sorry," she apologized. "I just thought that maybe you could send him a kite or something through the trustees."

"I don't think he's in this jail. After the COs busted up in the bathroom on us and found the weed, I heard them say that Supreme was on his way to the hole."

"Damn." Tenisha sighed. "I wonder how long they're gonna keep him there?"

"I don't know, but I want you to find out for me."

"All right," Tee replied.

She and I talked a little more, and then she clicked over to a clear line and called my parents. My mother answered the phone.

"Hey, Mom, how are you?" I asked.

"I'm doing fine, baby. How are you?"

I sighed heavily. "Not too good."

"What's wrong, baby?"

"Where's Dad?"

"He's stepped out for a moment, why?"

"I just asked."

"What's the matter, darling? And what's all that noise in the background?" My mom pressed the issue.

"Mom, I'm in jail."

"You're what?" her voice screeched. "Oh my God, for what?"

"It's a long story, so I really don't want to get into it right now. But I am calling you to let you know that I am all right."

"What jail are you in?"

"I'm in Chesapeake."

"What's your bail?"

"They didn't give me one."

My mother grew silent, and then I heard a muffled cry.

"Mom, are you crying?" I asked.

"Baby, why didn't they give you a bail?" she asked me. She sounded so pitiful, I had to break the real truth down to her. And after I was done, she had a few more questions for me, but I wasn't able to answer them because the time on my call was up. I called her back, though, and assured her that I would be all right since this was my first offense. She didn't sound so convinced, but hey, what could I do? I did, however, convince her that this would be the last time I put my life on the line, and that I was truly sorry for whatever heartache this situation caused her. After I was able to clear up a few things for her, I ended up giving her the address here so she could send me some mail. And before I hung up, she assured me that she would appear at my court hearing. By the time I got off the phone, I was in different spirits. Somehow my mother was able to put a smile on my face, even if it was only for one night. I called her back a couple days later so I could speak to my father. Since he already knew what time it was, talking to him about it wasn't so bad. Of course, I got the lecture of a lifetime, but all in all I knew he meant well.

"I'm gonna call y'all once a week, okay?"

"All right, darling. Take care."

"I will," I promised.

Chapter 11

Special delivery

My girl Tenisha came by to pay me a visit. It had been a week and a half since I last saw her. I remember the day I left her sitting on the living room sofa while I was on my way out the door. She was lying around in her pajamas, upset because her days of visiting Jay had come to a halt. So it seemed like every time I was on my way out to see Supreme, she would act like she was jealous or something. But I just brushed it off as if she was in one of her many mood swings and kept it moving. Today I could tell that she was in high spirits. She smiled from the time she saw me up until the time she left.

Sporting a beige BCBG Max Azira top and a pair of blue denim Chip & Pepper jeans, Tenisha sat down on the hard metal seat and faced the glass partition that separated us. I immediately took the phone off the hook and put it up to my ear. "Nice outfit," I complimented her.

"Thanks," she replied, dusting off imaginary lint balls from her blouse and her jeans.

"How was the drive here?" I asked, trying to start up a conversation.

"It was fine." She continued to smile as if she was tickled

pink about something. "But enough about me, how you doing?" she asked.

"I'm okay," I told her, even though I wasn't. I mean, what kind of question was that? She knew how I felt, period—end of story.

"Well, I'm glad because I've got some good news."

"Is it gonna get me out of jail?"

Tee cracked another smile. "No, but it'll put a smile on your face."

"What is it?"

"I got a letter from Supreme yesterday."

My eyes lit up. "What did it say?"

"He told me to tell you that he was all right. And that he goes up for his hearing next week, so don't worry about him because he'll be fine."

"Is that all he said? I mean, did he tell you to tell me that he loved and missed me?"

"Yeah, silly, you know he did," she said, and then she chuckled.

Hearing that definitely put a smile on my face. It seemed like all my burden went right out the window when Tee told me my baby loved and missed me. Finally I found a cat who cared about my well-being.

She and I finished the visit off with a couple of laughs. She also told me that she was leaving me a few dollars at the front desk, so I was pleased about that. And not only that, she told me that she was going to come see me every week until this thing was over, so that sealed the deal for me. I could finally say that I had two people who really loved me on my side.

Chapter 12

Judgment day

My parents were in the courtroom just as they promised. Tenisha was sitting on the bench right beside them. I was nervous as hell as I stood before Judge Lohan. He was in rare form today of all days, and he was handing down some harsh sentences. He gave this one guy twenty-one years for robbing an old lady of her purse. Homeboy was hurt when the judge handed him down that sentence. I felt sorry for him, but I quickly sobered up when I was told to step forward.

The clerk of the courts spoke. "Your Honor, your next case is # 98703-1A. It is the matter of Taylor versus the State. The defendant is charged with one felony count of possession with intent to distribute four grams of marijuana. On June twelve she entered in a plea of not guilty, and now she stands trial."

"Counselor for the defendant, are you ready to proceed?" the judge asked.

"Yes, Your Honor, we are," my court-appointed attorney said. And from that point everything became a complete blur. All I remember is when the judge looked directly into my face and told me he was sentencing me to twenty-two months in prison and banged his gavel down. I heard my mother cry out while the court's deputy escorted me back out of the courtroom. I felt her pain. Seeing her emotionally distraught like that gave me a nauseous feeling in my stomach. I believed she had suffered enough. So to know that her baby girl is going to be in prison for almost two whole years is definitely a hard blow to recover from. Before the deputy closed the door behind us, I managed to look back into the courtroom one last time. Tenisha was standing next to my mother. She looked like she was giving her some encouraging words because my mother smiled and gave her a big hug.

A couple days after I was sentenced, I called Tenisha, and she had an earful of information for me. I was kind of glad that someone was having better luck than me.

"Girl, I got a letter from Supreme, and he said that they finally gave him his hearing."

"What did they give him?"

"He said they only added six months onto this sentence, so he'll be out in less than a year."

"Oh really, that good," I replied nonchalantly. Because in the real sense of it all, I was fucking pissed. I mean, how in the hell did he get only six months added to his time, while I'm doing almost two years. What kind of shit is that? I am a first-time offender, and they treated me like I'm a fucking career criminal.

"I know, ain't it?"

"Yeah, I guess." Hoping she would catch on and shut the fuck up.

"He also said that he misses you and can't wait to see you when you get home."

"Did he tell you when they were going to let him out of the hole?"

"Yeah, he said he only had three months left and then they were going to put him back into population."

"Well, could you write him back and tell him I love him and that I can't wait until we can be together again?"

"I sure can. Anything for you, homegirl. You know I got your back," Tenisha said.

"I know you do, that's why you've been my girl for all these years. And can't nobody come between us either."

"You got that shit right!" she agreed.

She and I talked for the rest of my fifteen-minute call. But right before my time was up, I got her to call my cousin Kamryn on three-way, but she didn't answer her telephone, so I left her a message telling her I would be trying to call her a little later.

Chapter 13

Three months later

For the past couple of days I've been spotting, which is a bit abnormal for me, so I got the deputy to take me to see the doctor. It was a very quick visit, so after a brief check up, two Tylenol and a pregnancy test, I found out I was with child. I sat back on the hospital bed with my head buried in my hands and wondered how I was going to handle this situation. I mean, it wasn't much I could do. I can't have an abortion because none of the hospital staff in this place is licensed to terminate pregnancies. So I guess I can only make the best of this. After I left the clinic and was escorted back to my cell block, I called my parents, and then I called Tenisha to give her the news. My parents were really excited and started bragging about all the things they were going to buy. But for some reason Tenisha wasn't too pleased to hear the news. Everything that came out of her mouth was negative.

"Girl, you are going to have the worst pregnancy ever," she said. "Those doctors in there ain't gonna take care of you like the doctors out here."

"I know, that's why the CO told me that they're going to take me to an outside doctor."

"Girl, she lying! Do you think they gon' pay for you to go out and see a doctor on the streets when they got medical staff on call in there?"

"Well, I can only go on what the CO told me," I told her.

"She was just telling you that bullshit so you won't start complaining."

"Well, you know what, Tee, at this point it really doesn't matter. I could not care less where I go, just as long as my baby comes out healthy."

"Don't eat that food in there."

I sighed. "Tee, why are you being so negative?"

"I'm not being negative. I'm just giving you the facts," she said flatly. "Having a baby right now is going to be the worst decision you could ever make."

"What else am I going to do? I mean, it's not like I can go out and have an abortion."

"Why don't you try aborting the baby on your own?"

"What?" my voice screeched.

"Come on now, Rissa, you know you ain't ready for no damn baby. And besides, who is going to baby-sit for you when you want to go out with me to the club?"

"First of all, I am not killing my baby . . ."

"Why not? White chicks do it all the time," she interjected.

"Well, I'm not white. And another thing, having a baby is going to be a beautiful experience. But not only that, I know after I have this baby, Supreme is going to be all over me, which is why I can't wait to write him and tell him the good news."

"So you really think he's going to be happy?"

"Why, you don't think so?"

"That's not for me to answer."

"Well, if you want to know the truth, yes, I do. As a matter of fact, I believe he is going to be ecstatic, especially since we talked about marriage."

"When did y'all talk about that?"

"The visit right before this last one when me and him got busted."

"Why you just telling me about it now?"

"Because he told me not to tell anyone until he got out so we could announce it together."

"And you believed him?" Tenisha asked, as if she were gritting her teeth.

"Yes, I did. Why, you know something I don't?"

She hesitated for a moment, and then she said, "Nah, I don't know anything."

"Well, why have you been so negative throughout this whole conversation?"

Tenisha gave me the same spiel of why she wasn't being negative and how I needed to appreciate her being honest about all of this. In the end, she and I just squashed the whole conversation. I decided if she didn't have anything positive to say, then she didn't need to say anything at all. From that point on, I avoided all conversations with her when it involved my pregnancy. I felt bad enough being in prison, so I didn't need to be reminded over and over again about how fucked up my life is going to be when I get out of here. I would not have been able to deal with it, so I shut her completely down.

Chapter 14

It's a conspiracy

I've been sending my letters to Tenisha to send to Supreme, but somehow Supreme wasn't getting them. She said the mail was probably getting lost or something, so I started rerouting my mail to my parents down in South Carolina, and now all of a sudden he's getting my letters. I know now Tenisha has some major shit going on, and it's only a matter of time before I find out what it is.

Today at mail call I finally got a letter from Supreme, and when I opened it up and read the contents, I was really happy. He told me how happy he was because I was pregnant and that he is going to make sure that I will be taken care of. He also told me that he's making a couple of moves while he's in the hole so we can be straight when we both get out. But then he said that our wedding is going to have to be put on hold because he's not going to be around to play the hubby role. I was a little disappointed, but I know in time I will get over it.

In addition to the bad news about him postponing our wedding, he said that Tenisha had been up there to see him, but he had already had a visit from his sister. So a red flag went off in my head. Tenisha never told me she went up to the prison to try to visit him, so I'm now wondering what in the hell kind of motives she has.

Right after I finished reading my letter, I hopped off my bunk and grabbed one of the telephones in the phone booth stalls. Just my luck, though, she didn't answer. So I hung up the phone and thought to myself that maybe her visit was harmless. I mean, we are homegirls. I knew she wouldn't try to step on my toes. Well, whatever it was, I'm sure it was probably nothing. I might as well leave it alone. For now at least.

Chapter 15

Touchy situations

My parents have always been protective over me since I was the only child. And ever since I got in the situation, my dad has been really fucked up behind it. He wants me to move down south with them after I am released so they can get to know their grandchild. I told them both I would see if Supreme could get his parole transferred down there, but they weren't trying to hear that. So I had to stress to them that he is the father of this baby, so by right he should be able to have a say so where his child resides. My father had a different opinion.

"He shouldn't have a say so in anything, especially since he's the one who put you in that situation," my dad retorted.

"You are absolutely right, Dad, but I don't want to argue about this right now. I just called to see how you and Mom was doing."

"We are fine," his sarcasm continued. "You are the one we are worried about."

"I'm fine, too," I replied with assurance.

"Well, what's this talk about you giving your girlfriend temporary custody of the baby?" my father pressed on.

"Dad, I am only doing it because I feel like giving my baby to you guys would put a big strain on you, and besides, y'all live way down south, so it would be very hard for me to get to see my baby."

"You are carrying on like you got life in prison or something!" he snapped.

"Dad, that's not the point. I just want to be able to see my baby on a regular basis, so that's why I made the decision to give Tenisha custody."

"I really don't think that's a good move," he protested.

"Come on now, you're only saying that because you want your grandbaby with you and Mommy."

"You know this whole thing is breaking your mother's heart."

"Dad, please tell her it's for the best and not to worry. It's just a temporary solution, and when I come home everything is going to go right back the way it was."

I think it took me two rounds of fifteen-minute calls to convince my father that everything was going to be all right with my baby staying with Tenisha while I was away. My mother, on the other hand, wouldn't budge. She was adamant about where she stood on this issue, so I knew she wouldn't be moved. Now even though I felt like they were being biased about this whole ordeal, I had to respect them for their honesty. Time would tell how this thing played out.

Chapter 16

Dropping the load

"**P**ush!" the nurses and the doctor screamed. I put my chin to my chest and did as I was told.

"Aggggh!" I screamed as the baby's head made an appearance. It felt like a hot bowling ball coming out of my ass. I couldn't even grab on to anything because I was shackled to the bed. Giving birth as a prisoner was the worst. Chained to the bed like an animal, I gave birth in the most primitive way—no drugs, no help, no man, no support—and in the most primitive setting—the hard prison hospital bed.

I heard my baby boy cry for the first time, and the sound was music to my ears. I was given a short visit with him before the nurses came to take him away. He was beautiful, a small bundle of joy, and already looked just like Supreme. I closed my eyes and imagined what it would've been like giving birth with Supreme holding my hand. He would've probably kissed me on my forehead and told me the pain would go away. Supreme would've been so proud to have a son . . . a namesake to carry on his legacy. I gave him Supreme's full name and added junior to the end of it. Too bad Supreme wasn't around to sign the birth certificate because that would have truly made this experience worthwhile.

He's been home for about a month now, but I haven't heard from him yet. I've tried calling him on several occasions. I left messages for him at his people's house in Berkley, and I even left a few messages with Tenisha, but all I keep getting from her is the same ole excuses, *"I told him what you said, and he said that as soon as he gets himself together he's gonna come holler at you."* So I'm like, yeah right, tell me another lie because this one is getting old. But hey, what could I do?

Later on that night, after the delivery, the nurse told me that I would only get to see the baby for the two days that I was in the hospital. I can't lie, my heart exploded. I felt like killing myself. My son deserved a mother who was worth something . . . not a weak prisoner with nothing to give.

Today was the day that I had to say goodbye to my son. But before the social worker carried him away, she informed me that Tenisha was downstairs in the waiting area, filling out forms so she could take him in her custody. The woman also informed me that I would have to appear in juvenile court in the next few weeks to finalize all the paperwork. I said okay and watched her as she took him away.

In the back of my mind I had doubts about giving Sean Jr. to Tenisha, but at this point I didn't have any other alternatives. The main thing was that he was close so I would be able to see him as often as possible. In addition to that, Supreme would be able to see him, too, and then they would be able to bond like a father and son should.

Chapter 17

On the outside looking in

Tenisha brought my baby up to see me today. I was so excited when the CO called me and told me I had a visitor. I jumped straight off my top bunk in a matter of two seconds and was out the block and into the visiting room in less than three. My son was a month old today, so Tenisha and I decided that it would be best if she brought him up here so I could share this day with him. She had him bundled up in a stack of blankets due to the thirty-degree weather outside. She was dressed for the weather, too, in her cream-colored, turtleneck, wool sweater, a pair of blue denim jeans by bebe, and some funky cream-colored Fendi snow boots. Her hair wasn't done in one of her most fabulous styles; instead, she had it combed back into a ponytail.

"Here is your mommy," she said to my baby as she handed him to me.

I was smiling my ass off because this was the second time I saw him since he was born. Tenisha hadn't been able to bring him every week because of other shit she had to do, so I'm dealing with this little arrangement one day at a time.

"Come here, you little stinka!" I said, cradling him into my arms very tight.

"He's growing up, huh?" Tenisha started off.

"Yeah, he sure is," I replied, admiring him from head to toe.

"Just think that you only got thirteen months left to do in this joint and then you're back on the streets."

"I know, I can't wait," I said, focusing all my attention on my son.

"How is your commissary looking? You aiight?"

"Yeah, I'm fine. I got enough stuff to last me for another week."

"Aiight, well, I'ma see if I can get with Supreme so he can give me some money to send to you."

"What's up with him anyway?" I wanted to know. I had been getting really irritated by his absence. Everybody seemed to be able to get in contact with him but me. Now what kind of bullshit is that? And it seemed like every time I asked Tenisha to get him to either write me or come see me, she came back with one hundred and one excuses for him. I am truly fed up.

"I haven't seen him recently, but I heard he be hanging out in Diggs Park."

"Well, the next time you run into his ass, let him know that he has a son that needs him."

"He seen the baby."

"When?"

"A couple days after I took him from the hospital."

"Why didn't you tell me?"

"I thought I did." Tenisha looked dumbfounded.

"No, you didn't," I assured in the most irritated manner.

"I'm sorry, but I thought I did." Tenisha tried to convince me, but that shit she was saying went in one ear and right out the other.

"Well, the next time you see his ass, you let him know

that I am still sitting in prison behind his ass and I would appreciate it if he would drop me a line or something."

"I'll let him know," she assured me.

"What's up with Jay? Have you spoken with him lately?"

"Nope. I'm done with his ass," she began to say. "His baby momma can have him and all that shit he's got with him."

"Is he out yet?"

"Nah, but he doesn't have long."

"Are y'all still keeping in touch?"

"Not after I went up there and found out that his baby momma was up there, too. Shit, you know I'm not into playing the sideline chick. That shit just ain't me."

"Has he tried to get in touch with you?"

"Yep, he sure has, but he might as well cut his losses because I have. I mean, it was good while it lasted. But now the show must go on."

I smiled at Tee and had a chance to look at her really good. On the surface she looked like she had it all together, but then I could hear a totally different story going on through her voice. I can't say what she had going on, but whatever it was, it was eating away at her. I just hope my son doesn't suffer behind it.

Our visit lasted for four whole hours, and I enjoyed every single minute of it. But before she left, I had a chance to tell her how much I appreciated her and I also told her that I would forever be in her debt. She kissed me and reminded me that that's what friends are for.

Chapter 18

The surprise of a lifetime

It had been a long time since I heard Supreme's voice, so when he answered Tenisha's phone and accepted my call, I almost had a massive heart attack.

"What's good, love?" he asked, his voice sounding the way I had remembered.

I was flabbergasted. I really didn't know whether to curse his ass out for abandoning me or tell him I loved and missed him. I knew that I couldn't cry, though, because niggas like him feed off shit like that, so I played it safe and acted nonchalant. "I'm all right," I said.

"I miss you, Mommie!"

I sighed heavily because his words melted right through. But I knew I had to keep my guard up, so instead of telling him I missed him, too, I asked him where he had been all this time.

"I been around, you know, trying to handle my business."

"How come I haven't been able to get in touch with you?"

"That's because I haven't been stable. If you wanna know the truth, a whole lot of people haven't been able to keep in touch with me."

"But I am not a whole lot of people. I'm supposed to be your girl. And as of six weeks ago, I became the mother of your son. So how are you able to walk around out there like everything is okay while I am sitting behind bars for you?"

"Oh, don't put all that shit on me!" he snapped. "I didn't twist your arm and make you do that. You did it because you wanted to."

"I did it because you worried me to fucking death about it!" I roared back, losing every morsel of composure I had left in me.

"Hey, look, I ain't get on this phone to argue with you. All I wanted to do is say what's up!"

"That's it?" I said in disbelief. By this time I was trembling, and I truly believe that if I was in front of this motherfucker, I would've spit right in his face.

"What else do you want me to say?" he asked nonchalantly.

"If I got to tell you what to say, then this conversation is over."

"Aiight, well, I'ma holler at you another time."

"Don't holler at me, take care of your fucking son! I mean, you can at least do that."

"Oh, don't worry about him. He's straight." He became cocky.

"Yeah, that's what you said about me until I got caught up in all your bullshit. But you know what, Supreme, I am going to be all right. Everything is going to move in my favor, you watch and see."

"That's good. Keep your spirits up, and like I said before, I'll holler at you."

And before I could get another word in edgewise, he gave the telephone to Tenisha.

"Hello," she said, in a way to see if I was still on the other end.

"I'm still up here." I sighed heavily.

"You all right?"

"Girl, that motherfucker ain't shit! But that's all right, though. What goes around always comes back in full circle. And you know what?"

"What?"

"Whatever bitch he gets with is going to get it, too."

"Oh, Rissa, don't talk like that."

"I am dead serious. Whoever is around this nigga when he gets his payback is going to get blindsided, too. Watch what I say!" I continued.

But Tenisha quickly changed the subject by giving me a report on how quickly Lil' Sean was growing up. She told me he was in the stage now that he's beginning to lift up his head, and then she said that he grips her finger really tight, too.

I smiled and said, "Ahhh, that's so sweet! I am so proud of my baby." But deep down inside I was hurt because I wasn't there to see all these things for myself. But then I thought, *In time I will.*

Chapter 19

Love is blind

My cousin Kamryn sat on the opposite side of the glass partition and gave me a look I hadn't seen in a very long time. She was the eldest of the cousins on my mother's side of the family. In fact, she was five years older, and she made sure we gave her respect. Growing up, she would always be caught in the middle of somebody's drama. She kept shit going around our neighborhood, and if anybody wanted to know something about somebody she always had the answers for them. Today was no different, so as I sat before her dressed in my prison jumpsuit and hair braided back into two big cornrows, my facial expression immediately conformed to the nasty allegations she had begun to make.

"Stop lying to me, Kam," I said angrily. *Why is she saying the things she's saying?* I asked myself.

"I'm telling you. I saw them together. As clear as day, Supreme was holding hands with Tenisha while they were coming out of Nordstroms carrying tons of fucking shopping bags," Kamryn repeated. The words crashed through my skull like a wrecking ball and crushed my heart into pieces. "Everybody's been talking about it, but that was the first time I had seen them together. I mean, they were acting like they were married and shit. When I looked at your son's face while Supreme was pushing him in the stroller, he was asleep, but he looked so peaceful," she continued.

Now, I heard everything she had just said, but the part about Supreme being on the streets was what surprised me the most. At that very moment, I wasn't concerned about Supreme fucking around with Tenisha; I was more worried about the fact that he was out of prison and hadn't come to see how I was doing, or written me a letter for that matter.

"Wait a minute, you mean to tell me that that nigga is walking out on the streets playing family man with Tenisha and my motherfucking baby like I don't exist?"

"That's what it looked like to me," Kamryn assured me.

"Oh, so that's why that bitch stopped coming to see me and accepting my phone calls."

"Yep, it sure is," Kamryn said, encouraging me to listen to my own self.

"What kind of game they playing?" I wondered aloud.

"I don't know. But you should've seen him prancing around Tenisha and the baby like he was a fucking big shot. I swear, if I didn't have my kids with me I would've ran up on both of them and gave them a piece of my mind."

"It's okay, she'll get hers," I said, fighting back tears.

"She sure is. But I told you years ago that that bitch Tenisha was a snake. Whether you want to believe it or not, she has always been jealous of you. And I would bet a million dollars that she played those chicks against you so they could fuck your face up," Kamryn whispered harshly, her words stabbing me over and over again.

I shook my head in disbelief. "I can't believe this bullshit!" I snapped.

"Well, believe it because the ho is trying to bury your ass

alive, and as soon as she gives Supreme joint custody, it's going to be really hard for you to get your son back."

Hearing everything Kamryn had run down for me caused a lump the size of a golf ball to enlarge in my throat. And at that point I knew I could not hold back all the tears my eyes had built up, so I released them.

"That bitch betrayed me! She tricked me into giving her ass custody of my child," I mumbled, my words barely audible.

"Yeah, she did, but don't let that shit tear you down. You'll get that ho back, and best believe that I am going to help you."

For the very first time in my life Kamryn's words seemed believable. She was always known for fabricating a story, and she was also a selfish person which was why we never really got along growing up. So it was enlightening to hear her tell me that she would have my back in all of this. I honestly didn't know how to react to her initially, so I smiled and told her thanks.

Right at the end of the visit, Kamryn told me she heard that Tenisha was down at the club bragging to one of her stick girls that she was the one who set me up to get busted from the jump, and now that I am out of the way, she can finally have the family she always wanted.

"What did you just say?" I asked, trying to make sure I heard Kamryn correctly.

After she reiterated what she had just said, I slumped down in the chair and tried to make sense of everything. But then it all came to me. Tee wanted Supreme from the very beginning. I couldn't see it then, but every time I would visit him and he and I would be at our table kissing and stuff, I would catch her periodically frowning at us. Then after we'd leave from our visit, we would get on the road and she'd always ask me how good was his dick this time and what position did he put me in. She also used to ask me how big his dick was, but I wouldn't give her his exact measurements. All I would tell her was that he was *straight*. In addition to that, I remembered Tee couldn't ever have children. Every time she became pregnant, she was not able to carry the baby full term. Now it made sense, her acting jealous after I told her that I was pregnant. I guess she thought getting rid of me would be the best thing she could ever do. Why not kill two birds with one stone? Everybody else does it.

Kamryn continued to feed me all the gossip she got from her girlfriend, and when I couldn't stand to listen to that mess anymore, I put my head down and sobbed right there in front of over a hundred people. My life was over as I knew it, and my man and my best friend were living it up on the street.

I went back to my cell after my visit, but I couldn't keep still. All I could do was picture Tenisha kissing Supreme's lips. I imagined them walking through MacArthur Mall on a shopping spree, while I could hardly get money in my commissary. Then to think that those bastards were playing house with my son, that shit took me over the top. I grabbed everything off of the small table in front of my bunk and tossed it around my cell. I started screaming and destroying everything in my small prison home. I broke my mirror and ripped pictures that me and Tenisha had taken back in the day. This bitch had brought me pictures of us to remind me where we used to be . . . I guess. All those years everybody refused to be her friend . . . I was there for her stinking ass. Now she had my man. I couldn't understand it. Why would she even hook me up with him in the first place? It all didn't make sense . . . but then again maybe it did. I was the fall guy and I was the scapegoat while they both profited off of my hard work. I am so sick of people pretending to love me, when they have all sorts of other agendas. But you mark my words; I will get my just due. Both of them are going to pay for all the shit I went through in my life, especially the shit Todd took me through. I will have the last laugh.

Chapter 20

Do or die mission

After all the shit I had been hearing from the streets, I knew I had to put something into action so I could get out of this place. Living with the reality that Supreme and Tenisha had become one and that my child was their trophy baby, I knew I had to do something to shut them down, especially since it had been seven months since I had last seen him. Unbeknownst to all my family, I had signed up for the drug program, and after I had completed it, I got six months knocked off my sentence, which made me eligible for the halfway house, so I signed up for that, too. After the initial screening and the filing of the paperwork was completed, I finally got the okay from the halfway house coordinator. I was excited as hell because I knew that I was going to get me a little bit of freedom. This newfound freedom would allow me to get things rolling on the situation concerning Tenisha and Supreme. It would also allow me to check on my baby. It had been a while since I had last seen him. But now things are going to be different and the sweet taste of revenge is drawing closer.

To get the ball rolling, I called my cousins Marlo and Kamryn and told them the good news. Kamryn answered the phone, so she and I spoke first. Midway into the conversation, she got Marlo on three-way, so he and I chatted for a bit. I couldn't go into specifics about what I wanted him to do to Tenisha and Supreme, but I did express to him in so many words that I wanted nothing but to see them suffer and that I wanted it done sooner than later. He happily obliged, so a sense of calmness fell over me.

"Give me some time to work it out, though," he said.

"That's cool," I told him. "Take your time because I want it done right."

"Oh, it's gonna definitely be done right. Don't worry about that," he assured me.

"Well, I am gonna be getting out of here Friday morning, so come and scoop me up."

"Oh, no question. We are going to be there bright and early," Marlo said.

"All right, so I guess I'll see y'all then," I told them both.

"Aiight," he answered, and then we hung up.

Chapter 21

Get-out-of-jail-free card

I heard the bass from Marlo's Range Rover blasting Jay Z's "Heart of the City," as I ambled my way down the cold gray hallway of the prison. My heart skipped a beat from mere excitement because I knew he wouldn't let me down. As soon as I told him I was being released early with nowhere to go, no clothes, basically nothing to my name, Marlo assured me that he would take care of it. As I made my way out of the prison doors, the sun burned my eyes. I was so happy to breathe in the fresh air and to see that gleaming-ass Range.

"What up, baby?" Marlo beamed, grabbing me into a bear hug.

"Hey," I said in a low whisper, returning his embrace with tears in my eyes. I was so fucking happy to be back in the world.

"Why you cryin'? Shit, you are back in the world, baby girl, and it's about to be on, so don't let nothing make you cry," Marlo consoled.

"Hell to the nah . . . I know your ass ain't crying," Kamryn yelled out of the back window of her brother's SUV.

"Heyyyyy!" I squealed. I was so happy to see my family.

They were the only two that had my back while I was down. Even though it meant that my parents had to find out about my incarceration it was all good because everybody needs somebody when they are locked up.

"Girl, I'm so happy to see ya'll," I said as I slid onto the butter leather seats.

"Listen, baby girl, you gonna be aiight. We about to do things right," Marlo said as he pulled out. I looked back at the prison through the side mirror as the SUV tires kicked up dust. I was leaving that fucking place in the dust all right, and it was going to be a bittersweet homecoming.

As we rode, Marlo, Kamryn, and I caught up on old times. They both blew my mind with more stories of Supreme and Tenisha. Now the word on the street was that Tenisha had set up a dude named Junior from Campostella so that Supreme could take over Junior's spots. The thing is, Supreme is from Norfolk. Everyone knows that Norfolk niggas and Chesapeake niggas don't step on each other's toes. It's not like Norfolk and Chesapeake got beef, but there is a street understanding that hustlers from different cities stay in their own town. Supreme taking over a major section in Campostella didn't sit well with a lot of cats from Chesapeake. So not only did I have an axe to grind with Supreme and Tenisha . . . so did half of the niggas in Campostella . . . including Marlo because Junior used to work for Marlo. So when Junior went down it affected operations all over Norfolk. Marlo explained to me how he had lost three hundred thousand dollars when Junior went down. He said he fantasized about grabbing Tenisha around her skinny-ass throat and watching her squirm. Marlo and Kamryn held a strong dislike for Tenisha, because for one they were always convinced that she was jealous of me, and two, she did mess over Marlo pretty bad when she used to send his hard-earned dough to a cat she was still fucking with on the low. And even though she was wrong, I still stuck up for her, but now I knew that what everyone was trying to tell me for years was true—Tenisha wanted to be me. Now she was living the life I was supposed to be living with my man and my son.

I was lost in thought as Marlo and Kamryn rambled on and on about what was going on in the world while I was locked up. I didn't even watch where we were driving to; I was along for the luxury ride. Marlo stopped the car abruptly.

"Aiight, we here," he announced. I looked out of the window, confused.

"Where we at?" I asked, concerned. I just really wanted to go to Marlo's house and take a hot-ass shower.

"You didn't think I was taking you home without taking you shopping first, did you?" Marlo asked rhetorically, like I should've already known the answer. I blushed. I felt kind of ashamed.

"Let's go! You know there's some shit I want!" Kamryn screamed out. She was used to her brother spoiling her. I looked out at the huge newly built structure. MacArthur Mall was where we stopped.

"Come on, Larissa. All the ladies in Nordstroms know me," Kamryn said excitedly, grabbing my hand and rushing me into the mall.

"Yo, I'm going into my spot," Marlo announced, letting me and Kamryn know he was going to his favorite jewelry store. My heart was pounding. I hadn't been shopping in so long, and definitely not in MacArthur.

Once inside the Nordstrom store, I felt like I'd walked into a dream. I was Julia Roberts in the movie *Pretty Woman*. The store attendants were so attentive and nice. Kamryn was right . . . they all knew her. Marlo kept her pockets so laced, she visited this department store at least once a week, and she would always come out with a shopping bag of shit worth every bit of a grand or more. Now, the shit they had on hold for me hadn't been put out on display yet. I was amazed. My shopping trip with Marlo and Kamryn was all out. I felt like a princess by the time we made it back to the SUV.

"Marlo and Kam, I can't ever repay y'all for all this," I said.

"Nobody asked you to repay us. Just live," Marlo replied, looking at me through the rearview mirror. For real, if he wasn't my cousin, I would be in love with him. I was glad to be related to him.

"Aiight now, let's go eat like royalty," he said, turning up the music in his ride. I closed my eyes and smiled as he eased the car in front of Ruth's Chris Steak House. *I'm so glad to be home*, I said to myself, smiling wide.

After all the shopping and good eating, reality set back in. I was out on the street again, but I wasn't quite as free as I wanted to be. I had less than thirty minutes to report to the halfway house, so Marlo put his truck in full gear and that's where we headed. When we got there, the daytime counselor allowed both Marlo and Kamryn to help me bring my things inside, but our visiting time together was limited. So after everything was in place, I walked them back to the front entrance of the building and kissed them goodbye.

"Hit me up tomorrow and we'll go from there," Marlo instructed me. I knew he couldn't be talking anything other than our plans to get back at Tenisha and Supreme, so I nodded, giving him the okay.

Chapter 22

A week later

I have been in this halfway house for one week now. The residents here are funny as hell, so for the most part everybody is cool. I've been looking for a job every day but haven't been having any luck. So today I decided to sign out and go to the Department of Motor Vehicles so I could renew my driver's license. I called Marlo and got him to take me to the Military Highway location, which was less than a mile from Tenisha's apartment. I did this so I could make a personal trip over to her place right after I took care of my business. But according to Marlo, Supreme moved her out of her old apartment a little over five months ago and moved her ass into a three-story condo in downtown Ghent area of Norfolk. We took a stroll by there right after we left DMV.

The name of the complex was Ghent Estates, and believe me the word *estates* said it all. The fucking place was beautiful, and it was set off in a gated community, too. I almost got sick to my fucking stomach trying to picture that bitch Tenisha basking in glory while I'm sleeping on a damn bunk bed in a halfway house.

"This shit makes you mad, huh?" Marlo asked me, pointing to the front of one of the tall buildings.

"You damn right!" I snapped.

"Well, it should, because this is the shit that your home-girl did to you!" he said as he parked his truck alongside of the tall, iron, black gate. "See that Mercedes CLS-500 . . . that's hers, too," he continued, pointing toward a silver-colored Benz.

This bitch is living ghetto fabulous off my fucking hard work, I thought to myself. I kept my mouth shut because if I would've opened it, I would have screamed nonstop.

"Yo, you aiight?" Marlo asked me.

"Hell nah, I am not all right! I'm fucking fuming right now," I replied. Just as I finished my sentence, like something out of a movie, Tenisha and Supreme came out of the building. I watched as she sauntered arm in arm with my man as he carried my son. I glared at them as they walked toward her luxury car like one big happy family. Supreme held on to my son's feet, and the baby sat on his neck and held on to Supreme's head. The baby giggled as Tenisha tickled his leg. The sight of them made me sick. Hot vomit threatened to escape from the back of my throat, and my bowels tightened.

"You see that bitch living it up, right?" Marlo snarled. His facial expression told how much he hated both of them.

"I still can't believe it. Even though I'm seeing this shit, I still can't believe it," I said, tears streaming down my face. I couldn't hold it anymore. It hurt so bad. Supreme and Tenisha had left me in prison for dead. They set me up and stole my life. They used me to give them a pretty baby to play house with. Tenisha knew what the fuck she was doing. She planned my demise from the day Todd left me. Getting with Supreme was a scam from the very beginning. It was Tenisha's idea for him to use me as a mule so he could get back on his feet and have start-up money to get his feet wet when he got back on the streets. But it's all right because they will get what's coming to them. I will bet my life on it.

"Don't worry . . . they both gonna get theirs. Don't you worry one fucking bit," Marlo said, as if he had just read my mind. I watched them load into Tenisha's car and pull off. They looked like the perfect family.

"Let's go. I can't stand this," I said, lowering my head. I was burning inside.

Chapter 23

Bouncing right back

After seeing Supreme and Tenisha together like that, I decided that letting them know I was out right away wasn't a good move, so that was why I elected to keep them in the dark about it.

Now after another week, I finally found myself a job. I started working at this telemarketing firm, so Marlo let me use one of his cars to get back and forth. Everything was going well for the first few days until I started experiencing a lot of mixed emotions. I would shift between pure happiness at the good things that had happened for me and pure devastation at the betrayal I had suffered. I had officially counted men out of my life, and no matter how hard Kamryn tried to hook me up, I refused. That was until the day I met what I considered Mr. Right. It was a rainy morning, three weeks after my release. I was chilling at Kamryn's apartment on a weekend pass, and I heard three loud knocks on her front door.

"Who is it?" I screamed, surprised and concerned.

"Me, open up!" Marlo yelled from the other side of the door. I immediately yanked the door open.

"Wassup?" I huffed as I pulled back the door. Marlo was

standing there with another man. I was immediately flushed with embarrassment. My hair was sticking up on my head, I didn't have on a bra under my T-shirt, and my sweats were holey. I didn't look at the guy; instead, I looked at Marlo like he was crazy.

"Yo, cuz, sorry for barging in but we need to talk," Marlo said with urgency. "This is my man. Terrell, this is my cousin I was telling you about," Marlo introduced.

"Hey," I said, lowering my eyes and still not really looking at the man Marlo called Terrell. They both rushed into the apartment.

"What's going on?" I asked, looking at Marlo for an explanation.

"Yo, we need you for something. Terrell is from Junior's camp. Remember I told you Tenisha was fucking with Junior and had him set up? Well, I told Terrell about you and what Tenisha and Supreme did to you," Marlo started.

"A lot of people want your friend and your ex-man dead, ma," Terrell interjected. His voice was smooth and confident. I finally looked over at him. He was a caramel color with small slit almond-shaped eyes. He reminded me of a black Chinese person. His teeth were so straight they looked fake. "I hear you might be one of those people," Terrell continued as I stared in his handsome face. Although he was good looking, there was a hardness that permeated his face, as if he'd been through a lot in life, and he also had that "I ain't no joke" look.

"Yeah, I hate both of them for what they did to me, but they have my son right now," I replied.

"Ma, we ain't into hurting kids. My beef is with the adults, especially that bitch Tenisha. Junior did all kinds of shit for that sheisty-ass bitch. He told me that he respected her because she was a real chick and never asked him for shit. Little did that nigga know this bitch was setting him up. Junior was my man, like my brother. This can't go unanswered, and all the fingers point back to her. Then I found out that she was fucking with that nigga that moved in on Junior's spots. It can't go down like that," Terrell said, rubbing the perfect goatee that adorned his sharp chin.

"What am I supposed to do?" I asked. I wanted revenge myself, but I also wanted to get my son. I knew if Supreme and Tenisha were wiped out, the cops would have an all-out manhunt for my son.

"We gonna explain what your role is," Marlo interrupted.

"Ma, we gonna take care of you. You will get your son, and you won't have to worry financially," Terrell said. The more he spoke, the more I realized how attracted to him I was. I immediately put that shit out of my mind. I had written men off. After Todd and Supreme I wasn't thinking about a man.

Marlo and Terrell stayed and explained a bunch of things to me. It was agreed that we would move slow so that things would go as planned. I was comfortable with my role.

Two days after the first visit, I received two dozen red roses. The card said, *"I've never met someone as beautiful as you. A down-ass chick. From Mack."* I was confused and flattered at the same time. Terrell, aka Mack, was so serious and so cool during his visit I would've never thought he was attracted to me. I looked at the flowers and the card over and over again. In all my years I had never received flowers from a man. *Damn, should I call him to say thank you?* I asked myself. He had given me his cell phone number since we'd be working together. I walked around in a circle several times before I picked up the phone. I dialed Mack's number, but when the other line began ringing, I hung up. *Shit! Why am I so scared?* I wondered.

Buzz, Buzz . . . my cell phone vibrated in my hand. My heart thumped in my chest, it was him. That meant he knew I called him. I had to answer.

"Yo," Terrell barked through the receiver.

"Hello . . ." I answered apprehensively.

"You called me?" he replied. He didn't sound too happy.

"Um . . . yes. I called to thank you for the flowers," I mumbled.

"Ahhh, ma. That was nothing. After what I heard . . . you deserve them," he said.

"Thanks. I've never gotten flowers before," I admitted.

"Shit. Those niggas you were fucking with didn't know how to treat your pretty ass," Terrell said, pouring on the charm. I was blushing and smiling. "Ma, let me take you out tonight. It don't have to be all business. I got your cousin's blessing," Terrell announced.

"Okay, pick me up at eight," I said, burying my head in the couch pillows and smiling like crazy.

As the time for my first date with Terrell approached, I panicked. I tried on at least seven outfits and couldn't choose one. I must've looked at myself in the mirror a hundred times. I finally settled on a pair of fitted, straight-legged Citizens of Humanity jeans and a black bustier top with my favorite black Gucci stilettos. I let my hair down and flat ironed it straight. I put on my MAC makeup and I was ready. I peeped out my front window ten times before I saw a black BMW pull up and stop. My heart started beating when my cell phone rang. The caller ID read, "Terrell."

"Hello," I said, trying to remain cool.

"Hey, beautiful, I'm outside," Terrell said smoothly.

"I'm coming out," I replied. I waited exactly seven minutes before I even attempted to head for the front door. I had to make him wait for a minute, didn't want him to think I was too anxious.

After that first date Terrell and I were inseparable. Marlo and Kamryn teased me all the time, saying that I was glowing since I got some real man dick. I made Terrell wait three months before giving him some pussy. I wanted to fuck him from day one, but I wanted him to respect me. While we dated, we watched Tenisha and Supreme's almost every move. I made several calls to Tenisha making her think I was still locked up. She always said the same snake shit. "Oh, Rissa, I'm coming to see you," or "Rissa, I'ma bring the baby up there." I fronted like I didn't know shit. I wanted her to believe I was in the dark. All I needed was time to put plans in motion for my son; plans for Tenisha and Supreme were already in the works.

Chapter 24

Let the games begin

Terrell kissed me deeply and passionately. "Don't worry about shit, ma, we gotcha back," he said as he stroked my hair. We sat in his car in front of Tenisha's building, and his crew was huddled in an all-black van behind us.

"I'm not nervous. I just want my son," I replied.

"Listen, I would die before I let anything happen to that baby," Marlo said from the backseat.

"It's all good. Once you get inside, we coming in. You get that baby and get the fuck out of Dodge," Terrell instructed.

"Aiight, I'm ready," I said, rubbing my hands together to calm my nerves.

I wanted to see Supreme and Tenisha's faces when Terrell and the crew came up in there, but I knew I needed to get my baby and get out.

Knock! Knock! Knock! "Who is it?" Tenisha screamed. I could hear music playing through the door.

"It's Larissa," I yelled back.

"Who?" Tenisha screamed in response. I could hear that the music got lower.

"Tenisha, it's Larissa," I said again. Terrell and the guys were in the exit up the hallway. Tenisha looked through the peep hole. I heard whispering and shuffling around.

"Open the door, Tenisha. I'm home," I said calmly.

"Hold on a minute," she replied nervously. The bitch didn't know what to do. I could hear her and Supreme whispering.

Finally Tenisha pulled back the door. She still didn't let me in. "How you know I was living here?" Tenisha asked.

"Aren't you happy to see me?" I asked. That was the signal. Terrell, Marlo, and the crew came rushing toward the door. I pushed Tenisha in her chest and stormed into the apartment.

"What the fuck? Supreme!" Tenisha screamed. It was too late. I rushed to the living room and grabbed my sleeping baby.

"Y'all niggas know who I am!" Supreme yelled. That was the last thing I heard. I took my baby son and dashed outside to a car that was waiting for me.

"You got what you came for?" Kamryn asked as she sped from the block. My mind raced as I tried to console my screaming baby. He looked up at me and cried even more. It broke my heart . . . my baby didn't even know me.

The next morning I paced the floor, nervous as hell. I was waiting to hear from Terrell or Marlo . . . somebody. No phone calls ever came. I was worried to death and I felt sick. I didn't know if I should go through with the next phase of the plan or what. I had bathed and fed the baby, but I was nervous as hell to have my own son. *Rinng! Rinnng!*

"Shit!" I jumped when the phone rang. I was shook.

"Yo, it's all good. Go to the next step," Marlo said calmly.

"What happened?" I asked.

"Yo, I don't be doing no talking on the horn. Do you and I'll see you when the smoke clears," Marlo said.

"Where's the other half?" I asked, inquiring about my new love.

"In the cut. You'll get that half back soon," Marlo said in code.

I hung up and immediately dialed the number to my son's law guardian. I spoke to the white lady and told her what I'd planned to tell her. I explained that Tenisha had contacted my cousin Kamryn and said she needed a baby-sitter because she was going out on a date, so after Kamryn gave her the okay, Tenisha dropped him off. The woman asked for my cousin's address, so I gave it to her. Minutes later, she advised me that she would be meeting me over there to discuss guardianship in the A.M. I told her I would be there bright and early.

I tossed and turned that night. First, I didn't know if everything was taken care of. I didn't know what had happened to my former lover and former best friend, and more importantly, I didn't know how things would go at court.

As soon as one beam of light came through my window, I jumped out of bed. I turned on the TV to get the weather, and it happened, the news broadcast that changed my life.

"In breaking news today police in Norfolk found a gruesome scene at the Ghent Estates. A man and a woman had been tortured and murdered inside one of the building's apartments. Sources say the woman was so badly disfigured during the torture that medical examiners don't know how they will identify her. There were no fingers for fingerprints and no teeth for dental record identification. Police say that the woman suffered great and horrific pain before she finally expired. Sources also say the man was tortured simi-

larly and that his male organs were removed and stuffed into his throat."

I didn't hear anything else the reporter said. I was sick to my stomach. Although Tenisha and Supreme had done me dirty, I had no idea how much they were hated. When it was all said and done, I heard that Tenisha's nipples were cut off and they made Supreme eat them while she screamed. I heard they tortured her for hours before she finally died and they removed her fingertips and teeth. They beat the shit out of Supreme with metal knuckles; then they cut his knees and made him crawl around naked like a dog. After they were done torturing him and making him give up all his stash spots and all his workers' spots, they cut his dick off and stuffed it in his throat. He bled to death in less than ten minutes. I wanted to cry for them, but when I looked at my son, I couldn't even bring myself to shed a tear.

Chapter 25

This is some real shit

The very next day, the woman from Social Services showed up at Kamryn's place with a police escort. Now, I can't lie, I was nervous as a bitch! I assumed off the bat that he was there to arrest me and Kamryn both while the lady took my baby and put him into foster care. But I'm glad my assumptions were wrong, because after I let her in, she and the officer both ran everything down to me.

"Ms. Taylor, it was a good thing that your friend gave your son to your cousin because he might've been dead, too," the detective said as he sat across from me on Kamryn's living room sofa.

"I know, but I still can't believe my best friend and my boyfriend are dead." I sobbed with fake tears.

"And you might be like that for a while. When someone very close to you dies, it always takes some time for it to sink in. But take it one day at a time and everything will be all right."

"I will, thank you."

The detective stood to his feet and looked at the social worker who was sitting on the other side of the living room jotting something down on paper. "Do you have something you would like to add?" he asked her.

She looked over at me. "Seeing as though you are the biological mother, I am going to recommend that you get custody of your child," the law guardian chimed in.

"Thank you so much! I swear I will be a good mother." I cried some more.

"We know you will," the law guardian comforted. Kamryn sat at the table trying hard to hide her smile. I know she wanted to give me an Academy Award.

Needless to say, after the social worker made her recommendation, I got my baby back, which was what I had been waiting for.

"Come here, little boy," I called out to the new love of my life. My son hesitated for a bit, I guess because he didn't know who I was. He cried and cried at first, but I had to convince him that I was his real mother and that I wasn't gonna ever leave him again. After a while he finally got used to me, and then he started calling me Mommy, too. My payoff from the setup was pretty hefty, so I wasn't pressed to work long hours on my job at the telemarketing firm. All in all I was straight.

Two hours after the detective and the social worker left, I felt like taking my baby outside.

"Wanna go to the park?" I asked him while he was sitting on the living room floor in Kamryn's apartment.

"Phone," he said in baby talk.

"Phone? Who you talkin' to," I joked, and reached for my cell phone. I assumed he had been playing with it. I looked at the screen and realized he was really talking to someone.

"Oh, shit. Hello?" I said into the phone.

"How you doing?" the voice on the other end said. My heart melted because I knew who the voice belonged to.

"Terrell," I said, his name rolling off my tongue, hoping that this was in fact who I was talking to.

"Won't cha' come outside and see?"

My heart stopped, but my feet moved at the speed of lightning as I raced toward the front door. As soon as I opened up the door, Terrell was standing directly in front of me, bearing gifts. I wasn't concerned about the huge, crystal vase filled with red roses or the giant teddy he had underneath his armpits; all I was concerned about was him. So I rushed into his arms.

"Baby, I missed you," I squealed, excited.

"I missed you, too, but you know I had to get out of town for a minute. But I am here to stay this time," he replied.

Hearing his words sent chills all over my body. I looked down at my skin and saw that I had goose bumps. Just knowing that I had my man back gave me a sense of security. I now know that I am going to finally be all right because he is going to give me the life I always wanted. No more drama. My days of sleeping with the enemy are over!

Acknowledgments

Much love to my babies, Shaquira, Lil' J, and Kammy. I had a lot of projects on my plate this time last year but y'all stayed out of Mommy's way, so I want to thank you for that and tell you how much I love you.

To my agent, Crystal L. Winslow, you are one savvy businesswoman. You wear so many hats, half of the time I don't know how to address you. But, I do know that you have your finger on the pulse of what's going on in this industry. So keep doing your thing, sister!

Selena James, my editor, thanks so much for bringing me on board. You know I'm about to take this thing to the next level, right?

To my brother, Charles "Silk" Dunn @ FCI Elkton; sweetheart, you know what I've been through and the hurdles I had to cross, and through it all you were there to cheer me on. I can't express how much I love you for that.

To my family and friends, I love all of you guys. And to my girl, Wahida Clark, you know you got it going on, sister. When I was asked to get on this project with you, I didn't hesitate because you bring the heat. Now let's show the world what it's like with *Sleeping With the Enemy*.

A Letter to My Readers

I just want to let my readers know how much I appreciate you for your continued support. My books *Wifey, I'm Still Wifey, Life After Wifey*, and *The Candy Shop* have been selling like hot cakes because of you and I owe it all to you. So, to keep the momentum going, I am going to come harder and harder on everything I bring out from this day forward.

Thanks again for the love.

Yours truly,
Kiki Swinson

Want more Wahida Clark?
Turn the page for a preview of Wahida's hottest novels.
Now on sale at your local bookstore.

Thugs and the Women Who Love Them

"Thank you very much, Ms. Thompson, and please come again." The saleswoman smiled, shaking Angel's hand eagerly before she handed her three Wilson's Leather boutique shopping bags and a receipt.

"No, thank *you*," Angel replied. "And I'll be sure to tell all my friends about your store."

As she headed to the door, Angel turned to look at the woman, and she had to laugh. The salesgirl had picked up a calculator and was furiously punching in numbers, obviously calculating her commission on the $4,400.00 purchase Angel had just made. Too bad she had no idea that the check Angel had written was from a stolen checkbook, and the account had been closed for months. So Angel walked out of Wilson's with three big shopping bags filled with lots of items she would sell and a few for herself.

This was Angel's hustle to keep cash in her pockets. Going to law school was no easy task. It was a full-time job in itself. Trying to work *and* study just didn't work for her at all. There was no way she'd be able to finish school a semester early with a full-time job. She had to do one or the other, so she chose school. She'd already managed to get her bachelor's degree in three years. Now her goal was to graduate the same time as her homegirls: Roz, Kyra, and Jaz.

Angel did some window shopping on the way to her car. Oxford Valley Mall was the perfect place for Angel to run her game. The clerks were cordial and all the stores were very check friendly. She assumed the stores must have had some good insurance because she and every other hustler she knew had been wearing them out. Still, she knew her good luck couldn't last forever in this place. That's why she'd decided that after tonight she wouldn't be back. The last time she was at Oxford Valley she wrote almost $12,000.00 worth of bad checks. She planned on doing about the same tonight, if not more.

The merchandise she got from Wilson's would easily sell for between $1,800.00 and $2,200.00. Her fence, Rashid, usually bought all of the handbags and jewelry she could bring him. Way back, she and Rashid had been a couple, until Angel found out that she wasn't his only woman. Actually, she was one of three women who Rashid had scattered throughout the city. They'd only been involved for about six months, so it wasn't that tough for Angel to break things off. She still kept their business relationship open, though. After all, he was the best fence around, and she was looking forward to collecting from him after tonight.

Angel spotted a tennis bracelet in the window of Zales that she couldn't resist, but the Wilson's bags were starting to hurt her arms. So she decided to put the bags in her car and then come back for the bracelet. She had just squeezed onto the escalator that led to the first floor level when she noticed a woman staring at her from the up escalator. Angel did a double take as they passed each other. She realized the woman was a clerk who worked at one of the perfume counters at Macy's. Apparently, the woman remembered her, too.

A damn perfume clerk! Angel laughed to herself. Why couldn't it at least have been a jewelry store? Somewhere that she'd bilked for thousands of dollars instead of a couple of hundred. But when she looked up, Angel wasn't so amused anymore.

The tall, skinny clerk had stepped off the escalator at the second floor and was motioning to one of the mall's toy store cops. Angel was glad she had on some flat shoes. She stepped off the escalator and walked fast, in search of the nearest exit that would lead to her parked car. When she glanced back, she saw that the skinny clerk and a toy cop were on their way down the escalator. Angel got a firm grip on her bags and took off running.

"Excuse me! I need to catch my bus!" She was loud but polite as she swerved in and around the several crowds of people standing around the food court. "Sorry! Pardon me!" she apologized as she bumped a little boy in the head with her bags.

Angel ran right past the bus that was picking up the mall passengers. "Fuck!" she screamed as she realized that her car was parked way around the other side of the mall. She felt like crying, but she kept running. Her fingers and arms were burning from the heavy bags she was carrying. A red van provided a place for her to hide behind, to catch her breath, and see where the toy cop was. She went to the edge of the van and peeked around. A meddling shopper was standing next to a toy cop—she was pointing in her direction. *Goddamn Good Samaritan!* Angel ducked down and was moving between the parked cars as fast as she could. She had broken into a sweat.

"Shit!" she yelled as she set off a car alarm on a silver BMW. She stood up so she could run even faster. Behind her, the toy cop was fumbling with his radio, trying to talk into it and chase her at the same time. She was glad that he was fat, because he wasn't moving very fast.

"Where's my fuckin' car?" She was trying not to panic.

Her fingers and arms were now in super burn mode. The thought that she left the driver's side open for reasons like this one soothed her a little bit. A spare ignition key was stuffed in her bra.

I'd be aiight if I could just find my damn car now! she thought.

Toy cop was trying to gain on her.

"Yes! Yes! Thank you, Lord!" She spotted her green Honda Civic. "Fuck!" She breathed out fire when she saw orange dice hanging from the rearview mirror. "That's not my car!" She ran faster.

"Come here! I just want to . . . talk to you!" Toy cop barely got out those words.

Angel ran faster. She spotted another green Honda four cars over. "Please forgive me, Lord, for cussing. Please let this be my car!" This time she looked at the license plate. "Oh, fuck!" She had stolen tags. She noticed the strawberry air freshener hanging down and smiled. "That's my car."

She didn't even remember opening the door and stuffing the bags onto the passenger seat. She only knew that she had to start the car. She put the car in reverse. When she backed up, she hit a station wagon. Another Good Samaritan was performing their "civic duty" by blocking her in. Angel rolled the window down and screamed.

"Move the fuck outta my way or I'm gonna knock your doors in!" She rolled her car window back up just as toy cop grabbed the door handle and tried to open the door. Luckily it was locked. He started banging on the window and calling for help on his radio. Angel ignored him. She backed up again into the station wagon. This time the Good Samaritan was cursing as he moved the station wagon out of Angel's way. Toy cop was banging on the hood, commanding Angel to stop as she finally backed out of her parking space and floored it. She headed to the nearest exit, prayed, and thanked God for helping her out of that close call. If she got busted, then her man Keenan would know what she'd been up to—not to mention her mom. She couldn't afford for that to happen.

Every Thug Needs a Lady

Kyra showed the last of her baby shower guests to the door and thanked them again for the gifts. She closed the door and yelled, "Where my dawgs at?" She was hollering for Jaz, Angel, and Roz. The three of them had already flopped down on Kyra's Italian leather furniture.

"Where on earth are you going to put all of this stuff?" Roz asked Kyra. "The baby's bedroom already seems too crowded."

"Who are you telling? I don't think I have to buy anything," Kyra said, looking around at all of the gifts.

"That's what baby showers are for, to get *everything!*" Angel said. "And when are you allowing us to throw yours?" She pointed at Jaz.

Jaz yawned. "I'm not sure yet. Y'all the ones giving it. Just let me know when y'all ready. Even though I'd rather wait until after I have it."

"It was supposed to be a surprise," Roz said sarcastically. "And what do you mean after you have it?"

"I don't like surprises. And I haven't been in a festive mood." She turned toward the kitchen where Kyra was and yelled, "Can I have another piece of cake?"

When Kyra came out of the kitchen she was carrying a tray with a bottle of Dom, a bottle of sparkling grape juice, slices of cake, champagne glasses, and a bag of weed. "Roz, I know you got some paper," she said as she set the tray down.

"I sure do," Roz answered, rolling over and grabbing her Chanel bag from under the coffee table.

Kyra plopped down on the couch and poured two glasses of champagne and two glasses of the nonalcoholic bubbly for the pregnant sisters. "I'd like to say a few things to y'all," she announced. "For starters, I can't thank y'all enough for the beautiful baby shower. Y'all really went all out; the gifts are all of that. I don't know where everything is gonna go, but we'll figure something out. Second, I love y'all. Y'all are the sisters I never had. And for real, if it wasn't for everyone's support—not to mention your competitiveness—I wouldn't have finished school. I wouldn't be where I am right now." She stopped and smiled at them. "Of course, y'all didn't have anything to do with this big belly."

"I would hope not!" interrupted Roz. They all laughed.

"Anywho," continued Kyra, "even though I left y'all for a couple of years and got off track, you all still let me back in, accepted me with open arms, encouraged me, and pushed me to reach my goals. We did it, y'all! We stayed on track in spite of all the obstacles. Angel, all you have to do is pass the state bar and we'll have our own corporate lawyer to handle our business. Jaz, all you have to do is walk across the stage and get that first piece of paper before going on to medical school. Roz, you tackled two majors and are now prepared to take two state exams, one for physical therapy and the other for respiratory therapy. I gotta walk across that stage and get my piece of paper on my way to graduate school to study and become a doctor of psychology. Soon we'll be four sisters with bachelor's degrees or better, straight from the hood. None of us are drug addicts or carry ourselves as hos. We're happy for the most part. Two of us are engaged to good, strong brothas, and, hopefully, the other two won't be too far behind." They all agreed with Kyra. They were proud of their success and accomplishments.

"Roz, did you roll the weed?" Angel blurted. Roz dumped the joints on the table.

"Oh yeah," Jaz said. "I'd like to make an official toast." They all took a glass and raised it in the air for Jaz's toast. "A toast to life, love, peace, and happiness. Congrats to Angel, our own corporate and entertainment attorney. Congrats to Roz, who doubled up in physical therapy and respiratory therapy! Good luck in opening your own practice and healing all of those fine, rich-ass ball players. Congrats to me. I am now a fuckin' scientist with offers from five graduate schools. And congrats to Kyra, a future head doctor, a/k/a psychologist. And she got accepted at six graduate schools. My sisters, I think we all did pretty damn good. Even though we are all fine and beautiful we didn't get a man to depend on for food, clothing, and shelter. We handled our shit." They put the glasses to their lips and drank, continuing to congratulate themselves.

"We put us first," Kyra continued. "We can hold it down on our own if we have to. But, for real, having a good man—another half—sure makes things a lot smoother. This toast goes to us. I love y'all, my sisters forever!" They touched glasses again and finished their drinks.

"Um, can you fire it up, my sister?" Angel pleaded, looking at Roz, who passed everybody a joint except for Jaz.

"Where's mine?" Jaz whined.

"I ain't messin' with you and that crazy-ass Faheem. If he found out that I gave you and his unborn child some weed, I'd never hear the last of it."

"Give me the bag then. I'll roll my own."

"Nope!" Roz said, lighting her joint.

"Kyra got one and she's pregnant," Jaz whined.

"Marvin ain't gonna trip as bad as Faheem would," Roz explained.

"C'mon, Roz," Jaz begged.

"Here. We'll split this one." Kyra passed Jaz her joint. "If you get busted, you on ya own!" They all started laughing.

"Thank you, Kyra." She looked at Roz and stuck her tongue out at her. She took a drag. "I want to get my party on, too."

"Turn on some music," Angel ordered. Kyra picked up the remote and pointed at the stereo.

"Oooh! Turn that up! That's the shit!" Roz was bobbing her head. *"How did you get here? Nobody s'posed to be here. I tried that love thing for the last time. My heart says no, no. Nobody s'posed to be here, but you came along and changed my mind."* Roz was singing along with Debra Cox.

"What's up, Roz? Who is he?" Angel probed. All eyes were now on Roz.

"What?"

"You heard what I said."

"I'm too embarrassed to tell y'all," Roz answered.

"Who is he?" Angel probed again.

"His name is Trae."

"Trae! Oooh!" Jaz emphasized his name.

"You are scandalous," Kyra added.

"Who is Trae?" Angel was puzzled.

"This big-ass baller from New York," Jaz told her.

"You are scandalous!" Kyra repeated. "First of all, you know how fine Tyson Beckford is, right? Well Trae is finer than him. He has big, pretty eyes, thick eyelashes, thick, dark, eyebrows, and thick, pretty lips. Second of all—this is the kicker—he's Nikayah's partna. His boy. I repeat, his boy. That is downright scandalous, Roz. What is up with you? Tell me you're joking!"

"So that means he's paid then, right?" Angel was looking back and forth at Kyra and Jaz for an answer.

"Can I talk?" Roz asked.

"He got a coupl'a whips," Kyra said, ignoring Roz. "He mostly be in that fly-ass black Lincoln Navigator with the chrome. He always has his hair in braids. Dayum! I'm getting excited just talkin' about him. If I didn't have Marvin I would be trying to hit that my damn self!" They all laughed.

"Kyra! Can you stop lusting and shut up? Can I talk, please?" Roz asked, relighting her joint.

"The floor is yours," Kyra said. "I gots to hear this. Inquiring minds do want to know. Go ahead."

"Shut up, Kyra!" Jaz said. "Let the girl talk."

"Jaz, I don't know why you frontin'. You know I'm not lying," said Kyra, refusing to give up.

"She ain't lyin', y'all. The bitch ain't never lied!" Everybody burst out laughing. "If I wasn't crazy about Faheem, I'd be wanting to hit that myself. And yes, like Jaheim said, *'It would be because of the ice I see.'*" They all laughed again. "Naw, I'm playing. And for the record I said *if* I wasn't in love with Faheem."

"Can I talk now?" Roz made eye contact with everybody, and no one said a word. "Thank you! First of all, he's not just a baller."

"Bullshit!" Jaz interrupted. "Faheem only associates with ballers. I ain't bragging or nothing, but y'all know Faheem ain't nothing nice. He thinks he's the president of the ballers' club. He knows he's the shit, and that's how he carries himself. Plus, I saw that nigga at Faheem's apartment around the time my sister fucked up her life." Jaz noticed Roz staring at her. "I'm sorry. Go ahead, Roz. I didn't mean to interrupt."

"Yes, you did!" everybody yelled in unison.

"Anyway," Roz continued, "the brotha got a bachelor's degree from Long Island University. So he's not just a straight thug. And yes, the nigga is straight-up fine. I do have to give him that. His braids? I've been keeping his hair up for him. As a matter of fact, I've been doing that for the last couple of months. Did he hit it yet? Nope. Why? I know he wants to, but it's a couple of things making me hesitant. One, he's Nikayah's boy. Two, no more thugs for me. I lose too many peeps to that lifestyle. They either go six feet under or get locked down. I'm running from that shit. You want to know if I'm feeling him? Unfortunately, hell fuckin' yes! When he's around, the hair on my skin stands straight up. And he calls me by my middle name, Tash. He doesn't say Tasha. He calls me Tash."

"Dayum. It's like that?" Jaz asked.

"Yeah, baby, it's like that. He got my head spinning and it's scaring me. He got a small diamond on the tip of his tongue and I want to feel it, if you know what I mean!" She didn't mention kissing him at the club a few weeks ago.

"How much time did Nikayah get?" Angel asked.

"Twelve years. His appeal is about to get heard. At least that's what he told me."

"Dayum," everybody chimed in. They all liked Nikayah.

"So what's up with y'all? How you gonna just dog our boy out like that?" Angel asked.

"Puhleeze! Let me tell y'all about little, innocent-ass Nikayah. Y'all know we've been kickin' it for almost five years now. And for the last two of them I've been going down to that fucking prison faithfully, every weekend unless I have a semester where I have to take a Saturday class. Well, your boy apparently had my schedule screwed up. I pop up for a visit on a Saturday because I didn't have a class. I was all happy and shit at the opportunity to see him two days in a row. I go bouncing my happy ass up in there, and he's all hugged up and kissing on this other female."

"What?" yelled Kyra.

"That ain't all," added Roz, obviously choking up. "He was rubbin' her stomach. The bitch is pregnant!"

"You lyin'!" said Angel, hands covering her mouth.

"That's fucked up, dawg. I'm sorry to hear that shit," said Jaz. "So what happened?"

"First of all, it was so fucking embarrassing, mainly because everybody—the guards, the regular visitors, the inmates—know me up in there. I was wondering why it got so quiet and folks was whispering while I was walking by. I was trying to be cool and front like it wasn't no big deal. I grabbed a chair and sat right in front of them. I turned on my physical therapist voice and acted like I was interviewing a client. I got right up on her and said, 'Hello, I'm Rosalyn, and you are?' I think she said 'Simone' or something like that. Then I asked, 'Did Nikayah tell you that he has a woman, me, Roz, who has been his woman for the last five years and that I've been coming to see him in this rat hole ever since he's been here? That would be two years. I'm driving a 2000 Beamer that this nigga bought, and he pays my mortgage every month. I guess that's why he feels justified in thinking that he can act like a playa. You been kissing him, right?' She looks at me all crazy. 'Well, y'all was kissing when I walked in the door. You see that corner over there?' I pointed to where we usually get busy. 'Last Sunday he ate my pussy right over there.' The yellow bitch was turning red by now.

"Then I faced Nikayah and asked, 'Am I the other fuckin' woman, or is she? How long has she been coming down here, Nikayah?' He wouldn't answer so I pushed him. He said, 'Roz, what difference do it make? Why you trippin'? You my woman. I take care of you and she know that.' I said, 'Fuck that shit, Nikayah. Answer the fuckin' two-million-dollar question. How long you been playin' me?' So he says, 'Ain't nobody playin' nobody, Roz. She been comin' down here for a minute.'

"I screamed, 'For a minute? The bitch looks six months pregnant!' Then he says, 'Let me talk to you in private,' and grabs my arm. I fuckin' punched him in the head, screaming, 'Fuck you, Nikayah. I'm outta here.' Then I punched him in the face. Then I told her, 'You can have his sorry ass and all the visits.' I looked at him one more time and told him, 'I'm glad I didn't keep your babies!' as I headed for the door. That last comment slipped out. That nigga came running behind me, and I got scared and started walking faster until the guard told him to go sit down. He kept screaming, 'You got an abortion.' And that's the last time I seen or talked to him."

"Dayum," Jaz said. "When did all of this happen?"

"It's been three months."

"Why didn't you tell anyone?"

"Too fuckin' hurt to talk about it. Plus, I'd rather tell all of y'all at once instead of repeating it over and over. I'm trying to put him behind me."

"What's the matter with three-way?" Kyra asked. "We use it all the time."

"Kyra. Y'all just don't know. I didn't feel like talking about it until now—since all of us are here. I was hurt. Well, I'm still hurt but not as much. He fucked me up. I still can't get over the fact that he played me like that. I could see if I was fucking around on him, but he knew I wasn't. He got too many eyes and ears out here. Plus, he would have sensed something when he saw me. Niggas ain't stupid. So now it's fuck him! It's over. I don't accept his collect calls. I don't answer his mail. And if I didn't have so many peeps on lockdown, I would have put a block on my phone.

But most of them gonna have to go through so much drama if I changed the number. So I just decided to leave it."

"So tell us again how did Trae get in the picture?" Kyra wanted to know.

"Nikayah had Trae for a while bringing me money and checking on me to make sure I was okay."

"That was dumb," Jaz said.

"Obviously. But Trae is his boy—or supposed to be. So one day he stopped by to check on me and his hair was in a big-ass 'fro. He asked me if I could braid. I told him, 'yeah.' Then I hooked him up. Ever since then he's been makin' sure that I keep it up for him, using that as an excuse to come over. Of course we talk while I'm braiding. That's how I found out about his bachelor's in marketing and public relations. I like him . . . but why does he have to be Nikayah's boy? And why does he have to be so deep in the drug game? I chose to get away from that lifestyle. I got caught up before. I lost my pops to it, my mom, friends, relatives, and my man of five fucking years. Now this nigga is trying to invade my space . . . and it's fucked up because I like him . . . a lot."

"What do you mean, you got caught up before?" Angel quizzed.

"That's a whole 'nother story."

"We got time," Kyra added.

"I'll tell y'all, but first let me throw this out there."

"Oh, gosh. Now she's gettin' ready to get all philosophical and shit," Jaz joked.

"No, check this out," Roz said, puffing on her joint. "What's up with this picture? We are all intelligent sisters, right?"

"Right," they all agreed.

"We all are fine, right?"

"Right," they all said again.

"We all got college degrees, right?"

"Right."

"So why do we attract the niggas that's out there pimpin', slangin', bangin', and ballin'? You know what I mean? Why not the niggas who are professionals: doctors, lawyers, investment bankers, and niggas like that? Y'all feel me?"

Everyone was silent. They were replaying in their minds what Roz had just said. Angel puffed on her joint and looked around at everybody. "I think it's because we're young, we're fine, and the ballers . . . well, that's what they chase. But I am with Roz, I am through with that lifestyle."

"You got a point," Kyra said. "But we're attracted to them just as much as they're attracted to us. Y'all know them hustlin', thuggish niggas turn us on. So don't front."

"Yeah, that's true. But at the same time if we hung out around the professional brothers, we would be attracted to them. If they hung out around us, they would be attracted to us. It depends on what and who you want. It seems like most women look for the thug in every brother. Baller, hustla, slanger, or professional, thug me out, baby!" Jaz drooled. "Take charge, baby!"

"Right! Right! That's what I like about Trae. He likes to run shit. Take over. I don't know about the next ho, but that shit turns me on." Roz laughed. "I know I don't want no weak-ass, pushover nigga."

"Turns you on? Look at me. I was sprung over a pimp. I was crazy about him. He was always runnin' shit. And now Bilal has been trying to push up on me, but I've been duckin' him out big time. I'm scared of that nigga. I won't even tell him where I live. Plus, I'm a lawyer now, I can't be fucking with them criminal niggas anymore," Angel said.

"Yeah, he came over here a couple of times to see Marvin. He's a fine black brotha. I heard he's a ho with your baby momma drama, so you better keep ducking him out if you don't wanna get caught up. At least we attract all the fine niggas, even if they're thugs," Kyra said, bursting with laughter.

"Take the weed from her," Roz snarled. "Ain't shit funny. This is serious."

"It's funny to me!" she said and kept on laughing. Then they all started laughing. Roz crawled over to Kyra and took the joint, then went over to Jaz and took hers.

"Y'all not supposed to be smoking anyway," Roz snapped.

"Come on, *Tash*," Jaz joked, "this is the first time I got high since I've been pregnant."

"Don't call me Tash. Only one person is allowed to call me that."

"Well, excuse me, *Tash*, but since you're so serious, tell us about you getting caught up out there. How come you never told us that story?"

"The same reason you didn't tell us about you cooking meth for the last year or so. You feel me?"

"I feel you," Jaz whispered.

"What's up with your case anyway? I still can't believe you did that shit," said Angel, getting into lawyer mode.

"I was sentenced to seventeen years," Jaz answered. "Faheem paid a sentencing lawyer to make sure that I don't start my sentence until after I have the baby. Then I have to self-surrender." She leaned back into the recliner. "Then he paid a lawyer to handle my appeal to make sure that I can remain out on bond pending the outcome of the appeal. Just getting the damn thing heard can take anywhere from six months to two years." She took a gulp of her grape juice.

"Seventeen years? You didn't want to sign the fuckin' plea bargain?" Roz wanted to know.

"Girl, fuckin' with Faheem, his motto is 'death before dishonor.' He said to trust him and do it his way or take the highway. So here I be."

"I have to give it to you. You sure are handling it well," Roz told her. "Putting your life in a nigga's hands."

"Shit! I wasn't at first. I was stressing like crazy until Faheem threatened my ass. He told me that if something happens to his baby because of me stressing, it wasn't going to be nice. So I said, 'Fuck it. I'ma chill the fuck out. You want to run thangs? Then go right ahead, my brotha.' That's why I've been chillin'. If things don't turn out right, I'ma fuck him up and go to prison for some real shit!"

"Girl, you silly!" Roz told her.

"Silly? I am dead serious."

"Now see," Roz said, sitting up, "you and Kyra, y'all's shit is rare. Like some storybook shit. Dude gets in the game. Dude gets legal. Dude gets out of game. Dude gets girl. Dude marries girl. They have kids and live happily ever fuckin' after. Wait! Let me back up. Dude is a good man. Dude loves girl. Dude don't fuck around on girl, causing a whole lot of drama. That shit is one-in-a-million odds, like hitting the fuckin' lottery!"

"Wait!" Angel said, holding up both hands. "Don't leave out, dude can fuck! Dude can keep a hard-on until girl comes. And comes. And comes again." They all started laughing. "I ain't mad at y'all. Because I know I'ma get mines one of these days."

"Me neither. I ain't mad at y'all. I got a feeling that Trae is all of that," Roz said.

"Why is that, Tash?" Jaz asked jokingly.

"None of your business! But one thing for sho': if he ain't all of that, I'ma clown his ass big time. And stop calling me Tash!"

"Oh, so you do plan on allowing him to hit it?" Kyra asked. "Bitch, you need to slow your roll!"

"Chill out. I'm still investigating. Basically I'm just waiting until I'm ready. Plus, I want to see how bad he wants me, how patient he'll be. Shit, I don't know what the fuck I'm planning."

"Oh, so you got it like that?" Angel asked. "You need to make up your mind. You just said you were done with that lifestyle, but at the same time you're plotting and scheming. What, do you think you can have your cake and eat it, too?"

"Yes, I do. So when are y'all getting married?" Roz asked, putting her foot on Kyra's knee, trying to change the subject, because she really had mixed emotions on the situation.

Kyra pushed her foot down. "I'm not sure when I want to do it. Marvin told me to let him know when I'm ready. What about you?" Kyra looked at Jaz.

"We're waiting until Faheem's dad comes home next May. He'll have done nine years."

"Dayum," said Roz. "Everybody is trying to get their hustle on and they're just locking us away and throwing away the keys. And that's another thing. See . . ."

They cut Roz off. "Oh, gosh! Here she goes again," everybody sang at once.

"Naw, for real, y'all, listen. See, everybody is trying to survive. Them. Us. We go after the ballers because they're obviously trying to survive. Nobody wants to be all poor and shit, suffering. Folks are chasing that American dream that's on TV. Now, I'ma be quiet."

"Yeah, right! You said that two hours ago," Kyra said. "What about our graduation party? Y'all wanna have it here?"

"Of course, I thought that was already decided," Jaz responded.

"It was," Angel said. "Just don't invite the whole city. And, Kyra, don't have that baby until afterwards."

"I'll do my best," Kyra answered sarcastically.

"Okay, Tasha. We're giving you the floor again. Tell us this big secret that you keep trying to keep to yourself." Jaz leaned back and waited.

Everybody turned toward Roz. She fell back onto the floor and stretched her long legs onto the arm of the chair. "This shit better not leave this room," she warned.

Payback Is a Mutha

"**G**urrll, guess what?" Shan was almost jumping up and down as she shouted at her best friend Brianna through the phone.

"Why are you screaming?" Brianna asked with obvious agitation.

"I got the job, girl! I got the J-muthafuckin'-O-B!"

"Which one? You done interviewed with damn near fifty thousand people."

"The computer instructor for the prison, FCI Memphis. They just hung up."

Brianna sucked her teeth and rolled her eyes. "It took them long enough. I would have changed my mind. I don't see why you want to work for the prison system or work, period! All these niggas out here with money."

"Bitch, please! Everybody ain't a gold-diggin' ho like you. I need my own cash and I don't want to suck dicks to get it!"

"You better get with the program. What the fuck you think these niggas are for? There's absolutely no excuse for bitches like us to be broke!" Brianna shrieked in bewilderment. "And the last time I checked you were talking to two niggas! Where are they! You ditched them? Sometimes I don't understand your line of thinking." Then she frowned. "Working at a prison?"

"Bitch, just because you were in the BOP, and I choose to work for the BOP, don't hate. Congratulate! Plus, I've only been kickin' it with Calvin for a month. He likes me because he sees it ain't all about the cash with me. I'd rather get my own and have my own."

"Girlfriend, please! Do you hear yourself? Like I said, you better step up your game and get with the program. You can fall for that weak shit if you want. That nigga knows it's all about the cash. Niggas ain't nothin' but tricks."

"Do you, B, 'cause you know I'ma do me, so are you down to help me celebrate or what?"

"Like I said, if you were on top of your game—"

"Girl," Shan interrupted, "I bet you even hustle niggas in your sleep! Don't you?"

They both burst out laughing. Brianna knew for sure that Shan was telling the truth. "Let me make a few phone calls and I'll call you around nine. Dress to impress. You know I gotta kill two birds with one stone. I'ma celebrate with you and see who I can get with later," Brianna said.

"Yeah, I know how you do. But don't worry about me dressing to impress. You just make sure you are here by nine. Don't call at nine. Be here at nine! Peace out."

"Wait. What are you getting ready to do?" Brianna asked.

"Take a beauty nap. What you think?"

"Whatever, ho. Do you."

"I'm trying. Peace."

After Brianna hung up the phone she dialed Yolanda, her hairdresser. "Landa, what's up? This is Brianna."

"I know who this is," she snapped. "What do you want? I have two bitches under the dryer, two at the sinks, the one in my chair, and three waiting. You just came here two days ago, so no, I can't squeeze you in!" Yolanda rattled off.

Brianna sucked her teeth and rolled her eyes. "How do you know that's why I'm calling?"

Brianna was busted.

"Ho, I know you, so stop playing games. I told you I'm busy."

"Too busy for an eight-pack on top of what I usually pay?" Yolanda was thinking. Her regular fee plus an eight ball of coke? "Yeah. That's what I thought," Brianna snapped back. "What's the best time to come?"

"Be here at two, Brianna. Not two-fifteen, two-thirty. And bring my shit!"

Brianna hung up without responding.

She stood in front of the mirror as she pinned up her $1,200.00 weave. "Where should we go tonight?" she asked the mirror. It was Friday night, and she wanted to take full advantage of it. Her girl, Shan, loved the hip-hop clubs, but B's first preference was anything where the *real* ballers hung, so she knew she had to choose the spot.

She and Shan had been friends since the third grade. Everyone thought that they were family. Shan was closer to Brianna than her own blood sister. Unforeseen forces bound them closer together, like when Shan's parents were killed in that fatal car accident, and when Brianna got pregnant in the seventh grade and her mother put her out. They really leaned on one another. Even though Brianna lost the baby, her mother still wouldn't take her back. When Social Services came and took Shan and her brother, Peanut, away, Brianna was homeless. When a relative came and rescued them from the group home, that's when they took Brianna off the streets. Her mother didn't allow her back home until she went to the tenth grade.

Other than their copper complexions, they were night and day in just about every way. Brianna had those full pouty lips, while Shan had dainty sensuous ones. Brianna's nose was full; Shan's was a cute little button. Brianna's onion screamed, "Goddamn!" Shan's onion screamed, "Dayuum!" Brianna was tall and Shan was short. Brianna had to wear Gucci, Prada, and Chanel, while Shan preferred Sean John, Baby Phat, and FUBU. Brianna had the weave, fake nails, and boob job, while Shan had the locks, sported her real nails, and refused to do the makeup thing. Brianna went to prison, while Shan now chose to work at a prison. Brianna lived large off the ballers, while Shan preferred the legit business-man or blue collar worker. Which is why everyone couldn't figure out how they remained so close over the years.

During Brianna's eighteen-month prison bid, the only three people who stuck by her were Shan, Peanut, and one of her sugar daddys by the name of Nick. He kept money on her books and allowed her to run up his phone bill. She had mad love for Nick but she had been out now for almost a year and he felt like she still owed him. Brianna had re-cently told him that she gave him enough pussy to consider her debt paid in full.

Upon hearing the phone ring, Brianna snatched it up. "Hello."

"What up, B?"

"You."

"You don't even know who this is."

"Oh, I know who this is," she teased. "There is only one Shadee."

"Act like you know, girl! I thought I was gonna have to tap that ass. I need to swing by later on."

"Around what time? I got a hair appointment and me and my girl is going out. Can you come before six?"

"That'll work."

"Be on time, please."

"I got you."

She sucked her teeth. "Yeah, right." She hung up and immediately called Hook.

When Hook answered, Brianna said, "Okay, nigga, I don't owe you nothing else. Your boy said he'll be here around six, which means eight. So handle yours."

"Handle mines?" he asked, sounding pissed off. "We straight as long as it's worth *my* while."

"Look, nigga, that ain't got shit to do with me. I called you and it's on, so now we are even. *Ya heard?*"

Hook didn't say anything for a minute. "Bitch, it's over when I say it's over! *Ya heard?*"

Brianna sighed as she slammed down the phone. "How in the fuck did I ever get involved with a sorry, punk-ass nigga like that?" she said through clenched teeth.

Shadee didn't show up until a quarter after eight. When Brianna opened the door he grabbed her by her hair and gave her a big sloppy kiss. "What up, B?" he asked while squeezing her ass. His six-foot, two-inch rich chocolate frame filled up the doorway. His white du rag was tied so tight it was making his already chinky eyes look closed.

"I'm on my way out. My girl is waiting on me. When it comes to me you never have a concept of the time, do you?"

"Time is always on our side, B. And it's time to break me off a little sumthin' sumthin'." He grinned, causing that left dimple to wink.

"I don't think so. If you would have come a little earlier, time would have been on your side. But I'm dressed, ready to go, and my girl is waiting on me."

"So, B, it's like that?"

"Right this minute? Yeah!" She tried to move his hands off her ass. "You always puttin' me on the back burner."

"Let me break you off, then," he whispered into her ear. "You can spare a few minutes for that, can't you?"

Brianna really didn't have to think that one over because Shadee could give tha bomb head. It felt like he had two tongues and like he put his nose in it.

"That got your attention, huh?" He laughed, sucked on her luscious lips some more, then picked her up and took her to the bedroom. "When are you gonna settle down for me?"

She slipped off her dress as soon as he put her down. "When can you settle down for me?" She flipped it.

"Why you gotta always answer my question with a question?" He slapped her on the ass.

"Oowww! Why'd you do that?" She rolled her eyes at him.

"Answer my question." He watched her nipples stick out as he played with them.

"That feels good." She slid back onto the bed, spread her thighs and ran her feet across his chest. "Can I answer you later?" She moaned as he licked the inside of her thighs.

"Yeah, I guess you can do that," he said as he spread her swollen pussy lips, smiled at the sight of her clit sticking straight out, and sucked one of his favorite juicy pussies until he couldn't suck anymore.

As Brianna washed up, Shadee packed in a bag of six kilos of powder, 8Gs, and he took two of those and threw them on the coffee table for Brianna. "Yo, B!" he called. Brianna's apartment was one of the spots he used as a stash spot.

As Hook and his boy Rob sat in the car waiting for Shadee and watching his Benz, Shadee was kissing B on the lips. "Can I come by later?"

"Call me, okay?"

"Give me another kiss." He leaned over and kissed her, then headed out the door.

"Here comes our boy." Rob was anxious as hell as he grabbed his pipe and they sprang from the car. As Shadee went to unlock the car door, Rob smashed him over the head with the pipe, causing Shadee to let out a loud grunt as he fell over. Hook grabbed the black duffel bag, then he and Rob stuffed Shadee's limp body onto the backseat. Hook started the car, but as soon as he got it out of park, a forest green Hummer blocked him in and out jumped five of Shadee's boys.

Thug Matrimony

"Fuck the groom! I'm here for the bride, she's my woman. Can you tell her Snake is here and he needs to talk to her?" As if on cue his boys came inside. There were five of them and every one of them was strapped.

"Snake? You're Keenan, her ex!" Trina glared in disbelief. He gave her this look that said, *What the fuck you think?* When she got the message she made a mental note of all the niggas he had there for backup. "Aiight, then. Wait right here and I'll go get her."

"Yeah, you do that," he said to Trina's back as she walked away.

"Ooooohhh, shit! Ooooohhh, shit!" Trina kept mumbling as she wove around and in between the many hotel guests as she was trying to rush to the elevator. "Ooooohhh, shit! That nigga is alive and kicking!" She kept banging on the UP button as if that would make the elevator move quicker. She looked up to see what floor they were on, but only one of the elevators was moving. The other one appeared to be stuck on the eighteenth floor. She kept pressing the UP button. When it finally opened she pushed her way on without even giving the guests an opportunity to get off.

"Excuse you!" a young sister shouted at Trina as she mean-mugged her.

"Bitch, this is New York and you're excused!" Trina shot back.

"Trina, why you always gotta start some shit?" Jaz teased. "And what's up, who got your G-string all in a bunch?" Jaz was all hugged up on Faheem. They were the last two to step off the elevator.

Trina grabbed Jaz's arm. "Aw, shit. Come here, y'all. Y'all ain't gonna believe this shit! Guess who's here?" Jaz and Faheem just stared at her, both of them obviously not up for any guessing games. Sensing that, Trina yelled out, "Muthafuckin' Snake! That nigga is in the building!"

"Snake!" Jaz and Faheem said simultaneously. "Who the fuck is that!" Faheem needed to confirm. "Not Snake. You mean the pimp? I thought he was dead." Faheem had a puzzled look on his face.

"You and everybody else! It is on now!" Trina said, ready for some drama.

"You sure it's him?" Jaz was skeptical. "How do you know it's him?" she pressed. None of them noticed that they were just riding the elevator as if they had no destination. Surprisingly no one got on.

"It looks like him. He said it was him and he said for me to go get his girl."

"That's impossible." Jaz was shaking her head no. "What you been smokin'? You up here imagining things and shit."

"Imagining? I didn't imagine that he had five niggas with him and I know they're carrying some heat!"

"What?" That got Faheem on full alert. "Aw, hell no!" Faheem was looking at Trina to see if she was for real. Jaz could see Faheem's killer qualities kicking in.

"Faheem?" Jaz said as she squeezed his arm.

"Where's Kay?" he asked Trina, referring to Kaylin.

"I think in Angel's room."

"I need to go holla at him." He hit the button to the suite level. "Trina, go get Kyra. I'ma go tell Angel."

"Naw, you go get Kyra. I'ma go tell Angel. I'm not missing this!" Trina stood next to Faheem. "Later for Kyra. If I was you I'd go with the rest of us."

"Kyra is her cousin. She needs to be there." Jaz was getting agitated with Trina.

When the elevator doors opened they followed behind Faheem to Angel's suite. They heard laughter from behind the door. Faheem knocked as if he was the Po Po.

Kyra opened the door. She had tears in her eyes. Everyone looked behind her and immediately knew why she had tears of joy cascading down her cheeks. Angel looked simply stunning. She was glowing as the photographer snapped pictures of her and Kaylin, then the bride by herself, then the bride and groom with all of the parents.

"Yo, Kay! I need to holla at you, man." Faheem didn't care about interrupting as he stepped inside the suite.

"Hold up." Kaylin kissed his moms on the cheek and walked her to the door.

When Kaylin came back to the bar area, Faheem said, "Get your wife."

"Get me for what?" Angel was already right behind Faheem and immediately detected the tension in his voice.

"We got a problem."

"Damn. What now? We gonna start in exactly fifteen minutes," Kaylin said. "Whatever it is will have to wait until my day is over."

"Y'all got some unwanted guests and niggas is packin' that heat. I don't think that can wait. I suggest you get your squad ready," Faheem warned Kay.

"Them niggas stay ready. But I need to know who the fuck is tryna throw salt on my wedding and why I gotta get my squad in place."

"Me, too," Angel chimed in.

"That nigga Snake."

"Snake?" Angel and Kaylin both said, confused.

In the meantime on the eighteenth floor . . .

Tasha was riding with one of her twin sons, Shaheem, on her hip, while glad to be spending some time with her little brother, Kevin. "I miss you, you little punk," she teased.

"I miss you, too, you big punk." He looked at his sister in admiration.

"I worry about you all the time, Kevin."

"Don't do that, 'cause what's gonna happen is gonna happen." As soon as Kevin pressed the UP button the elevator doors opened, and their eyes went to Trae lying on the floor bleeding.

Kevin mumbled, "What the fuck?"

"Oh, my God! Trae!" She shoved Shaheem into Kevin's arms, who was just standing there. "Get my baby outta here. He can't see this!" she screamed. "Give me your cell phone. Oh, my God!" She kept her eyes on Trae as she dialed 911. "Trae baby." She knelt down beside him as she felt his weak pulse. "Trae baby, don't do this to me. Don't you do this to me! I need an ambulance to the Hyatt Regency." She spoke firmly into the cell. "We're on the eighteenth floor in the elevator. My husband is bleeding, his pulse rate is probably about thirty-eight, his breathing is very shallow, and . . ." As she put her ear to his chest, she said, "I can't tell if there is bubbling in his lungs. I think I'm losing him!" she screamed into the phone. "He was shot in the chest and leg and I think the shoulder or arm, I can't tell, there's so much blood." She noticed that his gun was lying next to him. She ran her finger over the barrel and it was still warm. "Please hurry!" She ended the call while tearing a strip off the bottom of her dress. She tied it as tight as she could around his arm, went under the armpit up to the shoulder. Then she tore another piece off and tied it tight around his leg. "Trae, if you can hear me, I love you, baby, and you're a fighter. I need you to fight. Fight for me, baby. Fight for me and our boys. We need you, baby. I can't do this without you. Don't make me do this without you. Do you hear me, Trae?"

I hear you, baby. Trae was talking to her, but no sound or words were coming out of his mouth. He felt as if he were floating out in orbit.

"Stay with me, baby."

I'm with you.

Just then hotel security came off the elevator. "Holy shit!" He pressed the TALK button on his walkie-talkie and said, "They're here on the eighteenth floor in the B elevator. Blood is everywhere."

The shooter obviously had pressed the emergency STOP button. So hotel security got on with them, hitting the same button. "We're coming down to basement level now," he said as he hit the B2 button. "The ambulance is waiting, ma'am," he said to a crying Tasha, who had Trae's head resting in her lap. He had never seen a live and up-close gunshot victim before.

"Okay," she mumbled. "Please, baby, don't die on me," she whispered.

When the elevator doors opened, the paramedics rushed inside. "Ma'am, we need you to step outside please." The older paramedic helped her up. "Is this your husband?" She nodded yes. "We need to get him stabilized. You said he was shot?" He noticed the tourniquets that she had made and was impressed.

"I think three times." She watched as they ripped his clothes off and set up an IV line, all with tremendous speed. She heard them say "One . . . two . . . three . . ." and he was on the gurney being loaded into the back of the ambulance. When Tasha tried to climb up onto the back with them the older paramedic shook his head no.

"What are you shaking your head no for? That is my husband and you best believe that I will be riding with him." Tasha was about to lose it.

"This is a high-trauma case, ma'am. We need to be alone with the victim," the older paramedic told her.

The two other paramedics were working on Trae as the female paramedic tried to calm Tasha down. But she was holding on tight to the back of the ambulance door.

"You're wasting precious time, ma'am."

"Fuck you! That is my husband and I'm not leaving him!"

"Ma, what the hell happened?" Omar, Trae's cousin, apparently had been running. So had Kevin and two other guests, because they were right behind him.

"They shot him, Omar, and these muthafuckers are tryna tell me I can't ride with him. They got me fucked up! I'm riding!" She climbed up onto the back of the ambulance. She screamed, "Don't you touch me! Don't fuckin' touch me! I am going with my husband!" She was spookin' the older paramedic, who was trying to grab her arm.

That's right, baby, Trae was saying.

"Kevin, I need my purse. Meet us at the hospital."

"Which one?" Omar looked at the older paramedic.

"Right down the street." And he closed the ambulance doors.

Omar took off to get his car. Kevin went to get Tasha's purse.

"Oh, God, please." She closed her eyes and prayed as they went to work on Trae. She hoped that when she opened her eyes this would have all been a nightmare.

"C'mon, people, we're losing him!" the older paramedic yelled, snapping Tasha out of her trance.

"Damn you, Trae, don't you do this! Don't you die on me!" she cried. "Fight, baby!"

I'm trying, baby. It burns. It feels so good when I don't fight. It feels like I'm floating.

"Fight for me and the boys. Don't forget we have another one on the way. I need you, baby. We all need you. You are my world," she said back as if she could hear his thoughts.

I love y'all more than anything. You are the best thing that ever happened to me. Y'all are what I live for, baby. But I did a lot of bad shit in the past so now I gotta reap all the bad shit that I've sown. I want you to stop crying. You know I don't like it when you cry. I love you forever.

"Trae, don't you do this! I need you to stay with me."

The heart monitor was getting slower, his vitals were dropping. She didn't want to believe that he was going downhill.

"This is too much of a blood loss!" the female paramedic said.

"Is he gonna make it? He's gonna make it, right?" Tasha was grasping for any ounce of hope.

"I can't promise you anything, ma'am. We're losing him fast."